CHAPEL LIBRARY CEN
1500 CHAPEL STRE
NEW HAVEN CONN. O

DATE DUE

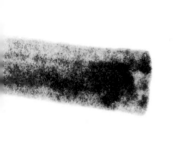

WEEP FOR HER

2

WEEP FOR HER

Sara Woods

What's Hecuba to him or he to Hecuba
That he should weep for her?

Hamlet, Act II, scene ii

ST. MARTIN'S PRESS, NEW YORK

Any work of fiction whose characters were of uniform excellence would rightly be condemned – by that fact if by no other – as being incredibly dull. Therefore no excuse can be considered necessary for the villainy or folly of the people appearing in this book. It seems extremely unlikely that any one of them should resemble a real person, alive or dead. Any such resemblance is completely unintentional and without malice.

S.W.

Library of Congress Cataloging in Publication Data

Woods, Sara, pseud.
    Weep for her.

    I.   Title.
PR6073.063W4   1980   823'.914   80-5308
ISBN 0-312-86019-6

I

'Antony,' said Sir Nicholas gravely, 'your aura isn't good.'

His nephew, Antony Maitland, started so violently that his coffee slopped over into his saucer, and glanced rather wildly at his still fairly new aunt-by-marriage, Vera, Lady Harding, who was sitting, placidly enough, in the corner of the sofa nearest her husband's chair.

'Don't think he suddenly went mad, Antony,' she assured him kindly. 'At least, if he has, that's the first intimation I've had of it.'

Jenny Maitland, curled up at the other end of the sofa, treated the matter more practically. 'What colour *is* his aura, Uncle Nick?' she asked. 'And what colour ought it to be?'

'It's a dull, chocolaty brown,' said Sir Nicholas, his attention still fixed on his nephew. 'As I understand it that means a grave disorder of some kind, either physical or mental. Perhaps he's bilious, though in that event the colour would, perhaps, more likely have been yellow.'

'Uncle Nick, you know Antony is never bilious!'

'Or more likely, I was going to say, my dear Jenny, in view of your excellent cuisine, it is his thoughts that are causing this very distressing emanation.'

'What sort of thoughts?' said Jenny, determined to get to the bottom of the matter.

'Unwholesome,' said Sir Nicholas, with a misleading air of candour.

'You didn't tell Jenny what colour it ought to be, Uncle Nick,' Antony pointed out.

'Oh, anything clear and cheerful,' said Sir Nicholas. His nephew was pretty sure his vagueness covered a complete lack of knowledge. 'It's the – the muddiness that I don't like.'

'Well as it happens you're quite wrong,' said Antony. 'I thought you'd have noticed, I'm feeling in a particularly good humour this evening.'

'There have been certain signs of euphoria,' said Sir Nicholas thoughtfully. 'But in view of the aura I spoke of I thought I must be mistaken about that.'

'Well, you're not. Mallory turned down a brief for me today – '

'I should have thought that was an occasion for regret rather than for rejoicing,' said his uncle, who had a pretty good idea of the Maitlands' financial situation – 'neat, but not gaudy,' Antony would have said, though the matter, of course, was never mentioned between them.

'Not in this case. It was to act for the defendant in a case of obscene libel, I didn't fancy it at all. But the beauty of it is that Mallory thought he was disobliging me by turning it down.' Old Mr Mallory was Sir Nicholas's clerk, and Antony had been in his uncle's chambers since he left his pupilage many years before.

'I suppose that was young Willett's doing,' said Sir Nicholas. 'Between the two of you, you'll get into trouble one of these days.' John Willett was the one of the junior clerks who most nearly identified himself with Maitland's concerns. Over the years he had discovered ways of manoeuvring Mr Mallory's decisions, a thing for which Antony could never be sufficiently grateful.

'I don't think so,' he said now, seriously. 'He saves me from going quite mad, that's all. I mean, if I were to take all the cases that Mallory wants to load me down with – '

'He's an older man than you,' said Sir Nicholas didactically, 'and wiser in the ways of the world. You might do worse than to listen to his advice.'

This was an old argument, but Antony had never in his life accepted Mr Mallory's opinion about anything, just as Mr Mallory had never for a moment relented in his attitude of disapproval towards his employer's nephew. Whether each of these feelings had sprung up simultaneously, or whether one had caused the other, was a point on which Sir Nicholas was occasionally inclined to dwell ... generally to the detriment of his nephew. Antony, who was beginning to feel the conversation was headed in the wrong direction, put his coffee cup down carefully and took the wing chair opposite the one that his uncle was occupying.

'What do you know about auras anyway, Uncle Nick?' he asked, with interest.

'Well, if you must have it, Antony, not very much so far. By the time I've finished studying my brief, however ...'

'Uncle Nick! You can't possibly be studying a brief that needs you to know anything at all about auras.'

'On the contrary, my dear boy, I can't help feeling that the knowledge is going to prove invaluable. I am surprised, however, that your friend and ally, Willett, hasn't apprised you of this particular matter. I thought he gave you all the gossip.'

Antony ignored this. 'It can only be something to do with spiritualism,' he said. 'But nobody prosecutes mediums nowadays, if that's what you're talking about,' he protested. 'They're – they're respectable.'

'The Fraudulent Mediums Act of 1951 –'

'Yes, I know all about that. But nobody prosecutes anybody under it any more,' Maitland repeated. 'Or do they?' he asked, suddenly suspicious.

'In this case, they certainly do.'

Antony got up and went to fetch the brandy bottle. 'I can't take this in,' he said, circulating. 'It can only be a tuppenny ha'penny affair, why should you bother with it?'

'There are points of interest,' said his uncle aggravatingly.

Antony completed his round, returned the bottle to its

place, and went to stand on the hearthrug a little to one side of the fire. 'Do you know anything about this, Vera?' he demanded.

'Not a thing,' said Vera placidly. 'I'm as curious as you are. And as Jenny is,' she added, smiling.

'Of course I am,' said Jenny. 'If someone had their fortune told and didn't like the result – '

'Nothing like that. This was a full-blown seance,' said Sir Nicholas. 'My client, I believe, is what is called a trance medium.'

'But what on earth . . . look here, Uncle Nick, are you sure you want to mix yourself up in this? I can see it might be possible to prove fraud, if that were taking place, but how on earth could *you* demonstrate that the manifestations – whatever they were – were genuine?'

'The difficulty had already occurred to me,' Sir Nicholas told him. 'On the other hand, you know, there must be positive proof of fraud. That is, it must be shown that the thing complained of – in this case a message from what I believe is known as the spirit world – has been put forward without belief in its truth, or even recklessly or carelessly, whether true or false.'

'You're talking about civil law. This isn't a police case then?'

'No, a private action.' He paused and sipped his cognac, and looked round his audience as though pleased to have got their undivided attention. Vera, whom he had married at the end of the previous Trinity term, was sitting back with her hands folded in her lap, obviously quite content to wait for whatever explanation he wished to give. She was a tall woman, rather heavily built, with greying hair that seemed impossible to arrange so that it stayed in place for more than two minutes at a time, and a predilection for sack-like clothes, which had survived her marriage; the only difference being that the sacks were now well cut, and the colours more cheerful than the drab shades she had favoured before. Jenny,

8

curled up in the other corner of the sofa, was obviously all agog to hear what Uncle Nick had to tell them, while Antony, though he would have died rather than say so, was almost as curious as his wife.

'It's rather a strange case,' said Sir Nicholas, determined not to be hurried. 'I haven't looked for precedents yet, but I doubt whether there are any. The man bringing the action is called Daniel Walpole. He's the chairman of the Board of Bramley's Bank. His wife, Emily, committed suicide about a month ago.'

'That doesn't explain anything,' Jenny objected.

'I'm coming to it, my dear. The Walpoles had two children, a son, Michael, and a daughter, Sally.'

'Had?' queried Antony. He turned to take up his brandy glass from the mantelpiece but immediately his eyes were on his uncle's face again.

'You're quite right, of course. One of them is dead, the son, Michael. He went with a friend to Canada during the Christmas vacation, to take a skiing holiday. There was an avalanche and they were both killed.'

'Was that why Mrs Walpole killed herself?' asked Jenny, ever ready to be sympathetic. Antony glanced at her, and saw that her serenity was momentarily troubled. 'I mean,' she explained, 'I'm terribly sorry for her, of course, but wasn't there the daughter to think about too, as well as her husband?'

'That's right as far as it goes,' Sir Nicholas conceded. 'But it isn't quite as simple as it seems. Very much against Daniel Walpole's wishes, Mrs Walpole, who seems to have taken her son's death very badly, began to attend seances. That's how she met my client, Mrs Dorothy Selden, whom I understand is well known in psychical circles.'

'If you can enunciate that tongue-twisting phrase clearly I think you need some more brandy,' said Antony. His uncle didn't reply, but placed a hand eloquently over the glass. 'You still haven't got to the point, you know,' Maitland added.

'If I'd been telling the story, you'd be grumbling by now about the lack of a connected narrative.'

Vera gave him an amused look. 'Patience, Antony,' she advised. 'I have a feeling that all is about to be made clear.'

'That's good,' said Antony, declining to be distracted from his grievance.

'During the six weeks or so between her son's death and her own,' said Sir Nicholas, quite unmoved by this exchange, 'Mrs Walpole went to see Mrs Selden several times. First, she went to a group session, and then privately. Mrs Selden is a medium by profession, by which I mean – in case you are in any doubt about this, Antony – that money passed on each occasion. At their final sitting – I think that's the correct phrase – Maurice Selden, the medium's husband, was also present. Mrs Selden went into a trance, and transmitted a message purporting to come from Michael Walpole.'

'But surely that was what Mrs Walpole wanted,' said Jenny. 'Unless, of course, it was something horrid that was said.'

'Horrid enough,' Sir Nicholas agreed. 'He said he was in a dark haunted place, and couldn't find his way out. There were shadows all about him, other people whom he couldn't recognise, but each of them found a guide and was able to go on ahead. There was a place of light beyond that he was longing to reach, but unless his mother joined him and they could go on together he was doomed to stay where he was.'

'I don't think I like this story,' said Jenny, with a shudder. 'It was a cruel thing to say.'

'But Mrs Selden maintains she has no knowledge of messages transmitted through her in that way.'

'Couldn't her husband have stopped her?' asked Vera.

'That's the last thing he would have done, it seems that to rouse a medium from a trance suddenly is very dangerous indeed. But, in fact, Mrs Selden came back to herself again just before Mrs Walpole left the house.'

'And she went home and killed herself? This Emily Walpole, I mean,' said Jenny.

'Not immediately, three days later.'

'How did she do it?' Maitland asked.

'Carbon-monoxide poisoning.'

'That's a bit unusual, isn't it?'

There was no doubt that Sir Nicholas was enjoying his story and was in no hurry to finish it. 'She fixed a tube over the exhaust of the car – which was a Daimler, as befits an important banker – and fed the gas in through the window, which was, of course, open to the smallest possible extent. I understand that it is quite a pleasant death,' he added, his eyes going from Vera's face to Jenny's. But it was Jenny who protested.

'I think it's horrible! I don't care how comfortable a death it was, think of the state of mind she must have been in.'

'There's that, of course,' Sir Nicholas agreed, and fell silent again, apparently considering this.

'When was she found?' asked Vera practically.

'Not until the following morning. Her husband had been away overnight, and the chauffeur came down to fetch the car to meet him at the airport. That's why she hadn't been missed before.'

'Doesn't Sally Walpole live at home?'

'Yes she does, but when she came in she assumed her mother had already retired, and was probably asleep, so she never knew her room was empty and the bed hadn't been slept in.'

'What happened?' asked Vera.

'All the usual things, including of course an inquest, where the jury found that she had committed suicide while the balance of her mind was disturbed. As good a verdict as they could possibly have given for Daniel Walpole's purpose.'

'He blames your client?'

'Indeed he does. He consulted Paul Collingwood, who told

him, quite properly, that an action would lie. All the prelim-
inaries have been taken care of –'

'Wait a bit! Who's briefing you, Uncle Nick?'

'Geoffrey Horton. So, as I say, you can rely on everything
having been taken care of properly.'

'How is Collingwood proceeding?'

'There are various lines he could have taken, and I think
Walpole's choice of Collingwood means that he had a private
action for murder in mind. It was probably Collingwood who
persuaded him that he had less chance of success that way.
He might have alleged negligence, on the grounds that my
client's action was one that no reasonable person would have
taken. But he has decided to proceed against her for fraud,
the act of 1951 leaves no doubt that this course is open to
him, and he is claiming substantial damages on the grounds
of injury to his client.'

'Well, if that isn't one for the book!' said Antony incau-
tiously. His uncle gave him a cold look. 'On what financial
grounds exactly does he base his claim?' Maitland added
hurriedly.

'Because of the loss of his wife.' He exchanged a smile
with Vera. 'And if I need to explain that to you, Antony,
Jenny isn't the girl I thought she was. On a more mundane
level there is the fact that Emily Walpole was a very successful business-woman, being a partner in Verlaine and Walpole.
I dare say you've heard of them, they're antique dealers.'

'Yes, I see the chap has got a case. You wouldn't have
thought a woman like that would be taken in though, would
you?'

'When you're as old as I am,' said Sir Nicholas, suddenly
becoming before their eyes a doddering octagenarian, 'you'll
know that there is no end to human folly. In any event, the
case that Collingwood has put together is quite ingenious.
He can bring witnesses to Emily Walpole's increasing depen-
dence on Dorothy Selden, and also to her extreme distress at
this last message. I think there can be no doubt that she was

to some degree obsessed with her son, but I dare say they won't stress that. It might seem to detract from Mrs Selden's responsibility in the matter.'

'And what sort of a defence will your Mr Horton put up?' asked Vera, getting in before Antony could. As a member of the bar before her marriage she was as fascinated as either of the two men by these legal discussions.

'The only defence possible, that no deception was involved. Nobody has ever suggested before that Dorothy Selden wasn't genuine, that's something to be thankful for, I suppose. Anyway, in addition to her husband, there's the secretary of the Society for the Investigation of Psychical Phenomena, and a woman whom I believe is an automatic writer, though I must admit I'm not very clear as to what that means.'

'Your education has been neglected, Uncle Nick. You sit down with a pencil in your hand, and something from outside takes control of you, and without knowing it you find a message written on the pad.'

'I don't like the sound of that,' said Jenny. 'Spooky,' she added, as though any explanation was needed. 'But let's get back to your medium. Do you think it will be a successful defence?'

'I think a great deal will depend on the jury. And that's where you come in, Antony.'

'I don't see how. It's a difficult thing to prove a negative,' he added slowly.

'It certainly is. On the other hand, as I said, the onus of proof is on the plaintiff.'

'That still doesn't explain how I come in to it,' said Antony.

'Horton is bringing this woman to chambers for a conference tomorrow morning,' said Sir Nicholas. 'I'd take it as a kindness if you'd sit in on the interview.'

Maitland's eyebrows went up at that. It would have been more like his uncle to command his presence. 'I can make it all right,' he said. 'Did Mallory tell you that Carling business has been settled out of court? But you can bet your boots

Geoffrey has got the whole thing at his fingertips. You don't need me.'

Sir Nicholas closed his eyes for a moment. 'I cannot imagine why you find it necessary to resort to such a vulgarism,' he said. After the temporarily mellowing effect of his marriage he was getting into his stride again. 'What I want of you is quite simple. It is merely your opinion of my client.'

'But, Uncle Nick! No really, if you can't make your mind up about her yourself – '

'She worries me,' said Sir Nicholas, suddenly coming down from his high horse.

'Why?'

'I don't believe in all this foolery. But I've met the lady, talked to her, and I'm not at all sure that she doesn't believe in what she's doing herself.'

'I see. But my opinion . . . well, it'll only be my opinion, you know.'

'Worth a good deal,' said Vera gruffly. 'Perceptive,' she added, looking around her, as though defying any of her audience to misunderstand what she meant.

'Well, of course, I'll help if I can.' Maitland was speaking directly to Vera now. 'But if Uncle Nick, with all his years of experience, can't make up his mind, I don't see what you can expect me to do.'

'It isn't a matter of doing anything,' said Jenny, 'only of saying what you think.'

'Well, if you two have made up your minds,' said Antony helplessly, 'who am I to argue? All right, Uncle Nick, what time is she coming? And is she likely to make personal remarks about my aura?'

'That I can't tell you.' Sir Nicholas, having got his own way, was relapsing into amiability again. 'Come to my room about ten o'clock and we can talk before they arrive. You may be interested in what Horton has sent me, after all it's an unusual case.'

II

'And I wish I knew,' said Antony to Jenny later, when the other two had gone, 'whether I should take him at face value, or whether this is some diabolical scheme of Uncle Nick's to involve me in the matter.'

Jenny was piling glasses and coffee cups on to a tray, and he watched her with satisfaction, the one fixed point in a world that could sometimes unexpectedly turn itself upside down. 'He can't involve you against your will,' she said. 'Anyway, I don't see that it matters, it's only a civil case.'

'Mediums,' said Antony in deep disgust. 'Spiritualists! People who do automatic writing!'

'There was that book,' said Jenny.

'*The Cambridge Experiment* . . . I know. And very impressive it was too. But if Uncle Nick can't make up his mind whether this woman is honest or not I don't see what I can do about it.'

'You know about people,' said Jenny simply.

'I wish I was as sure about that as you are, love.' He laughed suddenly. 'Well, who lives may learn,' he said. 'What Uncle Nick's intentions are, I mean. Do you think we ought to have found him a nice little wife without a thought in her head, Jenny? I don't know how you can bear the addition of another lawyer to this household.'

But Jenny only smiled at him. She was used to legal shop, had come to enjoy it. And she knew that Antony was as fond of Vera as she was. There was only one snag about their frequent get-togethers, they couldn't play any of the counter-tenor records, of which they were both particularly fond, because for some reason they set Vera's teeth on edge. Antony thought it had something to do with her being a natural contralto; Jenny had invented for herself some complicated psychological reason that he couldn't quite fathom. But it didn't really matter in the slightest, there were plenty of things that they could all enjoy, and Vera's collection of records, that she had brought with her from Chedcombe, were a definite gain.

Antony Maitland had lived in Sir Nicholas Harding's house in Kempenfeldt Square since he was thirteen years old, and in view of the housing shortage which prevailed at the time of their marriage separate quarters had been made for himself and Jenny from the two top floors. Everybody said it was a purely temporary arrangement, and it was only natural that there were times when one or the other of them found it irksome. But on the whole its convenience outweighed everything else, and over the years it had come to be regarded as permanent. When Sir Nicholas had surprised everybody (except Jenny, as she would have insisted on adding) by marrying Vera Langhorne, barrister-at-law, Antony had become doubtful of the propriety of continuing the *status quo*, though paradoxically at the same time he had for the first time realised how much he valued its benefits, including his uncle's company. But all that was in the past now, if any doubts remained to him he kept them to himself; Vera had become a part of all their traditions, and as she was the only person who had ever had any influence over Sir Nicholas's staff, had added considerably to everyone's comfort into the bargain.

The morning after Sir Nicholas's discussion of his latest case was a bright one, though still very cold. Maitland walked to chambers, and wondered as he went what his uncle really thought of this latest client of his. He had formed a mental picture of Dorothy Selden, a tall, thin woman in flowing

17

draperies, probably black. But when he tried to picture her talking with her counsel he had to admit the imagination boggled. He could only suppose that it was the bizarre aspect of the case that had attracted Sir Nicholas. For himself, he would have been inclined to dismiss the whole thing as nonsense, and had to remind himself that the woman – medium or not – was as much entitled to a defence as anybody else.

Sir Nicholas, who had taken a cab, had arrived in the Inner Temple before him, and was already ensconced behind his desk, on whose surface – carefully tidied up by old Mr Mallory before his arrival – he had already contrived to wreak havoc. He took off his glasses when his nephew arrived and favoured him with a sour look. 'You're late,' he said.

'Three minutes,' said Maitland equably. He wasn't going to start, at this time of his life, being put off by his uncle's manner; which in any case he attributed to a certain unwillingness to meet his latest client. 'You're wishing you hadn't taken the brief, aren't you?' he said, crossing the room to kick the fire into a blaze.

'Of course I'm not! Why should I be?' Sir Nicholas may have felt he was being too vehement. At any rate, uncharacteristically, he embarked on further explanation. 'I only told you about the matter because I thought you'd be interested, it's just the sort of unlikely affair you delight in.'

'I thought you wanted me to vet the good lady.' But he didn't wait for Sir Nicholas's reply to that, which would probably have been a scorching one. 'Tell me what Geoffrey thinks about her,' Antony invited. Geoffrey Horton was a solicitor, a few years younger than Maitland, who specialised mainly in criminal matters. They had been friends for many years, without prejudice – as Horton himself might have put it – to his feeling perfectly at liberty to disapprove of Maitland's actions whenever he wished.

'He thinks they'll have a job proving their case.'

'I wonder.' Maitland was thoughtful. 'Let's see, as you

18

reminded me, if she pretended to receive a message that would be enough, wouldn't it? Or if she gave the message recklessly, it wouldn't matter whether it was true or false.'

'We can hardly *subpoena* Michael Walpole,' said Sir Nicholas bitterly.

'I don't see why not. Come to think of it, that would be an excellent idea,' said Antony with intent to annoy. 'Have her going into a trance in court –'

'I doubt if the judge would allow it.'

'In any case, Uncle Nick, that wasn't what I meant and you know it. I meant, what did Geoffrey think of her as a person?'

'If you mean what does he think of our client, how should I know? We didn't discuss the matter, it was hardly germane to the issue.'

'You were sufficiently curious about her to ask me to meet her this morning.'

'You're accusing me of being illogical,' his uncle pointed out. And then, with one of his bewildering changes of mood, 'Well, I suppose I am. Damn it all, I've never met a medium before. I think it's all nonsense as I told you, but this woman . . . there's something about her, and if she really believes all this rubbish herself –'

'I seem to remember you once cautioning me against superstition, Uncle Nick.'

'I'm not saying that what she professes is genuine,' said Sir Nicholas testily, 'only that it's possible she may believe it herself. And now you've brought up the matter, do you remember the evening we talked about it?'

'About superstition?' Antony frowned over the memory, finding it elusive. Eventually, 'I wish I hadn't brought it up,' he said. 'That conversation is one I'd rather not remember, and I hoped you'd forgotten it by now.'

'If you think a little,' said Sir Nicholas caustically, 'you'll realise I'm not likely to do so. It was the only occasion, if my memory serves me, when you talked to me about your experiences in the war. I was going to say openly, but that wouldn't be altogether correct. Even then you were guarded.'

That sent Maitland to the window, where he stood looking out for a moment. 'What the devil started us on this subject?' he said at last, turning.

'A remark of your own,' Sir Nicholas pointed out.

'Well, anyway, it's nothing at all to do with spiritualism.'

'Nothing at all,' agreed his uncle. 'I'm sorry, Antony, I didn't mean to stir up your memories. I'd no idea, in fact, that they were quite so near the surface.' That was a deliberate untruth, and he refrained from adding that the subject of his nephew's sensitiveness was never very far from his own mind either. There are some scars that never heal, and Sir Nicholas had his share of them, but he sometimes wished that Antony would forget his self control and speak openly about the things that worried him.

Geoffrey Horton and his client arrived with commendable promptness at ten-thirty. Horton was a man of normally cheerful disposition, who nevertheless took his job with extreme seriousness. He was broad shouldered and of medium height, and his hair had more than a hint of red in it and more than a tendency to curl. As for Mrs Selden, Maitland took one look at her, and the creature of his imagination vanished forever. She was a little dumpling of a woman, with short, grey, curly hair and a round face adorned by very round spectacles. Her dress was sober and in good taste, a suburban matron come up to town for the day. As Horton paused to shut the door she advanced confidently into the room. 'Well, Sir Nicholas,' she said. 'Mr Horton couldn't tell me why you wanted to see me again.'

'There are a few more questions I should like you to answer, Mrs Selden,' said Sir Nicholas carefully. And then, with more precision, 'In fact I'd like you to go over the whole thing for me again. And in the meantime may I introduce my nephew, Antony Maitland? Mrs Dorothy Selden, Antony.'

'Is he a barrister too?' She was looking directly at Antony, who took it upon himself to reply.

'Yes, Mrs Selden, I am, and in my uncle's chambers.'

'It is sometimes convenient to have a second opinion,' said Sir Nicholas smoothly, 'which is why I asked him to be present. You must understand, Mrs Selden, that this is a complicated case.'

'Yes, I understand that.' Her eyes were still on Antony. She saw a tall man, as tall as his uncle but much less heavily built, with dark hair, grey eyes with laughter lines around them, and a sensitive mouth. 'Not a job you always find comes easily to you,' she said.

'On the contrary, I like my profession,' said Antony, a little taken aback.

'So you may, but there are times when you take it too seriously. You can't carry all the troubles of all the world, you know. And there are things . . . shall I say that come to haunt you, Mr Maitland? I don't think that's too strong a word.'

Coming on top of his talk with his uncle, there was something much too near the bone about this. It wasn't until later that he realised that Sir Nicholas's remarks had brought to the surface of his mind things that he usually kept buried; if this woman was a telepath, that would explain a lot.

Mrs Selden had a dreaming look in her eyes. 'A tall man, very fair,' she said. 'No, not Sir Nicholas, this man is dead. But I think he was someone you were afraid of, and not without cause.'

'Never mind that!' He tried not to snap the injunction at her, but wasn't very successful.

'Oh, but I do mind. I think that of all you here' – her eyes turned momentarily to Sir Nicholas and then to Geoffrey Horton – 'you're the one who's most likely to understand me. But I ought to warn you, don't get mixed up in my affairs, they can only bring you trouble. There is another big man involved, this one is older, nearly bald. What have you done to make him hate you, Mr Maitland?'

'I don't know what you're talking about,' said Antony, and Sir Nicholas judged it time to intervene.

'Does all this mean that you'd rather I didn't consult with my nephew?' he asked. 'There's no question of involving him directly, though I should like his opinion.'

'My warning was a personal one, Sir Nicholas. No harm can come to me through his intervention, but for him I can see difficulties ahead.'

'Antony?' said Sir Nicholas.

'I think perhaps Mrs Selden is exaggerating a little,' said Maitland, who had had time by now to recover himself. 'I should certainly like to hear what she has to tell us about this business of Mrs Walpole's suicide. After that, as you say, it will be no concern of mine.'

'Very well then, let us all sit down. Will you come here, madam, near the fire? That will be less formal than if I stay at my desk, and may make it easier for you to talk.'

'As you will,' she said composedly, and came forward to take the chair he indicated.

The three men seated themselves too, Geoffrey Horton with his inevitable bulging briefcase beside him. This habit of his always puzzled Antony, because the solicitor invariably seemed to have the facts he needed at his finger-tips, and therefore had no reason to consult the papers it presumably contained. He also had a habit of patting it from time to time, as though it was a dog that sat there, but perhaps this was merely to reassure himself of its continued presence.

But Sir Nicholas had no time to sit around while his nephew day-dreamed. 'I should like you to go back to the beginning of these – these manifestations,' he said, addressing his client. 'So far I know very little of your background.'

She looked quite lost in the big leather chair, but this didn't affect her self-possession. 'Mr Horton has impressed on me that I may not understand some of your questions, Sir Nicholas,' she said. 'I admit it's difficult to see how my earliest connection with the spirit world can affect this case.'

'Because, Mrs Selden, on the lines Mr Walpole's advisers have chosen to proceed, your credibility is very much in question.' That meant, as both Antony and Geoffrey realised, that he wanted to know how his client would stand up on the witness stand.

'I've been investigated before, you know,' she told him composedly. 'You realise, of course, that when I first practised my profession I was breaking the law.'

Sir Nicholas smiled at her. 'If it was before 1951, you were in direct contravention of the witchcraft act of 1735,' he agreed. 'Did you ever have any trouble?'

'No, never. Of course, I wasn't very well known in those days. But what I was going to explain was that since the Fraudulent Mediums Act the whole body of spiritualists has been more or less self-policing. The Society for the Investigation of Psychical Phenomena conducted a good many tests, and I'm sure their secretary, Mr Angus Fyleman –'

'Yes, Mrs Selden,' Geoffrey Horton interrupted her. 'I have Mr Fyleman's statement, and Sir Nicholas has seen it.'

'Then I really don't see –'

'Humour me, Mrs Selden,' said Sir Nicholas, with a sidelong glance at his nephew which Antony interpreted easily enough as calling for his congratulations on his patience with this difficult woman.

'Very well.' Sitting well back in her chair, her toes barely touched the ground. It occurred to Antony that they ought to have offered her a cushion for her back, but there wasn't one anywhere in chambers as far as he knew, and besides, now that she had agreed to speak it would have been a shame to interrupt her. 'Looking back,' said Mrs Selden, 'I am aware that my connection with the spirit world must have started long before I realised. Sometimes I would make a remark, quite casually, and people would demand of me, how could you possibly know that? It wasn't until I was eighteen or nineteen that I began to take an interest in spiritualism and read something about it. Even then I might never have attended a seance if a friend hadn't persuaded me. That, as far as I remember, was when I was twenty.'

'Had you had any special reason for becoming interested in spiritualism? For instance, had any of your family shown signs of psychical powers?'

'No, we were a very humdrum lot. My father was a grocer, and my mother had her hands full with a family of four, though she helped out in the shop when she was needed. I should perhaps explain that I'm fifty-four now, which means that I was born in 1918,' she added, as though they might have found the sum too difficult. 'So that first seance I attended was in 1938.'

'And were you immediately convinced by what you saw and heard?'

'It wasn't quite like that. We were sitting at my friend's home . . . her parents' home I should say, she still lived with them although she was a little older than I. There were about a dozen people present, and the room was very crowded. I hadn't an idea of what to expect, but I remember our hostess calling for silence and lowering the lights until the room was in shadow. And the next thing I knew I opened my eyes and found my friend Gloria bending over me with the rest of the party grouped behind her. I said, "Aren't we going to begin?" and Gloria said, "Thank goodness you're all right." And then she laughed, and added, "I think you could say it's all over".'

'What had happened?'

'I went into a trance myself before the official medium could do so. Apparently I had given Gloria's mother a message from her dead husband, and also a message to another member of the party whom I had never seen before, something about an uncle of hers who had just passed over. And — I'm afraid it wasn't very polite of me — I just said "That's nonsense!" '

'What happened afterwards?'

'Oh, they all started talking at once, trying to convince me. And the medium – her name was Madame Laura, she has passed on too now – came over and said to me, "My dear, you have a genuine gift, it will be the greatest waste if you don't cultivate it." I thought it was very nice of her, she might easily have been offended at what had happened.'

'Did they tell you?'

'Oh yes, of course they did. It took a bit of sorting out, because, as I say, they were all inclined to talk at once. They said the messages had been delivered by a spirit control called Angelo. I asked Madame Laura about that because I didn't quite understand it, but she said it was quite customary. A spirit friend who wanted to communicate from the other side would nearly always do so through some stronger personality, who would himself in a sense take possession of the medium.'

'And how did you feel about all this?'

'Well, you see, I didn't remember a thing about it, so naturally I was rather frightened. Also, I felt very tired. I went back home – I was book-keeping for my father then – and tried not to think any more about it. Madame Laura telephoned me several times, I understand now how she felt and why she was so kind and encouraging, but at the time I wanted to have nothing more to do with the whole business, just forget about it.'

'Yes, that's very understandable,' said Sir Nicholas, perhaps a little more vehemently than he should have done. 'But later, I gather, you changed your mind.'

'That was because of Maurice, my husband. I met him about two years after that seance, it was during the phoney-war period anyway, and he was already in uniform. We were married on his next leave, and managed a few days' honeymoon, and it was then I told him about going into trance, and what Madame Laura had said. It was odd really, because I'd never spoken about it to anybody, except of course that Gloria had sometimes brought the subject up.

But something seemed to impel me to confide in him. I thought he'd laugh at me, but that shows how wrong you can be about other people's reactions. Instead of that he was fascinated, and urged me to try again. I told him I didn't know how to set about it, but he said Madame Laura had been kind and would help me. But I still hadn't made up my mind to do anything when he went back to his regiment.'

'Something happened to make you feel differently about it?' asked Sir Nicholas.

'Yes, it did. He was home on several occasions, and each time he brought up the subject again. Then he was sent to North Africa, you remember how the fighting went there, backwards and forwards over the same ground. And one day I had a cable to say he was missing, believed killed.'

'That must have come as a shock to you. But I gather . . . this is your present husband, Maurice Selden, we're talking about, isn't it?'

'Yes, I'm coming to that. Even after the cable came I didn't make up my mind immediately, but then I thought perhaps I could find something out. If I could get messages for other people – and I still wasn't absolutely sure about that – why couldn't I get one for myself?'

'Did you go to this Madame Laura?'

'No, to tell you the truth I felt rather foolish about it. And I didn't want to try in a room full of people. So I went to my own bedroom, and took the most comfortable chair I could find, and left just the bedside lamp burning. Then I quite deliberately opened my mind to whatever might be waiting to enter it. Nothing happened at first, it's a wonder really that I didn't give up the idea altogether, but gradually a most extraordinary sense of peace came over me, and the firm conviction that Maurice was alive. That was the first time I was conscious of Angelo's presence, though no words passed between us. Anyway, I was so sure that Maurice was safe that I even told my parents, and they didn't contradict me, though my mother told me afterwards they thought I was deceiving myself. And then a week later we heard that Maurice had been found. At least, he hadn't been lost really, but he had had amnesia, and only just recovered. So that, of course, was a new beginning for me in more ways than one.'

'You mean, I think, that that was when you decided to become a professional medium.'

'That's going a little too fast. I decided there must be many other people in need of reassurance, just as I had been, and that if I could help them it was my duty to do so. So that's when I went to see Madame Laura. I should have said my father's shop was on the South Coast, and she lived in London. We had a few sittings together, and she introduced me to some groups of people who were interested. After a while I became self-confident enough to sit on my own. And it was just as I had supposed. There were many people troubled in their minds in those days, if I could help only a little I was happy to do so.'

'Yes, I can see how you must have felt. You were quite at ease with the seances now, no worries about what you were doing?'

'No worries at all. It's difficult to describe, because I think you are an unbeliever, but I seemed to be living in the spirit world as much as in this one. And Angelo was back with me.'

'Your – what did you call him? – control.'

'My control, my spirit guide, however you like to put it. He scolded me a little – this will sound strange to you too, Sir Nicholas – about not allowing him to help me before.'

'Who is Angelo?' Antony put in.

'He was a retired civil servant,' said Dorothy Selden, with perfect seriousness. Antony changed a laugh quickly into a cough, but not before his uncle had had time to glare at him. Geoffrey Horton looked preternaturally serious. 'I mean, of course,' said Mrs Selden, taking no notice of these reactions at all, 'that that was what he was before he passed over,'

'When did – er – when did he do that?'

'Early in the sixteenth century.'

'Good lord! As long ago as that? He doesn't sound like a civil servant, you know,' said Antony thoughtfully.

'England doesn't have exclusive rights to servants of the state.' For the first time Mrs Selden sounded a little stiff, as though his comment had annoyed her. 'He was an Italian, as you might have guessed. I'm sure he uses the term "civil servant" because it's one that is familiar to me.'

'Machiavelli in person,' said Antony under his breath. Again his uncle quelled him with a look.

'You were telling us about – er – the development of your powers,' Sir Nicholas prompted his client.

'There were so many people who needed help and reassurance,' repeated Dorothy Selden, turning back to him with some relief. 'I didn't advertise, of course, not then, it's Maurice who has the head for business, but I suppose word got around from one person telling another. Anyway, by the time he came home, which of course was after the war was over, I was holding regular seances.'

'Public or private?' Sir Nicholas asked.

'In our own home. There might be as many as twelve people there, or it might be a private sitting for somebody in particular distress.'

'Were you – you'll forgive me, Mrs Selden, but this is a question that must be asked – were you taking money for your services?'

'Not then,' she told him, and smiled again, this time including all three men in her confidence. 'Though I admit I was sometimes tempted. My allowance wasn't very large, and you know how difficult things were at that time. But all that changed when Maurice came home.'

'In what way?'

'He was able to go back to his own work for one thing.'

'What is his profession?'

'He's a photographer. Self-employed,' she added. 'I suppose it would have been more sensible for him to go to work for

28

somebody else, but he was anxious to build up his own business. And that, of course, took time.'

'So the idea occurred to you that you too might be gainfully employed?'

'That's right.'

'Excuse me, Mrs Selden, was that your idea or your husband's?' Antony put in.

'It's so long ago I don't really remember. But certainly Maurice looked after everything. He said I had a great gift, which should be shared with anyone who was interested in the truth, not just with the small circle of people who happened to have heard of me by word of mouth. So he advertised, but I must impress on you, Mr Maitland, that everything was done in the best of taste. When the numbers of people attending became more than we could conveniently handle we moved to a larger house, the one we are in at present, and set aside one room for what I should prefer to call consultations.'

'And did the venture prove profitable?'

'Yes, Sir Nicholas, it did. Though I must impress on you, and on your rather cynical companions, that I still gave many sittings for no other reason than to be helpful, for no gain.'

'Before the law was changed, did you have any difficulties?'

'We were, of course, discreet. But you've asked me that before, Sir Nicholas.'

'So I have. But – '

'Certainly we had no difficulties with the law. Maurice had his own studio now, but he could arrange sittings for his clients whenever it suited himself, so he has remained my . . . I suppose I should say my business manager and agent.'

'In other words, madam,' – Sir Nicholas's smile robbed the words of offence – 'your business venture, if I may call it such, was the more profitable of the two.'

'Yes, I have to admit that. It has remained so all this time.

Maurice is happy, he can pick and choose his own subjects. He really is a very clever photographer,' she added unnecessarily.

'I'm sure he is,' Sir Nicholas murmured. But again Antony had a question of his own.

'What did Mac – Angelo have to say about this new departure?'

'Almost word for word what Maurice had told me. At least it would have been if his English were better. He has difficulty in communicating in our language sometimes. But he said certainly I had a gift and a duty to the world, and it was right that this should be made known.'

'What sort of things do people ask you?' asked Maitland curiously.

She smiled again, rather as though she found a certain naivety in the question. 'You'd be surprised, Mr Maitland,' she assured him. 'There are questions on your own subject, for instance.'

'On legal matters?'

'Certainly. And on medical matters too. Then there are people who worry about business decisions they have to make, or who have marital problems. And sometimes it is religion that is worrying them.'

'I don't quite understand. Can you answer questions about all these things?'

'Only in the light of the help that is given to me by my spirit friends.'

'Do you hear the questions before you go into a trance, or are they asked afterwards?'

'Sometimes the one, sometimes the other. Sometimes I don't go into a trance at all during a sitting.'

'When that happens, can you help your clients?'

'Sometimes the vibrations come through very strongly, as they did when first we met, Mr Maitland. Sometimes it is all a blank, there is nothing for it but to call the sitting off and try again on an other occasion.'

'I see. Thank you for bearing with my curiosity, Mrs Selden, you must understand that all this is rather outside my normal experience.'

'And you're here to weigh me up.' That was a statement, not a question. Antony ignored it.

'You have spoken of talking with Angelo, Mrs Selden. Yet I understand you remember nothing that happens when you are in trance.'

'Maurice always reports to me most fully. But there are other occasions when I open my mind and Angelo communicates with me very clearly. Not in words, of course.'

'Of course,' Maitland echoed. Sir Nicholas intervened rather hastily.

'There are many aspects of the situation to be considered,' he said. 'I think now, madam, we must come to your relationship with Mrs Emily Walpole.'

Mrs Selden closed her eyes for a moment. 'You will understand,' she said carefully, 'that in view of what has happened this is a very painful subject.'

'I understand that, madam, but nevertheless it is essential for us to go into it. I can't go into court without hearing your side of the story, can I?'

'But I have no story! I was in trance when the message from Michael came through. I have no knowledge of it myself.'

'From the beginning, Mrs Selden,' Sir Nicholas urged.

'Very well. Mrs Walpole first came to my house to a group sitting on Monday, 10th of January. I went into trance on that occasion, so again my evidence can be of no use to you.'

'Just tell me what you know and what you have been told, Mrs Selden. Leave it to us to worry about the evidential value.'

'Maurice told me there were messages for several of our regular sitters. He also said that Angelo seemed to wish to continue, and suggested there was another message to come, but I came out of trance too soon.'

'What happened then?'

'The party began to break up, but when she arrived I had had a strong sense of Mrs Walpole's distress, and when I saw her hesitating in the doorway I went across to speak to her. When everyone else had gone she broke down and told me her son had been killed a little over a week ago. She admitted that she had never been interested in spiritualism before, but now she was desperate to get in touch with him.'

'How did it happen that she had come to you?'

'She said she had heard my name spoken of among her friends, long before she ever considered consulting me. I asked her, of course, who had spoken of me, but she couldn't remember, only that what they said was favourable. She seemed very vague, it might not even have been a close friend, perhaps an acquaintance she met at a party. As I said, at the time she wasn't interested.'

'But now things were changed?'

'Yes, of course. She spoke quite simply. She wanted to talk to Michael, to assure herself that he hadn't left her altogether. I did my best to tell her that he was somewhere in the spirit world, but that people from the other side sometimes found difficulty in communicating. But she pleaded with me to try.'

'Had she heard what Angelo had said?' Antony put in.

'Yes, she told me about that, just as Maurice did a little later on. She said she was sure the message was for her, Michael would never leave her without a word.'

'Did she give you any details of his accident?'

'No, she didn't. I think it upset her just to talk about it. But she said Michael loved her and would want to be in touch . . . that's how she put it, as though it was just a matter of catching the late post. So I promised to arrange for some private sittings.'

'How many times did you see her in all?'

'Five more times, including the last time. That was every Monday evening until the 14th of February.'

'Your recollection seems to be remarkably accurate.'

'Oh, that's Maurice. He keeps a full record, of course. I should stress, Sir Nicholas, that Mrs Walpole would have come more often if I had let her. In fact I think she would have liked to have talked to her son every day.'

'But you didn't think that advisable?'

'I have other commitments. Besides, she told me that her husband was very much against her coming to me, I didn't want to stir up trouble.'

'That was thoughtful of you. What do you remember about the intermediate sessions?'

'For the most part, I don't remember anything. We would talk a little when she first arrived, but each time the vibrations were extremely strong, and I went into trance more quickly than I usually do. Maurice tells me that on the first private visit there was no very clear message, but Angelo seemed to be trying to put us in touch with someone, and to be having difficulty about it.'

'And the final sitting?'

'Again, I can tell you nothing about what went on while I was in trance.'

'Does your husband confirm what Mr Walpole alleges?'

'Yes, he does.'

'And how do *you* explain it.'

'I think – no, I know – that it was a message from her son who had passed over, who was himself genuinely in great distress. There must have been some extraordinary bond between them. Non-believers may say it was a cruel thing, but I feel it came from his heart.'

'Do you agree with the action that Mr Walpole is taking?' That was Maitland again, and again her answer came rather sharply.

'Of course I don't! The basis of his case is that I'm a fraud. But they can't find against me unless they can prove that, can they?'

'I think not,' said Sir Nicholas cautiously. 'But you must understand that the jury, being less well instructed in these matters than you are, may feel that Mr Walpole has a genuine claim against you. It will be my task to explain to them the legal position. But let me put my question in another way. Do you agree that the message you gave Mrs Walpole was the cause of her suicide?'

'I must agree to that, mustn't I?' For the first time her composure seemed a little shaken. 'But the message was from her son, now in spirit, and I'm sure he must have considered carefully before he said what he did.'

'You mean he wanted her to kill herself?'

'To join him on the other side,' she corrected him.

'You approve of what she did then?'

'I have faith in our spirit friends. I believe very strongly that they have our best interests at heart.'

Sir Nicholas intercepted an eloquent look from his nephew. 'On that last occasion,' he said, 'did you come out of your trance before Mrs Walpole left the house?'

'Yes, I did.'

'What was your impression of her state of mind?'

'She was sipping a glass of water when I came to myself. I suppose Maurice had fetched it for her. She got up almost immediately and came across the room and took my hands and thanked me for all the help I had given her. I suppose you could say she seemed a little distraught, but there was nothing strange about that. It was only after she left, which was almost immediately, that Maurice told me what had been said.'

Sir Nicholas glanced from Maitland to Geoffrey Horton. 'Have either of you anything else to ask Mrs Selden?' he enquired.

Antony shook his head in silence; the solicitor muttered, 'Nothing more,' and came to his feet. 'If you can spare me a few more minutes, Sir Nicholas,' he added formally, 'I'll find a cab for Mrs Selden and then come back.'

'Yes, I think that will be best. I'm quite at your disposal,' said Sir Nicholas amiably, but turned on his nephew the moment the door was closed behind the other two. 'Well?' he demanded.

'I liked her.'

'Oh, for heaven's sake. Antony, that wasn't what I asked you.'

'You're rushing things rather, aren't you, Uncle Nick?'

'If I know you, you made up your mind within five minutes of her coming into the room. She had some pointed remarks to make to you, for instance.'

'As for that, I should say there's no doubt she's a telepath. I believe that goes without saying, with people in her line of business, whether they are genuine about the rest of it or not. But there was nothing she couldn't have taken out of my mind, if you remember what we'd been talking about, Uncle Nick. Things that ought to be buried quite securely in the past,' he added, in case his uncle had any idea of raising the subject again.

'And how do you interpret her reference to the big, balding man?'

'Briggs,' said Antony promptly.

'Were you thinking about him?'

'I never do if I can help it,' Maitland admitted.

'Then how do you explain – ?'

'I don't. But I still maintain that, on the evidence, all we can say is that she most probably has telepathic powers.'

Horton came back into the room just then. 'Willett took her over,' he said, and smiled at Antony. 'I think he didn't want Mr Maitland to be kept waiting.'

'That's a sign of grace anyway.' That was Maitland, perfectly well aware that his uncle's opinion probably didn't coincide with his. 'What about it, Geoffrey,' he went on, 'you've seen more of the lady than either of us. What do *you* think of her?'

'According to my instructions, she's a genuine medium,

and therefore no charge of fraud can be substantiated.'

'I asked for your opinion,' said Antony. 'Don't be so bloody cautious.'

'Well then,' said Geoffrey, and the look he gave Sir Nicholas was a trifle apologetic, 'I think the whole thing is nonsense. It didn't come out while we were talking, but do you know she professes to believe in reincarnation too? I nearly asked her, if that were the case, what this Angelo of hers was doing still hanging about on the other side.'

'Angelo has obviously found himself a good job and is sticking to it,' said Sir Nicholas gravely. 'We have just decided that a certain amount of extrasensory perception must be part of her makeup. I agree with you that the rest is nonsense, but I'm not at all sure she hasn't persuaded herself that it's true.'

'And what do you think, Antony?' Horton wanted to know.

'I've been trying to persuade him to tell me,' said Sir Nicholas, a little tartly. 'He seems strangely reluctant to do so.'

'No, it isn't that. It's only . . . well, she may or may not be genuine, I haven't made up my mind. But I do believe in the possibility that there is something in this spiritualism business, and if there is, it's dangerous.'

'She had a warning for you,' said Geoffrey, eyeing him curiously. But Sir Nicholas was following his own train of thought.

'You reminded me today that I once warned you against superstition, Antony,' he said.

'Yes, well, we won't go into that again,' said Maitland hastily. 'You asked for my opinion, and I've given it to you to the best of my ability. I'll tell you one thing, though, I'd like to meet this chap Maurice. I've got a few ideas in my head about him.'

'I was about to suggest that perhaps you would like to do so,' said Sir Nicholas cordially.

'Are you sure that wasn't what you intended all along, Uncle Nick?'

'Nothing was further from my mind. But I can see that your curiosity is aroused, and I should hate to be responsible for any frustration you might suffer,' said Sir Nicholas gently. 'Can you arrange for such a meeting, Geoffrey?'

'Nothing easier, as long as I'm included in the party,' said Horton firmly.

'I wouldn't suggest anything else.' That was said blandly, and Antony and Geoffrey exchanged a look. They could both remember occasions when Sir Nicholas, for his own ends, had suffered, and even encouraged, his nephew's unorthodox ways. 'Now, Geoffrey, perhaps you can tell us, what witnesses is Mr Walpole calling?'

At this point, if he had been briefing Maitland, Horton would certainly have said, 'It's all in your brief.' As it was, he embarked on his recital without protest. 'Medical evidence concerning his wife's death, police evidence about the same thing. The coroner's officer, concerning the result of the inquest. His own evidence will deal with Michael's accident, its effects on the boy's mother, Walpole's own disapproval of her action in consulting Mrs Selden, and what she told him of the message she had received at that last sitting. Also, I suppose, he'll tell the court something about the last few days of her life. In corroboration he's calling two witnesses, Mrs Walpole's old nurse, who lives with them and runs the household, and in whom Mrs Walpole apparently was in the habit of confiding, and the chauffeur who took her to and from the Seldens for the last seance. She didn't tell him what had transpired, of course, but he observed her demeanour when she left the house.'

'I should say,' said Antony, 'that that would do nicely. Unless the jury is composed entirely of spiritualists – '

'That's not quite all,' Geoffrey interrupted him. 'He's got hold of a couple of Mrs Selden's clients who for some reason or other were feeling dissatisfied with the results they got through her. However, I think we can counter that all right. I've got a couple of people who swear by her. One lot should cancel the other out.'

Sir Nicholas had been making notes. Now he lay down his pencil, took off his spectacles, and asked with interest, 'What else have we got?'

'Our client, who, as Antony pointed out, would probably not convince anybody but a confirmed believer. Her husband – '

'Who won't be able to deny that there were cash transactions,' Sir Nicholas pointed out.

'No, but we need him to try to put a good face on what was said at that last sitting. There's also a man called Fyleman, who is the secretary of the Society for the Investigation of Psychical Phenomena. He's an old friend of the Seldens, and is convinced that her powers are genuine. There is also a Miss Newbolt, whom he calls an automatic writer. I haven't seen her yet and I'm not quite sure what it is she does, but Fyleman seems to think her belief in Dorothy Selden would make a good impression on the jury.'

'And that's all?'

'That's all.'

'Then those are two more people you might care to talk to, Antony. Not that I'm not more in sympathy with *your* position on this, Geoffrey,' Sir Nicholas added, 'but another opinion can't do any harm.'

'I shall be glad of it too,' said Horton, 'as long as you don't feel too put off by the gypsy's warning, Antony.'

Antony smiled. 'I'll risk it,' he said. 'You haven't told us what damages he's asking, by the way.'

'That's why I think he's being rather clever,' said Geoffrey. 'If he made too big a claim it might alienate the jury's sympathies, and as one of you pointed out he's going to need those, in the absence of any definite proof of fraud. So what he's asking is fifty thousand pounds, and basing it on the unsentimental reason of loss of his wife's earning power. I get the impression he's not really interested in the money at all, but wants very badly to get back at Mrs Selden.'

'That seems likely,' said Maitland consideringly. 'You're going to have to tell us a little more about the Walpoles, though. Uncle Nick tells me that Daniel Walpole is the chairman of the Board of Bramley's Bank.'

'Yes that's right.'

'Yet his wife also worked?'

'Not from necessity, I suppose, though I dare say her efforts were profitable. She was in the antique business, Verlaine and Walpole.'

'Yes, Uncle Nick told me.'

'I understand that her speciality was paintings, that she was regarded as an expert.'

'That sounds as though she was an active partner?'

'Quite active, I understand. Of course, I don't know anything about the kind of money they've been making, all that artistic stuff is a closed book to me. Naturally I'm having the matter looked into, but I don't see how Walpole's claim can fail to be regarded as reasonable.'

'Unless they were actually losing money,' Antony suggested.

'Oh well, in that case . . . we shall just have to see.' He got up again, and Maitland followed his example. Sir Nicholas was fidgeting with his spectacles, which his nephew took to be a sign that for the moment he had tired of Dorothy Selden and her affairs. 'Have I got it right?' Geoffrey asked. 'You want Antony to see Maurice Selden, Angus Fyleman, and Miss Rose Newbolt. Would tomorrow be convenient for you?' he added, turning to the younger of his two companions.

'I can make it convenient,' said Maitland, suppressing in the interests of peace any dislike he may have felt for the proposal. 'I'll come down with you,' he added, and heaved a long sigh as his uncle's door closed behind him. 'And that, my dear Geoffrey, will be the end of the affair as far as I'm concerned,' he said positively.

'Nervous?' asked Geoffrey, grinning.

'If you mean, does Mrs Selden's warning worry me, no it doesn't. This is a civil action, what could Chief Superintendent Briggs have to do with it?'

'You think it was he she was referring to?' Horton sounded surprised.

'I do. Of course you weren't in the room when I was talking to Uncle Nick about it, I'd forgotten that. It was the description that made me think of him, after she spoke. He wasn't in my mind at the time, so *that* couldn't be taken as a proof of telepathy.'

'But perhaps of clairvoyance.' Geoffrey gave him a rather odd look, perhaps he was struggling with a desire to refer to the other part of the warning. However, he obviously thought better of it if that had been his intention. 'All right, all right, we'll say no more about it,' he said, almost as testily as Sir Nicholas might have done. 'I'll do what I can about arrangements, and ring you later in the day.'

I

Geoffrey Horton was as good as his word, and ten o'clock the following morning found them both on the doorstep of the Seldens' house in Hampstead. A large, handsome house, as Dorothy Selden had implied, plenty of space for the seance room she had mentioned, an office for her husband perhaps, and still more than enough accommodation for the two of them.

Maurice Selden himself let them in, a tallish rather handsome man who for some reason reminded Antony of an ostrich. Selden had, of course, met the solicitor before. Geoffrey introduced his companion as one of Sir Nicholas's associates, and the other man gave Antony a hard look but made no immediate comment. 'We'll go into the library,' he said and led the way to a room at the back of the house.

It was a comfortable room, with deep leather chairs, a rather over-ornate fireplace, dark panelling, and bookshelves – also of dark wood – that were nowhere near full. Maitland caught a glimpse of some handbooks on psychical research, but had no time to explore further. Selden said, 'Please sit down, gentlemen,' and somehow the mode of address didn't sound natural. It was as though he had adopted it for the occasion. Antony committed himself to one of the armchairs with the distinct feeling that he might never emerge alive from its embrace again. 'I gather you don't want to see my wife this morning, Mr Horton,' Maurice Selden went on.

'No, Mrs Selden was kind enough to come with me yesterday to Sir Nicholas Harding's chambers. For the present I've nothing more to ask her, but you must realise that there are things of which she professes to be unable to speak of her own knowledge. I'm referring to the times when she is in trance.'

'Mr Maitland is Sir Nicholas's nephew as well as his associate,' said Selden. 'Dorothy told me that she had met you, Mr Maitland. There were things about your aura that troubled her. She also said that she thought you were in considerable pain.'

'Heaven and earth! Let's leave my aura out of it,' Antony suggested. But truth to tell, it was the reference to his injured shoulder that troubled him. It was something that occasionally he could forget for an hour together, when his interest was caught; but which otherwise he was conscious of as an incessant dull ache in the background of his thoughts. And when he was tired ...

'Does it offend you?' Selden enquired interestedly. 'Dorothy felt you would make a good subject, in fact that you might have some powers yourself if you cared to develop them.'

'That's the last thing I want to do, and I'm not interested in raising any spirits either,' Antony assured him. But he had got a grip on himself again, and his tone was easy. 'You'll be one of my uncle's chief witnesses, you know, so it's natural that Mr Horton has some questions for you.'

'I suppose so.' He turned to Geoffrey. 'What do you want to know?'

'First of all, I should like to know about your wife's relationship with Mrs Walpole, from your point of view.'

'That's easily told. Mrs Walpole came here as any other sitter might have done, for one of the group sessions.'

'How was that arranged?'

'She phoned on the Monday morning, that was January the tenth. I've got all the dates at my finger-tips, because I've been looking them up for my wife. Mrs Walpole said she'd heard of Dorothy Selden and would like to see her at the first available opportunity. I suggested the sitting that afternoon, we don't usually encourage people to come privately until they have been here as part of a group.'

'Why is that?' asked Antony.

'I don't know about other sensitives, but Dorothy finds she has to have a certain rapport with her subjects, before any results can be achieved. A private sitting is more expensive, naturally, so it seems only fair to make sure that it will be worth the sitter's while.'

'I see. So it was arranged that she should come?'

'She agreed, a little reluctantly.'

'What did she tell you about herself?'

'Why, nothing.'

'Neither then nor when she came to the house?' Antony insisted.

Maurice Selden leant back in his chair with a deliberate assumption of ease. 'I wonder what you're thinking, Mr Maitland,' he said.

'It is a very simple question, surely.'

'Yes, but why did you ask it?'

'Curiosity, nothing more.'

'Well, the answer is simple too, she told me nothing about herself either then or later. Except, if I must go into details, that she was very anxious to see my wife.'

'What did you suppose that to mean?'

'Most of our sitters are anxious.'

'And most of them have lost someone dear to them,' said Antony, to whom it was natural as breathing to take on colour from his companions' modes of speech.

'Yes, I must admit that's what I thought had happened. She sounded distressed, and her distress was very obvious when she arrived here.'

'But there was no message for her that day?'

'No, though several communications were received from the other side.'

43

'Did Mrs Walpole seem disappointed? I understand Mrs Selden came out of her trance more quickly than usual.'

'Yes, she did.'

'But still Mrs Walpole seemed to think she had some cause to hope,' Antony insisted.

'It seemed that there should have been another message. You must understand, Mr Maitland, that it isn't always easy for a spirit that has newly passed over to communicate with us. My wife's control – '

'Ah, yes, Machiavelli.'

'I beg your pardon?'

'A slip of the tongue. Angelo. Did he say there was some-one else trying to get through? That makes it sound more like a telephone conversation than anything,' he added, with an amused look.

'But don't you see, that's exactly what it is? Something completely natural.'

'Come now, Mr Selden. Supernormal, surely?'

'That is a technical term, but the other describes it very simply, and is perhaps more easily understandable to a non-believer.'

'Where do you stand in this?'

Selden got up and kicked the fire. 'When I first met my wife I was as sceptical as you are,' he said. 'But so many things happened that couldn't be explained away, finally I had no choice but to believe in her powers.'

'You were telling me about the group seance on January the 10th,' said Maitland. He seemed to have forgotten that he had said it was Geoffrey Horton who had the questions to ask. 'Mrs Selden's control indicated that there was some-one else trying to get through – there's that phrase again! – and Mrs Walpole was encouraged to think it might be her son, Michael.'

'Encouraged? Not by me.'

'Encouraged by circumstances,' said Maitland smoothly. 'Is that how it was?'

'I think I should rather put it that it was by her own needs, her desires. She insisted on waiting to talk to my wife, and I think, well I'm sure, that Dorothy felt she could help her. She said she would see her the following week if she came in the evening, alone.'

'Mrs Selden indicated that Mrs Walpole would have liked to have come more often.'

'Yes, that's a state of mind we often encounter.'

'So by now you were sure, at least, that she had lost someone dear to her?'

'Mr Maitland, what are you insinuating?'

Antony merely smiled at that, and made a gesture in Geoffrey's direction. Horton said hastily, 'Mr Maitland is only thinking that we must anticipate the most awkward questions that Mr Walpole's counsel can ask in court.'

'So it would be a good idea if you answered my question,' said Maitland into the silence that followed Geoffrey's explanation.

'Yes, I see.' He didn't sound too confident about that. 'The answer is of course that I did think that was what must have happened, but as for being sure . . . it wasn't until Dorothy and I were discussing Mr Walpole's action that I learned exactly what had been said on that first day.'

'Tell us about the rest of the seances then. Mrs Walpole came every week, didn't she?'

'Every Monday until the 14th of February.'

'And spoke with her son?'

'With somebody called Michael. I know now that it was her son, but at the time I was rather of the opinion that it was her husband who had died. In fact, now that I realise it wasn't, I must say there was something odd . . . well, something unhealthy, about the messages.'

Antony stored that away for future consideration. 'What happens on these occasions? That's something I am completely in the dark about,' he said.

'It varies. There are times when Dorothy doesn't go into

trance at all, the sitter will ask questions, and if the vibrations are right she may be able to give the answers. But when she is in trance, the most familiar voice is Angelo's, of course. In a sense I've known him for years. But with the others of our spirit friends, once he has helped them to communicate with their loved ones on this side, the voice I hear is at first strange to me. Sometimes we've never identified the sender of the message, but mostly the sitter or sitters are able to do so.'

'Mrs Selden doesn't speak in her own voice then?'

'Certainly not!' He sounded offended by the suggestion.

'And Mrs Walpole seemed satisfied that the voice she heard was Michael's?'

'Oh yes, she was quite certain of that. And I can assure you it was the same voice on each occasion that Dorothy sat with her.'

'Tell me about the messages.'

'That's too big a word for them, until the last day. Expressions of love, of reassurance that he was near her, that kind of thing.'

'And on the last day that Mrs Selden came here?'

'There was only a word from Angelo. It seemed as though . . . as though some stronger personality pushed him to one side before he could say anything to us. Then there was Michael's voice, quite clear and recognisable.'

'I should like you to repeat to me, as nearly as possible, what he said.'

Maurice Selden hesitated. 'You'll be asked that in court,' Horton told him.

'Yes, but . . . it's what Daniel Walpole is basing his claim for damages on, isn't it? Do I have to answer?'

'Mrs Walpole told her husband what was said, and also her old nurse,' Geoffrey explained patiently, 'If you refuse to answer in court you'll be laying yourself open to a charge of contempt, and if you answer untruly you'll be committing perjury. So I think on the whole your best bet is the truth.'

Selden thought about that for a moment. 'Well, I do

remember,' he admitted. 'It was upsetting in a way. Michael said he was in a dark, haunted place and couldn't find his way out. There were shadows of other people all around him and sometimes they went on with a guide and left him alone again. There was a place of light beyond that he was longing to reach, but unless his mother joined him and they could go on together he had no hope of doing so.'

'At that stage, then, you knew it was Mrs Walpole's son who was purported to be communicating?'

'No, I said that because I know now who Michael was. His words were: Unless you join me.'

'And what was their effect on Mrs Walpole?'

'I thought she was going to faint, so I fetched a glass of water. Dorothy came to herself unusually quickly, while Mrs Walpole was still drinking as far as I remember, but, of course, she knew nothing of what had happened.'

'Did anything more pass between them?'

'Mrs Walpole thanked her before she left.'

'As though she was saying goodbye?'

'That never occurred to me. In fact, I think she mentioned a sitting the following week.'

'Did you think she would act on Michael's suggestion?'

'No, of course I didn't.'

'What did you think of the message?'

'It distressed me of course.'

'But you didn't think there was anything you should do about it?'

'If I'd known more about her, if I'd known her husband was alive, for instance, I might have been tempted to tell him.'

'Mrs Selden knew, she mentioned to us that Mr Walpole disapproved of his wife consulting her.'

'Yes, but as I explained to you I only knew that later. And we really can't take responsibility for messages from the spirit world, you know.'

'I suppose not.' Maitland sounded doubtful, then he smiled

47

and turned to his friend. 'I seem to have been monopolising the witness, Geoffrey,' he apologised. 'What about your questions?'

'They're simplicity itself compared with yours,' Horton assured him. 'But important, Mr Selden, in fact the crux of the whole matter. I understand that, in addition to your own profession as a photographer, you act as Mrs Selden's business manager, agent, whatever you like to call it.'

'Yes, I do. It seems a natural arrangement. Dorothy is so very unworldly.'

'And it was at your suggestion that she originally took to using her powers professionally?'

'You're getting round to the subject of money,' said Selden, with a rather rueful look. 'She was quite determined to go on with her work, felt it was her duty, but if you knew what these sittings took out of her, it was only fair that she should be recompensed.'

'That isn't quite the point. You felt confident enough of the success of the venture to buy this house. That was not so long after you came out of the army, I think. Did you mind taking on a heavy mortgage?'

'No, I was confident that between us we could make a go of things. As for the mortgage, it was paid off five or six years ago.'

'I realise all this may seem impertinent to you,' said Geoffrey doggedly, 'but the question of whether money passed between Mrs Walpole and Mrs Selden is a material one.'

'She paid me, actually, each time she came.'

'She paid you, in your capacity as your wife's agent?'

'That's perfectly correct. But because she paid for Dorothy's time it doesn't mean that the messages were a fake, you know.'

'The question of remuneration is one that Mr Walpole's counsel is bound to bring up. Can you produce your books, to show what money changed hands, and when?'

'Oh yes, no difficulty about that. This is a business like any other, I conduct it in a business-like way.'

'Thank you, then, I think that's all for the moment.' Antony was already on his feet, and Geoffrey followed his example more slowly. 'I'll be in touch with you or with Mrs Selden in a few days,' Horton added.

'You might tell me, how does the case stand? Are you hopeful about it?'

'Legally, the onus of proof is with the prosecution,' said Geoffrey evasively.

'They can't prove Dorothy is a fraud, because she isn't.'

'Well, that's something to be thankful for. Give me a chance to get a little more familiar with the situation, Mr Selden, and then I may be able to be more helpful. And I was doubtful whether we could get out of there with a whole skin, Antony,' he added severely when they were out in the street again, their farewells said. 'Selden didn't like your questions, not one little bit.'

'He wasn't meant to,' said Antony vaguely, and began to move down the road to where Geoffrey's car was waiting.

'Well, did his answers help you to reach a decision?'

'Not about your client. I'm still in two minds about her. But I'd say her husband is as crooked a customer as you'd meet on a day's march. Getting the truth out of him about anything was exactly like pulling teeth.'

'Let's get this straight. You think she may be genuine and he may be a fraud?'

'I think he may be manipulating the situation to his own advantage,' said Antony precisely. 'One thing I didn't like was the fact that each private sitter has had to attend a group session first. That could well be to give the Seldens a chance to sum him or her up.'

'It certainly could. You're coming round to my idea about Mrs Selden,' said Geoffrey.

'Don't go so fast! I told you I think she uses ESP, telepathy, whatever you like to call it. If her husband does a

49

little detective work on their prospective sitters, she might then read his mind and quite unconsciously give the sort of messages the sitter wanted to hear.'

'That's getting a bit complicated. But there is one other thing, Antony – '

'Yes, I know. Mrs Selden certainly knew that Mrs Walpole's husband was alive, but I think that's only another example of Maurice's twisting the story to suit his own ends.'

'Perhaps you're right. I don't see how any of it helps us in any case,' said Geoffrey, rather forlornly.

'That's something we shall have to leave to Uncle Nick. I'm sorry for him really, having to deal with this chap Selden in court, I mean. He might as well try to cross-examine a corkscrew.'

Geoffrey was unlocking the car. 'Angus Fyleman said he would see us at two o'clock,' he remarked.

'Then for heaven's sake let's get back to town and have some lunch,' Antony suggested. 'If we have to spend the afternoon in the spirit world, and then deal with this automatic writer female, we'd better have some sustenance first.'

II

Angus Fyleman, whom they found in the offices of the Society for the Investigation of Psychical Phenomena – two shabby rooms at the top of an equally shabby building – was a little man with an egg-shaped head and an Adolf Hitler moustache. Any unpleasant memories this may have evoked, however, were offset by his manner . . . kindly, polite, even a little fluttery, as though his dealings with the law had been few and far between, and the sudden incursion of two members of the profession – one from the senior, and one from the junior branch – had completely put him off his stroke. 'You must understand I don't like this business, I don't like it at all,' he said fussily. 'Gives the profession a bad name.'

'But if you can help Mrs Selden to prove that her gift is genuine,' said Geoffrey, seating himself on one of the hard, wooden chairs near the desk, 'surely that would be all to the good.'

'Indeed it would, and there's no question about it, no question at all. But going into court,' – this was obviously the main point of his complaint – 'that's quite another matter.'

'I dare say you'll find it more simple than you imagine,' said Geoffrey soothingly. 'But it's partly because some people find it an ordeal that we want to ask you some questions now, to prepare the way so to speak. Mr Maitland is an associate of Sir Nicholas Harding, who will be representing Mrs Selden.'

'This profession of yours, Mr Fyleman,' said Antony, who was still standing behind the chair that seemed to have been allotted to him, 'how would you describe it?'

'For myself, I'm an investigator. But there are so many different kinds of gift.'

'Perhaps you could tell us a little about some of them. We are both very ignorant, I'm afraid.'

For some reason, the question seemed to put Angus Fyleman more at his ease. He sat back in his chair and put the tips of his fingers together (like a lawyer in a Victorian novel, Antony thought) and prepared to enlighten them. 'The dictionary defines a medium as a person by whom supernormal phenomena are produced, whether the supposed cause is spiritistic or not. But the word is very often used in a more restricted sense, to include only those who produce physical phenomena, or give trance communications. So many things are involved . . . telepathy, clairvoyance, trance utterance, automatic writing, premonition, xenoglossy, psychometry, and cryptaesthesia.'

'Wait a bit!' Maitland held up a hand. 'Psychometry I know, but – what did you say? – xenoglossy and cryptaes- thesia, are new to me.' Geoffrey said nothing, but gave his friend a look as though deploring the depths into which his questions were leading them.

'Xenoglossy,' said Mr Fyleman, 'is the gift of making communications in a language unknown to the medium.'

'And the other?'

'Cryptaesthesia. That refers to any supernormal knowledge, whether obtained by telepathy or clairvoyance.'

'I see.' Maitland sounded doubtful. 'And under which of these headings do Mrs Selden's powers fall?'

'She is certainly clairvoyant, which means that her clients can question her directly on any subject they wish, even when she isn't in trance, and it is very likely that she will be able to help them. But I should class her mainly as a trance medium. Her connection with our spirit friends is very strong.'

'But at her seances there are no physical manifestations?'

'No, only communications by word of mouth.'

'Communications from the dead?'

'From those who have passed on,' Fyleman corrected him. 'Mrs Selden is a very modest person, you know, and she has often told me how much she regrets that she cannot help her sitters any further, by letting them see their loved ones as well as hear them. But I understand there has never been any manifestation like that.'

'You didn't mention telepathy as being among her gifts.'

'No, and I know what you're thinking.' He was worried again. 'You're thinking a genuine telepath could easily deceive her sitters. Well I have seen evidence in other people of an ability in this direction, but I assure you that the messages that were given at the seances of hers I attended were far too detailed to have been obtained in that way.'

'That brings up another question. How long have you known Mrs Selden?'

'For about ten years, roughly.'

'Since you became secretary of the Society perhaps?'

'No, I've held this position for nearly fifteen years. The

occasion of my getting in touch with Dorothy was her appearance on a television programme. What I had seen seemed interesting, and I telephoned her to ask if she would mind my sitting in on one or more of her seances.'

'Did she understand that you were investigating her?'

'That fact wasn't mentioned specifically, of course, but I'm sure she understood. Any medium would have done. As a matter of fact it was her husband I dealt with in the beginning, he came up to town to see me before he agreed to my request, but I think I was able to show him that it would be in her own interests.'

'There's something that has been puzzling me. Have you any connection with the Society for Psychical Research?'

Angus Fyleman glanced round the office and smiled. 'No, indeed,' he said. 'They are a rather more prestigious institution. Though I understand our aims are the same.'

'How would you define those aims?'

'Speaking for myself only, they are purely investigative.'

'But if you came to believe a certain medium was fraudulent — '

'I don't think you quite understand, Mr Maitland. Genuine phenomena are recorded and compared. If they were fraudulent they would be of no interest to us.'

'Do you know whether Mrs Selden had any contact with the Psychical Research people?'

'Yes, she told me so one day. They got in touch with her at about the same time I did, I suppose inspired by the same programme on television.'

'Did she, in fact, admit them to one of her sittings?'

As Maitland spoke Geoffrey Horton stirred uneasily; he had gone over all this ground before, and knew the answer already.

'No, not to my knowledge,' said Fyleman.

'Why was that, do you think?'

'Dorothy didn't say, except that Maurice wouldn't hear of it. I got the impression, though I may be wrong about this, that he had met with the Society's representative and taken a dislike to him.'

'But you attended . . . how many of her seances?'

'I've been looking at my records, four in all. Though, of course, since then I've come to know both Dorothy and Maurice very much better. She is very sympathetic person, and it's refreshing to be able to talk over one's work with someone who understands.'

'About these four seances now – '

'The first three were group sittings. The first time I went out to Hampstead Dorothy was very nervous, she didn't go into trance, but allowed her clients to question her. The results were staggering. There was one woman, I remember, who had a health problem. Dorothy knows nothing of medical matters, but she diagnosed the complaint correctly, told the lady what remedies had been prescribed for her, and advised that they be changed.'

'You'll forgive me,' said Maitland, 'but do you know anything about this woman's later history? Whether she followed the advice she was given, for instance, and what the result was?'

'Naturally, that didn't come within my sphere.'

'You would take this as evidence of clairvoyance?'

'Indeed I should. It was not the only example. As I told Mr Horton, I can produce the notes I made at the time.'

'The woman with the medical problem will do to be going on with. What happened at the next sitting you attended?'

'Dorothy went into trance. On that first occasion her control, Angelo, spoke directly to me, saying he could understand and sympathise with my doubts, but that I need have no fear at all of trusting her honesty.'

'Did you have any particular questions for her?'

'No, I was content to listen. And, as on the previous occasion, I was very much impressed by what I heard. You will understand, Mr Horton,' he added, turning to Geoffrey, 'that I cannot name names, even in court. Such things are completely confidential. But I can attest to the different voices I heard, to the fact that each one was identified by one of the sitters, and that there were numerous instances of facts being disclosed that could not possibly have been within Dorothy's knowledge.'

'Will you let me have your notes to go over at leisure?' Geoffrey asked.

'If you will allow me to make certain excisions first,' Fyleman told him. 'Nothing material, just the names of the people concerned.'

'Thank you. I'm sure the court will respect your scruples. That will be very helpful, and then we can discuss your evidence again.'

'Meanwhile,' said Antony, 'there remains the fourth sitting. Did I understand you to say it was a private one?'

'Yes, it was. Of course we had the sitter's permission, but I think he was flattered by being part of what he called an experiment.'

'The sitter on that occasion was a man, then?'

'Yes.' He ruminated for a moment. 'This is very difficult,' he said at last. 'If I tell you his name –'

'He might be willing to permit us to use it, and, of course, his own evidence would be helpful,' said Geoffrey.

'That's out of the question, I'm afraid. He died two years ago.'

'But in his day he was a well known figure?' said Antony, guessing. 'In that case, and as all this took place ten years ago, surely there can be no objection to your telling us at least what was said?'

'I suppose not.' He still spoke doubtfully. 'The thing was, you see, his wife had died only six months before. He was already thinking of marrying again and he felt guilty about it.'

'So it was his deceased wife he wanted to get in touch with.'

'It was. I thought at first we were going to be unsuccessful, the spirits were restless, and though Angelo obviously knew with whom we wanted to communicate, he had difficulty in achieving contact.'

'Just a moment. Did you know all this about the sitter at the beginning of the seance?'

'Of course I didn't. Nor did Dorothy, it was the first time he had been there alone.'

'But he had been there before to a group sitting?'

'That was Dorothy's normal policy. She didn't want to take people's money, unless she felt there was some prospect of helping them. So all we knew then was that there was someone he wanted to get in touch with, and when I had just about given up hope of anything happening, she spoke.'

'A woman's voice?'

'Not Dorothy's, if that's what you mean. The sitter recognised it instantly and said, "Margaret is that you?" Something like that. I'm not quoting verbatim, but I have my notes, as I said.'

'And what did the spirit say?'

'Without any prompting at all, she said, "Yes my dear. and I know why you want to talk to me. About Ann".'

'You're sure that name was mentioned by Mrs Selden in trance, not by the sitter?'

'Of course I'm sure. This kind of thing is my business, Mr Maitland, I'm trained to observe any hint of falsity. And he – the sitter – said, "Yes Margaret, I want to know – " but she interrupted him there. She said, very lovingly, "Silly old thing, don't you know I want you to be happy. As I'm happy here. And when you pass over I shall be waiting to welcome you . . . you and Ann".'

'Comforting,' said Maitland noncommittally.

'Indeed, he found it so. So he waited to see Dorothy after she came out of her trance, to thank her, and then he told us all the exact position. I know you gentlemen are sceptical, but that was quite enough proof for me.'

'And the later occasions when you met Mrs Selden were purely social ones?'

'That's right. I can talk over my problems with her . . . well, I told you that. It's really very comforting.'

'So you are quite willing,' said Geoffrey, 'to endorse Mrs Selden's claims to clairvoyance and to being a trance medium, in court?'

'If I said anything else I should be lying. Though as I told you,' he added ruefully, 'I'm not too keen on the witness box.'

'I hope you won't let that deter you. Perhaps I ought to warn you that a couple of Mrs Selden's dissatisfied sitters will be giving evidence for the other side. What would you say to that?'

'They are not professionals, as I am. Not trained in investigating this type of supernormal activity.'

'Thank you, that's very satisfactory. And you'll let me have those notes?' He glanced at Antony, who was still on his feet, and got up to join him. 'We're going to see a Miss Newbolt now,' he added. 'Is she also known to you?'

'Indeed she is, a most reliable person and works closely with us. I may say we've had some remarkable results.'

'So you would endorse her qualifications too?'

'I certainly would.'

'Thank you, Mr Fyleman. I shall look forward to seeing you again, when we can go into the question of your evidence more thoroughly.' Geoffrey was on his way to the door, but Antony had not moved.

'There's just one more question from me, Mr Fyleman,' he said. 'Have you heard what happened at the last seance Mrs Selden gave for Emily Walpole? The basis, in fact, for Mr Walpole's claim.'

'Yes, I have. Maurice Selden told me when he mentioned that he was putting me in touch with Mr Horton.'

'What do you think of the message from Michael Walpole?'

'It was not a matter over which Dorothy had any control,' said Fyleman firmly. 'No fraud was involved, I can assure you of that, and she can't possibly be held accountable for what the spirits say.'

'So that's that,' said Geoffrey, when they reached the street again. This time the car was further away, but both of them welcomed a walk. Spring was early that year, even the cold weather that had persisted up to a couple of days ago had given way to a gentle warmth. So that now it was not just a matter of the small signs that snowdrops and crocuses give, even in the middle of the worst weather, that winter is coming to an end that they were conscious of, but a genuine feeling of renewal. 'And no thanks to you,' Horton went on, introducing a sour note. 'that he's still willing to give evidence at all.'

'You didn't think my questions were tactful,' asked Antony, amused.

'Anything but!'

'Well you see, I wanted to know,' Maitland apologised.

'What do you think now?'

'About Mrs Selden? I wouldn't be inclined to accept Fyleman's assessment of her. He said – what was it? – that he was trained to observe any hint of falseness. I'm not disposed to question his sincerity, but he's certainly too predisposed to believe what he sees and hears. As for Machiavelli's endorsement of your client's honesty –'

'For heaven's sake remember to call the thing Angelo,' said Geoffrey crossly.

'If you prefer it. I was going to say that the recommendation comes well from a sixteenth-century Italian, and a civil servant at that.'

'I see what you mean,' said Geoffrey, relaxing his severity for a moment. 'But I think a more important point, and one that I don't like at all, is the fact that Maurice wouldn't allow the representative of the Society for Psychical Research anywhere near his wife. Didn't that make you think?'

'To quote our friend, indeed it did. If I were a fraud I know who I'd rather have investigating me, and it wouldn't be one of their highly reputable representatives. The credulous Mr Fyleman, however –'

'Are you saying he's a fraud too?'

'No, I don't think that follows. I'm merely saying he's more credulous,' Maitland repeated. 'And it doesn't follow either that Mrs Selden's powers aren't genuine –'

'Come now, Antony!'

'I still think they may be. In which case she's playing a dangerous game, far more dangerous in my opinion than fooling her clients. Or she may, which is what Uncle Nick is wondering, be fooling herself as well. But what I was saying was that she may be genuine, or may think she is, and her husband still be a rogue. As we decided.'

'It won't sound well in court,' said Geoffrey unhappily.

'No,' Antony agreed.

'Do you think I shouldn't call him?'

'Fyleman? No, I think you're right about that. Though, as you indicated to him, you'll have to go over his evidence very carefully first. But the Society for the Investigation of Psychical Phenomena has a good ring to it, and may impress the jury, even if the witness himself doesn't. And actually, you know,' he added thoughtfully, 'I like the man, even though I wouldn't give you tuppence for his opinion.'

'The next stop is Kensington,' said Geoffrey, glancing at his watch. 'Are you sure you still want to come with me?'

'It isn't what *I* want in this case,' said Antony humorously, 'but what Uncle Nick will accept in the way of a report. You know,' he added, thoughtful again, 'I was accusing poor old Fyleman of being predisposed to believe, but I think exactly the opposite is true about me.'

'What do you mean?'

'That I'm not terribly willing to accept Miss Newbolt's opinion. I mean, if she's any good at her job why isn't she working for the more reputable society instead of the rather fly-by-night outfit that Fyleman runs?'

'That's a thought, certainly. Oh well, all we can do is hope the jury will be impressed by its title,' said Geoffrey, slackening his pace as they approached the car. 'Maurice Selden gave me explicit directions,' he added, going round to the driver's side to open the door. 'Let's hope he knew what he was talking about.'

III

The directions proved to be accurate, and they found themselves in a cul-de-sac with a small private hotel on the right-hand side. Antony, who had been expecting more shabbiness, was surprised at its neatness and elegance and said as much as they stood on the pavement together and surveyed it. 'What of it?' asked Geoffrey, a little impatiently.

'It's a question of how she pays her bills,' said Maitland. 'Fyleman said she works closely with him, but I shouldn't think he would be able to pay her very much.'

'I dare say we shall find out soon enough,' said Geoffrey placidly. 'Come on!'

Inside it was a pleasant place. Miss Newbolt was expecting them, the receptionist said as soon as they spoke to her, and they would find her in the small lounge. This was at the back of the hall, on the left, and there was only one woman there when they went in. She got up immediately and crossed the room to meet them. 'Mr Horton?' she said, dividing the query between them.

Geoffrey introduced himself and his companion. 'I'm Rose Newbolt,' she said when he had finished. 'Come and sit down, both of you. Would you like me to ring for tea?'

'That would be very nice,' said Antony, sinking into a chintz-covered chair and stretching out his long legs. Geoffrey Horton broke off what he had been going to say to glare at him, he had been thinking it might be nice to get home early for once. 'I'm sure we can all talk more comfortably over a cup of tea,' said Antony firmly, beaming at his hostess, and turned the conversation deftly to the weather until the desired refreshment arrived.

Rose Newbolt was a tall woman, very thin, with iron-grey hair set in a style that had probably been fashionable when she was young, and a scrawny neck. Certainly not beautiful, or pretty, or handsome, or anything approaching any of those desirable states, but Antony found himself immediately drawn to her. There was a good-humoured look about her, a certain placidity. He thought she would make a better witness than Angus Fyleman. If she had anything to say, of course.

They got down to cases as soon as the tea was poured. 'This is very pleasant,' she told them, 'but I mustn't keep you busy men any longer than is necessary. From what you told me, Mr Horton, it's a matter of this dreadful case that has been brought against Dorothy Selden.'

'Has she told you about that?'

'Oh yes, we're very good friends. I think I may say she confides in me. In fact, I think I must have been the first person she turned to – except of course for Maurice – after she received the summons. If it was a summons,' she added doubtfully. 'I'm very ill-informed about legal matters, I'm afraid.'

'And we're very ill-informed about your and Mrs Selden's profession,' said Antony quickly, seeing the words of explanation hovering on Geoffrey's lips.

'Oh, but I'm the merest amateur compared with Dorothy, not in her class at all.'

'I see. You're going to have to forgive some pretty blunt questions, Miss Newbolt. Will you bear with us?' ('Bear with you, you mean,' muttered Geoffrey rebelliously).

'I'll do anything that will help Dorothy.'

'It's a matter, you see, not just of your opinion, but of your qualifications for expressing it.'

'You mean, it would be no good my saying to the court that Dorothy isn't a fraud, if I'm one myself?'

'No, that wasn't what I meant at all. I mean that it would be necessary to convince the jury that you knew what you were talking about, that's all.'

'I am a spiritualist of course,' said Miss Newbolt slowly, 'and have been since my father died when I was in my teens. Is that the kind of thing you mean?'

'It makes a beginning,' Antony assured her.

'Well, I started by attending seances, and sometimes – I'm not a fool, you know – I wasn't at all satisfied with what was going on. But there were many instances, far too many to be explained normally, that simply took my breath away.'

'Did you get any communications yourself from the spirit world?'

'Only once, but that didn't matter.'

'A message from your father?' asked Antony, smiling.

'How did you know that? Yes, of course, it was from him. Nothing much, just to say that he was happy and that I mustn't grieve. That was before I met Dorothy, you know.'

'And when was that?'

'About fifteen years ago.'

'Have you had any personal experience with her powers of clairvoyance?'

'Oh yes, if ever I have a problem I go to her with it and she always knows what to do.'

'I'm afraid if you say that in court, Miss Newbolt, the jury may think it's no more than common sense on her part.'

'Oh no, how could she be so right every time? I've asked her about . . . oh, dietary problems, and what to do about the young man in the next flat giving noisy parties. Now that's a good instance of what I mean. She said, without thinking about it at all, "You could go to the police, of course, but I shouldn't do that if I were you. He won't be there long

62

to worry you." I thought she just meant he would be giving notice and leaving, but he was killed a month later in a motor accident.'

Geoffrey began to look a little happier. 'I'm sure you have also experienced her work as a trance medium,' he suggested.

'Oh yes, I've been to many of her seances, and even had a few private sittings.'

'Were they satisfactory?'

'Yes, I think I can say they were in an unexpected sort of way. When I first sat with her alone, it was obvious that Angelo was doing his best but he seemed rather worried that he couldn't put me in touch with my father. Then, at the third sitting, he said he had been able to trace what had happened, and my father had been reincarnated.'

'The devil he had!' said Antony, surprised into an indiscretion, and was relieved to receive a forgiving smile. 'That must have been of particular interest to you,' he added more sedately.

'Of course it was, but the trouble is I've never been able to find out exactly where or when. Angelo didn't know, and though there were a number of other spirit friends coming through, they were never able to answer that question. That was really what started me trying to see if I had any powers myself. I could spend more time on it than Dorothy could give me, and perhaps I might be able to find out.'

'What did Mrs Selden think of the idea?'

'She encouraged me. She told me how she had started, alone, just quietly sitting and – and being receptive. So I tried it too.'

'And what happened?'

'Nothing at first. Nothing for six weeks at least. Then – I wasn't in trance you know, or anything like that, I've never been in trance in my life – but when I came out of my preoccupation I found that I had a pencil in my hand, and had picked up the pad from the telephone table, and there was

63

writing on it. Not much writing,' she admitted, 'but I had no recollection at all of putting anything down.'

'What had you written?'

'It wasn't exactly important,' said Miss Newbolt apologetically. 'It just said, There will be rain on Thursday. But it was so queer, it didn't even look like my handwriting, so I took it to Dorothy to see what she made of it.'

'And what had she to say?'

'She was tremendously excited, and said I must go and see her friend Angus Fyleman.'

'This was some years after you first met, then?'

'Six or seven years.'

'So what happened?'

'Oh, Angus was excited too, and encouraged me to sit regularly by myself, and always to have a pad and pencil handy. It was strange at first, but after a while the messages began to come more easily.'

'What sort of messages?'

'You don't really understand about automatic writing, do you?'

'I told you I was ignorant about all this sort of thing.'

'Well I know there are people, on a higher plane than I am – I've got a suspicion that I'm a new soul, Mr Maitland – who can sit as Dorothy does when she isn't in trance and very often get the answers to specific questions. My job is much more mundane than that, the messages I get don't seem to make any sense at all, but I pass them on to Angus, and he collates them with other samples of automatic writing that he receives. He says he's going to write a book about it, and is nearly ready to begin. That will be splendid, won't it?'

Antony had to smile at her enthusiasm. 'Quite splendid,' he agreed. And then, 'Miss Newbolt, you say Mrs Selden was in the habit of confiding in you. Do you know the gist of the message that purported to come from Michael Walpole?'

'Dorothy only knew what Maurice had told her, of course,

but I think when she came out of trance she realised that Mrs Walpole was upset, and asked him what had happened as soon as she had gone.'

'Was she – was Mrs Selden upset herself?'

'I think,' said Rose Newbolt, obviously trying to be accurate, 'that she was a little shaken. But I told her she wasn't responsible for what our spirit friends had to say, and of course she realised the truth of that.'

'Of course,' Antony echoed, doing his best to sound convincing. 'Will you forgive me if I ask you one further, rather important question?'

'I think I told you I'll do anything to help Dorothy.'

'You said you were – I think you said the merest amateur.'

'You mean, does Angus pay me for what I do? No, it's a hobby for me, an interest since I retired.'

'What work did you do, Miss Newbolt?'

'I ran the typing pool at the head office of the Imperial Insurance Company. And if you're wondering what I live on, Mr Maitland,' she added with the quiver of a smile, 'I have my savings and what my father left me, as well as my pension. I'm really very comfortable.'

'You see,' he explained, 'it will make your evidence so much more convincing, that you're not gaining in any way from your beliefs.'

'I could still be a fraud,' she pointed out. 'Wanting attention, something like that.'

'You couldn't legally be accused of fraud unless some consideration had passed,' said Antony, as seriously as Geoffrey might have done. 'One last question, and then we'll finish our tea and leave you in peace. When did your father die?'

'He passed over fifty years ago.'

'So he might be forty, or forty-five years old now in his new incarnation,' said Antony. 'It's quite a thought, isn't it?' He smiled at her again and passed his cup for a refill.

'You shouldn't have encouraged the woman,' said Geoffrey

reprovingly, a quarter of an hour later when they had left the hotel.

'Why not? I liked her.'

'All this reincarnation business,' Geoffrey grumbled. 'What's a new soul, anyway?'

'I'm not sure, that's something else I ought to have asked her. I think it means one who's just starting out, and hasn't been through any purifying process, if that's what they believe in. The idea is, you get a bit better each time, isn't it?'

'I suppose it is, unless you're very wicked, and then I dare say you go back to the beginning again,' said Geoffrey. 'And if I was whoever arranges these things, I should regard wilful aggravation as just as bad as wickedness,' he added.

'You can't say I wasn't tactful with her,' Antony protested.

'No, I suppose not. At least we can be thankful she isn't paid for her rather odd efforts. But this business of not being responsible for what the spirits say . . . it's a good enough excuse, I suppose, if you believe all this bunk, but what are the jury going to think about it?'

'That, my dear Geoffrey, is what you're being paid to worry about,' Antony told him. 'If, of course, that rather shady husband of your client's ever pays his bills.' He stopped then and made his way to the edge of the the pavement. 'I'll get a cab, shall I? It's no good going out of your way to take me home.'

'Just as you like. I don't mind, you know. Will you be seeing Sir Nicholas this evening?'

'I don't think I'll have a chance of avoiding him.'

'Then you can give him your impressions. He wants another conference tomorrow, so it will save time if you put him in the picture first.'

'I'll do that.' He saw a taxi in the distance with its light on and began to wave energetically. 'I wish you joy of this business, Geoffrey, but I've a nasty feeling you're not going to get much pleasure out of it. Thank goodness *I* don't have to worry myself any further about Dorothy Selden's affairs.'

<h2 style="text-align:center">IV</h2>

It was still early, but Maitland wasn't surprised to find Gibbs hovering at the back of the hall of the Kempenfeldt Square house, to greet him with the information that Sir Nicholas had not yet returned. Ignoring the implication that some men did a full day's work, while others had no sense of duty at all and merely frittered their time away, Antony asked only, 'Is Lady Harding in?'

'In the study, Mr Maitland,' the butler informed him. Gibbs was an anachronism, in this day and age, and a bad-tempered anachronism at that. He had served Sir Nicholas's father, and stubbornly refused to be retired, though none of them could quite make out how old he was now. The trouble was, he made a martyrdom of his continued service, and obviously enjoyed doing so. Things had improved a little since Vera joined the household, he no longer toiled upstairs with messages instead of using the house phone, for instance. But he still did only just as much work as suited him, and retired promptly at ten o'clock. And he didn't approve of his employer's nephew, any more than Mr Mallory did in chambers, and it was improbable now that he would ever change his mind about that.

Antony said, 'Thank you,' and crossed the hall to the study door. Vera was alone, with a book open on her lap, but staring into the fire. 'Gibbs thinks I'm slacking,' said Antony in an amused tone, as he closed the door behind him.

'And have you been?' asked Vera, looking up at him with a smile.

'Heaven forbid! I've been working my fingers to the bone on this case of Uncle Nick's.'

'The medium?'

'The very same. As a matter of fact, Vera, I've damn all to tell him, but I expect he'll want a full report all the same. Could you come up for coffee after dinner, or have you other plans?'

'Sounds a very good idea,' said Vera. 'Interesting business,' she added, 'but better not tell me about it now. You've got visitors, or didn't Gibbs tell you?'

'No, he didn't, but perhaps I asked where you were before he had the time,' said Antony. 'Is it Roger and Meg? It's a bit early for Roger to be home though.'

'No, a very young couple,' Vera informed him. 'Happened to be crossing the hall when they arrived, that's how I know.'

Maitland was already on his way to the door. 'What time was this?' he asked.

'About half an hour ago.' She smiled at his retreating back. 'Evidently Gibbs isn't the only one who thinks you're leading a pretty leisurely life,' she added.

The old man was still in the hall, and Antony paused a moment to question him. 'Lady Harding says we have guests,' he said.

'If you had given me time I would have informed you, Mr Maitland,' said Gibbs repressively.

'Who are they?'

'A Miss Sally Walpole and Mr Paul Bryan.'

'Miss Walpole?' said Antony incredulously.

'I am not in the habit of being imprecise about such things, Mr Maitland.' But Antony was already halfway up the first flight of stairs.

Jenny met him in the hall. 'I know,' he said. 'Vera told me, and Gibbs told me. I shouldn't have said I'd heard the last of this business when I parted from Geoffrey this afternoon.'

'What's upsetting you, Antony?'

'The name Walpole,' he told her.

'They're both very young,' said Jenny, as though her husband might find this an extenuating circumstance. 'I didn't ask what they wanted, of course, but I suppose she must be related to that man who's suing Uncle Nick's client.'

'I suppose so too. Though why she should come here – ! Oh well, I dare say I'll soon get rid of them. Uncle Nick and Vera are coming up for coffee after dinner, by the way.'

In the big living-room, where no piece of furniture matched its neighbours because they had been put together haphazardly in a time of shortage, he found his two visitors seated side by side on the sofa. They both got up to face him, and it wasn't difficult to sense in their attitude something defensive.

Sally Walpole was a slim, dark-haired girl who couldn't, he thought, be a day over twenty. Her hair waved tightly about her head, and she was pale – far paler than was really becoming – but on less stressful occasions she must be a very pretty girl. The thought was confirmed a moment later when she smiled at him. 'You must be Mr Maitland,' she said. 'This is Paul Bryan, we're engaged to be married.'

Antony had stopped halfway across the room to survey his unwelcome guests. Bryan was probably in his mid twenties, a tough looking young man with sandy hair, rather of the texture of a door mat, steady blue eyes, and a mouth and chin that might be considered to express some degree of determination. 'I'm pleased to meet you, of course,' said Maitland, over-formal because he couldn't quite think how to deal with the situation, 'but I don't really understand – '

'Of course you don't, how could you? Please ask Mrs Maitland to come back,' she added. 'There's nothing private about what I have to say to you. At least, that's not quite true, but nothing I'd mind her hearing. She was so kind, letting us wait for you.'

'Very well.' He summoned Jenny, and came back with her to join the others by the fireside. 'Are you sure you're not making a mistake?' he asked when they were all seated. After all, he couldn't throw them out completely unheard. 'My uncle – '

69

'Has Sir Nicholas talked to you about the case my father is bringing against Mrs Dorothy Selden?' Sally asked eagerly.

That was his worst fear confirmed, though what else could she have wanted to see him about, after all? He hesitated a moment before replying, and then, 'Yes, to a certain extent he has,' he admitted cautiously.

'Then you do understand!'

'Not what you're doing here, I'm afraid.' He caught Paul Bryan's eye and smiled. 'But I'm sure you're going to tell me,' he added.

Paul returned the smile, and for the first time took a part in the conversation. 'You can rely on that,' he said, 'but I think I should tell you I quite agree with what Sally is doing.'

'I see.' He looked back at the girl. 'But I can't help your father, you know. My loyalties are with my uncle.'

'Of course they are!' she said impatiently. 'That isn't why I've come here at all. The thing is, Mr Maitland, do you believe in justice?'

'I believe in – in striving after it,' said Antony, cautious again. 'Whether we always succeed or not is another matter.'

Sally heaved a sigh. 'That's what Clare said,' she remarked 'About your doing your best, I mean.'

That, had she but known it, was an unfortunate phrase to use. It only served to underline Maitland's feeling of inadequacy. 'If you mean Clare Canning,' he said, and insensibly his tone had stiffened, 'how does she come into this?'

'Yes, I do mean Clare, but she's married now.'

'I know.'

'She left the art school – the Napier School of Art, where I'm still studying – about a year ago, but we were good friends before that and she told me all about you.'

'Let's be thankful then that she didn't really know all,' said Antony, striving for a lighter note. Clare whom they had known since she was a child, was a very special person to both him and Jenny, and he could feel himself becoming enmeshed in Sally Walpole's affairs against all his instincts.

'Well, she told me how you had cleared her aunt of a murder charge,' said Sally, concentrating single-mindedly on her purpose, 'and she said you understood people. So I thought perhaps I could make you understand about Mother.'

'I should have been offering you my condolences, Miss Walpole, on your mother's death, and Michael's.'

'Thank you.' There was no more than the slightest tremor in her voice to betray her emotion, but Paul's hand came out to cover hers. 'But do call me Sally, everybody does.'

Antony laughed. 'As we seem destined to become friends,' he said, 'perhaps I'd better. But you still haven't explained, you know, what you're doing here.'

'Haven't I?' She turned to the young man beside her. 'I thought I had made it all quite clear,' she said in a bewildered tone.

Paul shook his head at her. 'As clear as mud,' he said. Then he turned to Antony and took up the explanation. 'You know about Mrs Walpole's death, Mr Maitland, and what the verdict was at the inquest. In the circumstances, you can't blame Mr Walpole for what he thinks. But Sally doesn't agree with him. She's sure her mother was murdered, and she doesn't want the wrong person to be blamed for what happened.'

'That's exactly it,' said Sally earnestly. 'Except that I also want to know who did it. It isn't a Crime and Punishment syndrome,' she added, 'it's that it surely must be someone we know. And that's too horrible to contemplate. Going through life, wondering.'

'Yes, I can see that. I still think you should be talking to my uncle, Sally.'

'Clare told me about him too,' said Sally. 'He's terribly clever, and rather frightening.'

'Not a bit of it, a child could play with him,' said Antony, and exchanged a glance with his wife. Against his will he was beginning to see some humour in the situation, even if the joke was against himself. 'However, if you'd really rather – '

'If I can convince you, you can convince him,' said Sally, with disarming simplicity.

Jenny, who had been sitting in the chair usually reserved for Sir Nicholas, where she looked singularly out of place, jumped to her feet at this point and said, 'If this is going to take some time, I think we'd better have a drink to help the story along. What will you have, Sally?'

Antony waited until she had finished her ministrations, and then turned back to Sally Walpole again. 'To begin with,' he said, 'you're going to have to tell me why you think it was murder.'

'I'm going to have to explain about us first. I mean, about the family.'

'In whatever way seems easiest to you,' he agreed.

Sally glanced at Paul uncertainly. 'The thing is, Mr Maitland,' he said, 'she has to begin by admitting that on the subject of Michael her mother wasn't altogether . . . reasonable.'

'Now, what do you mean by that?'

Sally began to speak rather quickly. 'He means Mother was obsessed by Michael,' she said. 'You know how some people say, she's more a wife than a mother. Well, in this case it was the other way round, only I think all her maternal instinct was centred on my brother. Please don't think I was jealous about that, I was used to it all my life. Even when I was quite young it was painfully obvious, but of course I heard my parents arguing sometimes, so even if I hadn't been very observant I'd have realised how she felt.'

'Then it's not really surprising that your father believed the verdict at the inquest.'

'I was afraid you'd say that, but I have to explain. You can imagine, when Michael was killed it was much worse for Mother than for my father and myself, though we felt it terribly too. Then she got the idea that she could get in

72

touch with him. Father was furious, but he couldn't stop her doing what she wanted. There were rather a lot of quarrels during those last few weeks, which didn't make things any better. But ... I don't believe in that sort of thing at all, Mr Maitland, but I have to say Mother seemed comforted by what she heard. She couldn't talk to Father, so she used to tell me about it. It was pathetic really.'

'You're making out a very good case against your own views. Do you realise that?'

'Yes, of course I do, but I had to tell you, it was only fair. But you see, in spite of what I told you, Mother was above all a very honest person.'

'What has that to do with it?'

'They say suicides always leave a letter, don't they, and especially women? And there was nothing, no word at all. She'd have felt she owed it to my father to leave him some sort of explanation, I know she would.'

'You know the phrase that was used at the inquest, don't you, Sally? Forgive me for reminding you, but the verdict specified that the balance of her mind was disturbed. That might have accounted for her acting in what seems to you like an uncharacteristic way.'

'No, I simply don't believe it. You didn't see her those last few days, I did.'

'Are you telling me she wasn't upset by what happened at the seance?'

'Abysmally, at first. Well, I didn't know then what was worrying her, of course, only that she came back from her sitting with Mrs Selden in a state of nerves. But afterwards she seemed to grow a lot calmer.'

'It has occurred to me that it was a strange way for a woman to kill herself,' said Maitland slowly. And then, 'Forgive me again, I'm reminding you of unhappy things.'

'It doesn't matter, I wanted to talk to you about it. And that's what I think too,' she added eagerly. 'That's the other point I wanted to make to you about Mother ... she was intensely impractical. Father explains that by saying that she read a lot of mysteries and real crime stories, she and Uncle Julian had a common interest in those.'

'Who?' said Maitland, and then answered his own question. 'Oh, her partner, Mr Verlaine.'

'Yes, but don't you see, it's a long way from knowing a thing *can* be done to being able to do it yourself.'

'You're suggesting murder, Miss – Sally. Have you any particular person in mind?'

'No. That's part of the trouble really, I can't bear not knowing.'

'But you yourself are completely convinced?'

'Completely ... utterly ... absolutely!'

'Then at least you must have some motive in mind.'

'No,' she said again, more hesitantly this time. 'But there was something troubling her, that's another point I wanted to make to you. Something beyond Michael's death, I mean.'

'Are you sure about that?' The sharpness of Maitland's tone brought Paul's eyes back to his face, but perhaps what the young man saw there reassured him, in any event he made no attempt to intervene. 'It seems strange,' Antony added more gently, 'in view of what you've told me about Mrs Walpole's feeling for your brother, that she had room in her mind for anything else at all.'

'I've been thinking about that, because I thought you'd ask me,' said Sally, with a sort of quiet satisfaction. 'If I implied to you that Mother went completely to pieces when Michael died, that wasn't completely accurate. After the first week she went back to the gallery again each day. I don't quite know how to put it,' – she glanced at Paul, as though she found his presence reassuring – 'her world had come to an end, but she went through the motions of living.'

For some reason there was something in those rather trite phrases that Antony found almost unbearable. 'A brave woman,' he said slowly.

'Yes she was, that's another reason –'

'Have you talked to your father about this, Sally?'

'Yes, I've tried to. He wouldn't listen, though. Perhaps he had always had a – a sort of thing about spiritualism. It was never discussed at home, but he was absolutely appalled when he heard Mother was going to see Mrs Selden. That, I think, is why he's so angry now, apart from missing Mother I mean, and determined to get back at the medium if he can.'

'If Mrs Walpole really had something on her mind – '

'I think she did,' said Paul, unexpectedly. 'I was there for dinner on the Wednesday night, and though I don't believe if she'd lived to be a hundred she'd ever have got over Michael's death, I think there was something else as well.'

'All right then, you say you've been thinking about this, Sally. Let's have the benefit of your ideas.'

'You were right in saying it would have to be something terribly important to her. Something that concerned my father perhaps, or me – though that's very unlikely – or to do with her business.'

'Have you talked to Mr Verlaine about that?'

'Uncle Julian? No, I haven't talked to him.' And all at once she was explaining again, the words tumbling out on top of each other. 'I don't know if you can understand, when I'm being so frank with you Mr Maitland, but it seems like treachery to talk about Mother to anyone who knew her.'

And Antony thought, So she suspects this chap Verlaine and doesn't want to say so. But wisely he didn't speak his thought aloud.

'The business was antiques, and your mother's particular interest was paintings, so I understand. Is that right?'

'Yes, quite right.' She stopped and smiled faintly. 'I was going to say she was obsessed by them too, but I seem to be using the word too much.'

'Was she in the habit of bringing business worries home with her?'

'Not really. After all, why should she? She had no need to work, it was just that she loved what she was doing.'

'We'll leave that for the moment, then.' Maitland got up restlessly, and took up his favourite position with one shoulder leaning against the high mantel. After a moment he retrieved his glass, and put it beside the clock. 'Supposing you're right about this,' he said. 'If we assume that you are, I think we must also assume that a deliberate attempt was made to make your mother's death look like suicide. There was an obvious motive, the last seance, and the message she thought she had received from her son. But in that case, the question arises: who knew about the spirit message?'

'I hadn't thought about that.' Again there was the quick glance at the young man beside her. 'You think it must have all been thought out in advance then, so that it could be made to look as if she killed herself?'

'I said, if you remember, *if* you're right. But in that case, yes, I do think it must have been meant to look like suicide. Can you think of any other reason for adopting such a clumsy method of murder?'

'I suppose not.'

'That brings us back to my question again, who knew about Michael's message? Your father did, of course, and a lady whose name I don't know, whom I have only heard mentioned as your mother's old nurse. Did she tell you, and did you tell Mr Bryan perhaps?'

'I think I told you Mother didn't say anything at all at first. Not to me, at any rate. Only on the Wednesday evening there was a dinner-party, some of our closest friends. I think my father had asked them, arranged the party without telling her, to try and cheer her up a little. She told us all while we were at dinner.'

'Some of your closest friends,' said Maitland consideringly. 'Do you think she told anybody else besides the people who were there?'

'She said she didn't. I think I can remember her exact words. She said, "I couldn't bring myself to talk about it before, only to Daniel and of course to Nan. She knows me so well there's no keeping anything from her. But now I feel I'd like you all to know about it." '

'Do you think that meant she was feeling . . . well, not quite so upset as she had been ?'

'That's what she said after she told us. Somebody exclaimed – I think it was Mrs Chorley – "how perfectly appalling for you, darling! Weren't you devastated ?" (Antony took time to wonder whether those were really the unknown Mrs Chorley's words, or Sally's interpretation of them.) And Mother said something like, "What do you think, my dear ? It was a shock, a dreadful shock, but it has been such a comfort to me to know that death is not the end of everything. So when I thought it over I was just grateful that my dear boy was still thinking of me and needing me." Those weren't her exact words, of course.'

'Was anything else said on the subject ?'

'Father said, "Nonsense!" very loudly. And then he assured them all that Mother was still extremely upset, whatever she might choose to say about it. She was only trying to stick up for that woman – he meant Mrs Selden – but he, Father, knew where to put the blame. And, of course, there was a lot of exclaiming, and saying how sorry they were, but it was all mixed up, I can't really remember who said what.'

'This was on Wednesday night. Did either of you tell anybody else about the message ?'

'I didn't, and Paul says he didn't either.' Antony glanced in the young man's direction and got a confirmatory nod.

'It wasn't the sort of thing one would repeat,' said Paul, 'even if it was just a casual story you heard about someone you hardly knew. But when it was my future mother-in-law – '

'Yes, I can see you wouldn't feel like talking about it. So we come back to the other people who were at dinner that night. Unless you think that . . . did you say Nan, Sally ?'

Sally returned his smile. 'Oh, that's quite impossible,' she said. 'Nan is nearly seventy, and devoted to Mother. Besides, why should she?' But then she was immediately serious again. 'For that matter, I don't see why any of them should, Mr Maitland. Now it comes to the point . . . I know I said someone we knew, but I didn't think of anyone quite as close as this.'

'But you must see that Mr Maitland has a point when he says that somebody must have known your mother had an ostensible reason for killing herself.' Paul took a hand in the argument. 'And that being so, Sally, I think you'd better tell him who was present. Or shall I?'

'You don't really know much more about them than their names,' said Sally. She seemed inclined now to be a little tearful. 'I'll tell you if I must, but I just know that none of them could have had a motive for killing Mother.'

Antony waited. After a moment Jenny leaned forward and spoke for the first time. 'Having come so far, don't you think you'd better go the whole way, Sally?' she asked. 'You've asked for my husband's help.'

'Yes, I know I'm being silly. I can trust you, Mr Maitland. You'll see for yourself that none of them could have wanted to do it.'

Antony closed his eyes briefly, seeing only too clearly where this was leading. First there would come sympathy, and then the feeling that even the most unlikely theory deserved an airing, and after that an unwelcome sense of responsibility. He moved from his place near the fire and went back to his chair again, and this time his glass remained ignored on the mantelpiece. 'In that case, there's no logical reason why you can't tell me,' he pointed out.

'I mentioned Uncle Julian. Julian Verlaine. You know he was Mother's partner, and they always got on tremendously well together. In fact, if I must be honest, I think they had more in common than Mother and my father had.'

'Their interest in art, for instance?'

'Yes, that of course. Mother always said Father was a bit of a Philistine, though I'm not quite sure what she meant

78

by that. They were also both intensely interested in crime, Uncle Julian more so than Mother, I think, at least more seriously. He was always reading famous trials, things like that, while she liked something lighter, and stuck mainly to fiction, unless he assured her that a particular true-crime book was really easily read. They talked endlessly about cases that were reported in the papers too, your cases sometimes, Mr Maitland.' (Antony had a private grimace for that.) 'Of course, I was more interested after Clare had talked to me about you, but I didn't dream up all this because murder fascinates me, if that's what you're thinking. I think it rather revolting on the whole.'

'Revolting in the extreme,' Antony agreed, solemnly, but there was a gleam in his eye that might have indicated amusement. 'Is there a Mrs Verlaine?'

'Yes, Aunt Harriet. She doesn't do anything except being Mrs Verlaine, and I know Paul tells me there's no more noble vocation than being a wife and mother, but in her case it does make her rather dull.'

'They have children, then?'

'Yes, but none of them were there.'

'Are they really your aunt and uncle?'

'No, only of course we've always seen an awful lot of them, Michael and I have known them forever really. That's how we came to call them that.'

'And who else was present?'

'Mr and Mrs Chorley.' Antony was feeling in his pocket, and she waited until he had produced a stub of pencil and a tattered envelope. 'He's rather a pushy man, really, and runs an advertising agency. She writes sentimental verse for one of the evening newspapers, and sometimes the poems are put out in a little booklet with flowers on the front for people to send instead of Christmas cards.'

Antony was scribbling. 'What are their Christian names?'

'David and Louise.'

'And they completed the party?'

'No, there were the Hazlitts. Theodore and Alfreda,' she said clearly, and paused for him to write it down. 'Everyone calls him Ted, of course. She's a dress designer, and actually terribly clever, I think. He's one of the senior partners in a firm of chartered accountants. And that really is the end of the list.'

Antony wrote for a moment more, and then sat and contemplated his efforts for a moment. 'Mr Verlaine is a student of crime,' he said then, consideringly. 'What about Mr Chorley and Mr Hazlitt? Are they, for instance, practical men?'

'I don't know about Mr Chorley, he's as mad about art as Mother and Uncle Julian, and always said he was trapped in the wrong profession, though he makes a joke of it. As for Mr Hazlitt, he owns three cars, but I don't know if he understands anything about them. And he once discovered where to turn the water off when we had a burst pipe, would you say that makes him practical?'

'About as practical as I am,' said Antony. 'But – '

'You're interested in the three cars?'

'Don't go reading anything into my questions, Sally. At this point I'm interested in everything, and nothing. Tell me, does your father know you're here?'

This time she avoided his eye. 'I didn't tell him,' she admitted. 'He'll be very angry when he knows.'

'You do realise that he'll have to know sooner or later if we go forward with this? And that brings me to another question, what exactly is it that you want me to do?'

'I want you to find out who killed Mother, of course.' She gave him again the attractive smile he had noticed when he greeted her. 'You ought to be glad to do that, Mr Maitland, it would clear Mrs Selden, who's Sir Nicholas's client. And it would set my mind at rest.'

'And which of those things am I expected to feel is more important?' he asked, teasing her. Before this conversation reached its logical conclusion, there were some pretty upsetting questions to be asked, and for the moment his only concern was to lighten the atmosphere.

She ignored the question. 'You'll do what I want?' she demanded.

'My dear child, how can I possibly promise you that? You may or may not be right, but even if you are it's a hundred to one against my being able to prove it, still less to bring it home to any particular person. Why don't you relax for a moment, and tell me a little about yourselves?' He got up as he spoke, to pick up his glass, and raised it in a silent salute first to Jenny and then to the young couple on the sofa.

'There's nothing to tell about us,' Sally protested. 'I'm at the art school, as I told you, but I am not good at it like Clare. I dare say I'll take some commercial work later, just for something to do. And Paul is going to be a doctor, an ordinary GP he says, and he will qualify in just over a year's time. We shan't get married until then, which I think is being rather sensible. Father doesn't like the idea at all, but I don't think Mother cared either way.'

'Thank you,' said Antony, smiling at her, 'that's very comprehensive. Do you mind talking about Michael?'

'Not really. I'm used to it by now.' (Now why do I have the impression that she cares more about her brother's death than about her mother's?) 'He was still at Oxford, and was one of those unlucky people who hadn't the faintest idea what he wanted to do. Father would have liked him to go into the bank, but he said that was dull, dull, dull. I rather think he was right. I expect he'd have made up his own mind in time, only he didn't have any time, you see.'

Maitland drank some of the scotch that he had chosen instead of sherry that evening. He looked for a long moment at Sally and then turned to Paul. 'I don't want to upset her,' he said.

'I think now she's here,' said Paul, 'and has gone so far with her story, we'd better get it over with. You want to ask her – don't you? – about the night of her mother's death.'

'I'm afraid I do.'

'She's quite ready to tell you,' said Paul, but once again his hand went out protectively to cover the girl's. 'That's right, isn't it, Sally?'

'Of course it is.'

'You must remember,' said Antony gently, 'that I don't know anything about it except the verdict at the inquest. So you'll have to tell me everything you know.'

'That isn't really very much,' said Sally steadily. 'I was out that night with Paul, it was Thursday, the evening after the dinner-party. And Father was out of town, attending a meeting in Birmingham. That was why she wasn't missed sooner, because when I came home it was quite late, and I never thought to go to her room.'

'But you can tell me more about it than that.'

'It will only be hearsay,' said Paul unexpectedly.

'Yes, I know, but that will have to do for the moment. I can get the information from Geoffrey Horton, who as you may know is Mrs Selden's solicitor, but why wait for that?'

'I just thought –' Paul began.

'You thought I might be snubbing about the lack of evidential value. We're hardly considering evidence at this point though, are we? Just feelings.'

'Well, of course, I can tell you what Nan and Soper had to say,' said Sally. 'Mother said she didn't want any dinner, but Nan took her some soup all the same. She said she only ate a spoonful though. Nan likes to go to bed early, but that evening she said Mother seemed restless and she offered to stay up with her. Mother wouldn't hear of it though, so she took herself off sometime between half past nine and ten. Her bedroom is on the top floor, so she wouldn't expect to hear Mother come up to bed, or hear me arrive home for that matter. The next thing she knew was when she took in Mother's morning tea at about eight o'clock, and almost before she had time to take in the fact that the bed hadn't been slept in Soper was hammering on the front door.'

'Is Soper the chauffeur?'

'Yes.'

'You'd better explain the relative positions of the house and the garage, and whether he lives in,' said Antony.

'Yes of course, you don't know about that, do you? We're in Bruton Mews, do you know it?'

'Yes, I pass it whenever I walk to work. Does that mean you have a flat over the garage?'

'Oh no, something more elegant than that.' She smiled at him again. 'You don't know my mother and father, or you wouldn't even ask about it. There are five houses on the left hand side, and each one owns the garage opposite to it. Father bought at the time the conversion was done, so he had things arranged as he wanted them. There could be a flat over the garage, but he preferred to keep that for storage space. Soper lives nearby. Actually, I think he has rather an easy life, so I don't suppose he minds that too much.'

'That would explain why he heard nothing, when the engine was running all night.'

'Yes, he came in early to polish the car before meeting Father when he came back from Birmingham. He knew what was wrong as soon as he pushed up the door, of course, but he had to wait a moment or two because the carbon-monoxide fumes had spread beyond the car, and almost filled the garage too. As soon as he could he turned off the engine, but I think it was quite obvious by then that Mother was past help. In any case there was nothing else he could do but come across to the house to telephone.' Her voice trembled a little as she finished her story, but she went on bravely. 'After that it was all ambulance men and police, and then Father came home and gave them his side of the story. But I don't suppose you want to hear all about that.'

'I think I can imagine it well enough. There's one thing that's puzzling me though. Why didn't your father use the evidence of one of these friends of his as to your mother's state of mind?'

'He thought if he did they might repeat what Mother had said too, about feeling better once she had thought it over, and that the coroner might believe she meant it, even if Father didn't. I *know* that, because I asked him that question myself, and he told me, but the next bit is guesswork. I think perhaps he also felt that people would consider her open discussion of what had happened to be good therapy, which would make her suicide less rather than more likely.'

'That's well thought out. Now, can you give me the addresses of these people we've been talking about?'

'Of course I can, but you're not really thinking – ?'

'I'm not thinking anything at the moment,' he assured her, much as he had done before. 'Here,' – he fished out another envelope – 'you can write them on this if you will.'

Sally obliged, and after a moment or two handed back the envelope. 'Will you do one thing for me, both of you?' said Maitland, pocketing it. 'Will you leave it to me to do anything that can be done. Forget all about this theory of yours if you can.'

Sally's eyes on his face were troubled. 'I think you're trying to tell me you don't believe a word of it,' she said.

'I think both you and I will be happier if I look into the matter a little. But don't expect anything to come of my enquiries, then you won't be disappointed. *I'm* not a clairvoyant, you know.'

'You've been very kind.' Sally finished her sherry and came to her feet. 'Come along, Paul, we've been trouble enough to Mr and Mrs Maitland for one evening.'

Paul got up too, but he hesitated before following her. 'We really are grateful,' he said. 'To Mrs Maitland for letting us use her drawing room, and to both of you for listening.'

'Wait a bit!' Maitland stopped them with a gesture. 'You haven't told me what you think about the message Mrs Walpole received, Mr Bryan.'

'Not a message from Michael,' said Paul firmly.

'Is that because you think it wasn't like him, or because you don't believe in messages from the dead?'

'Both I suppose, but it was the latter point that was in my mind when I answered you. The only thing is, why would a medium make up such a thing?'

'If she did do that, her intention might have been to stimulate curiosity, to ensure that Mrs Walpole clamoured for more and more sittings. But I still should like to know,' he added to Jenny, when he came upstairs again from seeing the visitors out, 'whether Mrs Selden is really a genuine medium or not.'

'I don't believe Uncle Nick thinks she can possibly be,' said Jenny.

'But even he thinks she may be deluding herself. However, that's beside the point.'

'Are you really going to try to do something about it?' asked Jenny.

'I think so. Sally made me uneasy,' Antony admitted. 'Of course, there's one great difficulty to be got over.'

'I thought there were two,' said Jenny.

'Did you, love? The one I'm thinking of, is how anyone could have got her to go out to the garage? What excuse could they have made?'

'That was one of my questions too.'

'For the moment I can't answer it. What is your other question, Jenny?'

'It seems such a . . . such a clumsy way of murder. I mean, even if they could have persuaded her to go out to the garage, to sit in the driving seat of the car, she wouldn't have stayed there quietly while the murderer fixed a tube from the exhaust of the car and fed it in through the window. If there had been any sign of violence, surely the autopsy would have revealed it.'

'I'm afraid that isn't really an objection, love. Pressure to the carotid artery – '

'Oh dear, that's what Superintendent Briggs thought you'd done to that poor little man Albert something,' said Jenny.

'Yes, exactly. It would have left no mark, and produced unconsciousness within a moment or two.'

'But are you sure it would have kept her unconscious long enough?'

'No, I'm not. I never – '

'Never what, Antony?'

He looked at her helplessly, but she was obviously quite determined to have an answer. 'Never left it at that,' he said in a despairing tone. And then, bewildered, 'That doesn't shock you?'

'I don't ask questions,' she told him; which, concerning the subject under discussion, was very nearly true. 'But do you imagine I thought you were playing Boy Scouts all those years you were in Military Intelligence?'

'My dearest love,' he started, in a shaken tone, but broke off when he saw her smile. 'I wasn't killing people *all* the time,' he assured her.

'Of course not,' said Jenny briskly. 'So what are you going to do about Sally's ideas?'

'Talk to Uncle Nick, of course, and . . . is Roger coming around tonight, do you know?'

'No, he has a dinner to attend in the City. Do you want him for something?'

'A little advice, that's all.' He glanced at his watch. 'I dare say he'll still be at home dressing if I phone him now.' Roger Farrell, whose wife, Meg, was better known to the theatre-going public as Margaret Hamilton, was in the habit of spending some time with the Maitlands most evenings between dropping his wife off at the theatre and collecting her again after the performance. The two of them were perhaps Antony's and Jenny's closest friends, and Antony was not above taking advantage of the fact when he wanted some advice on matters that fell into Roger's orbit rather than his own. Roger was a stockbroker, and – in general – what he didn't know about financial matters, or things connected with the City, he could easily find out. So that evening Antony, having got through to the Chelsea house without difficulty, didn't hesitate in putting in the query, 'What do you know about Verlaine and Walpole?'

That brought a momentary silence. 'When I saw you last night,' said Roger, 'you didn't mention being mixed up in that business '

'What business?'

'This case that Daniel Walpole is bringing against some medium or other. Isn't that why you're asking?'

'Yes, it is.'

'I thought you couldn't mean anything else.'

'There have been developments,' said Antony, not too lucidly.

'Are you prosecuting or defending?'

'Neither. It's Uncle Nick's case. I only came into it because, though he doesn't believe a medium can possibly be genuine, he has some doubts as to whether Mrs Selden thinks she is.'

'That sounds a little complicated.'

'It isn't really. I'll tell you about it when I see you next. In the meantime, answer my question, there's a good chap.'

'Verlaine and Walpole,' said Roger consideringly. 'They're a private company, of course, and as far as I know their reputation is extremely high.'

'Their financial reputation, or their reputation for professional probity?'

'Both, so far as I know. That picture of Meg's – you know, the one over the fireplace – was bought through Emily Walpole. I believe she knows her subject upside down and inside out, and I dare say Verlaine is equally knowledgeable on the antiques side.'

'There is also the question of how they stood financially. You haven't exactly answered that.'

'No, I can't. But think a minute, Antony. Do you know who her husband is?'

'Yes, he's the chairman of Bramley's Bank.'

'Then if you're thinking of trying to introduce an alternative motive for her suicide, I don't think business difficulties would wash. He's perfectly capable of supporting a wife and family, without any assistance from her. And if you're going to ask me now if Bramley's Bank is in trouble, the answer is a resounding No.'

'That's all I wanted to know,' said Antony. 'Thank you, Roger. Shall we see you tomorrow night?'

'Tomorrow night and a good many other nights, if this wretched play of Meg's goes on running,' said Roger. It was a perpetual source of grievance with him, though except with someone as close to him as Antony he wouldn't have dreamed of showing it, that as soon as one play's run was over another opportunity for Meg to display her talents came along. She could no more resist the lure of a good part than a cat can resist a caressing hand.

As he turned from the writing-table, after replacing the receiver, Antony found that Jenny had already poured them both another drink. She was back in her favourite corner of the sofa, but he, still restless, placed his on the mantelpiece again, and took up his stand beside it. 'I like that chap, Bryan,' he said. 'But what do you think he makes of all this?'

'I couldn't quite decide,' said Jenny. 'I liked them both you know –'

'Well, so did I.'

' – and in the modern phrase, so long as Uncle Nick isn't here to object to it, he was extremely supportive of her. But whether he believes that Mrs Walpole was really murdered or not I haven't the faintest idea.'

'Nor I. However, he's not likely to let her down, I think, even if she's in for a disappointment. Which is a comfort, because I can foresee fireworks when her father knows what she's done.'

'So can I,' said Jenny sadly, 'So can I.'

After that they had their drink more or less in silence;

Antony was occupied with his thoughts and was deciding how best he should word his narrative to his uncle and Vera later in the evening. But they ate in good time, and had everything cleared away tidily and the brandy bottle rescued from its place of seclusion, before this fresh wave of visitors arrived.

The coffee had also finished dripping. Jenny, carefully filling Sir Nicholas's cup to precisely one quarter of an inch below the rim, a thing about which he was inclined to be fussy, said airily, 'Things have been happening.'

'So I suppose,' said Sir Nicholas. 'Or so Antony led your aunt to believe.'

That was only the second time that Antony could remember Sir Nicholas referring to Vera in that way, and he took a moment to wonder whether he was only now becoming certain that his nephew had accepted her. Jenny showed no signs of such qualms. 'Since Antony talked to Vera,' she insisted.

Sir Nicholas gave his nephew a long look. 'I think that for the moment an account of the interviews you and Geoffrey have conducted today will suffice,' he said. 'I cannot imagine that anything very startling emerged.'

'It didn't,' said Antony, 'but I can tell you about that all right.' Truth to tell, he was glad of the reprieve, being by no means certain how his uncle would take his account of Sally's visit. 'First there was Maurice Selden . . .'

'You don't sound as if you like the gentleman,' said Sir Nicholas, when his nephew had finished speaking.

'I didn't exactly *dis*like him,' said Antony, anxious to get the record straight. 'But I didn't trust him an inch either.'

'The question is,' said Vera, 'are you any nearer believing or disbelieving Mrs Selden's credentials?' Equally with her husband and nephew, she had the lawyer's trick of returning to a point she considered essential, however far the conversation might have strayed.

'I'm sorry, no nearer at all, though there were things that

struck me as suspicious. For instance, it wasn't until Maurice Selden came home from the war that the idea of putting the whole thing on a business footing was first mooted, but when it was old Machiavelli got in on the act and confirmed to her that it would be a good idea.'

'You mean her control, or whatever they call them,' said Sir Nicholas coldly.

'Yes, yes, I should have said Angelo. That might mean her subconscious took over, wanting to agree with her husband. That might mean a genuine message from a spirit with some business sense, or it might mean cold, calculated fraud.'

'From what you and Nicholas have told me,' said Vera, 'I'm inclined to the first possibility you mentioned.'

'You may be right. I have to admit I haven't the remotest idea. And Angus Fyleman, with the long-winded title of Secretary of the Society for the Investigation of Psychical Phenomena, didn't enlighten me much either. If you're wondering how he'll shape up as a witness, Uncle Nick, I think he'll be hopeless.' He went on to recount something of their conversation. 'Another point is, you see, Maurice Selden declined to let his wife sit for the more reputable Society for Psychical Research, but welcomed this dubious, rather hole-in-the-corner investigation. And Miss Rose Newbolt, whom I rather fell for to tell you the truth, will make no better an impression on the jury. Personally she would, but it's what she has to say! This automatic writing business, apparently she doesn't even know what it means, just passes her results over to Fyleman, and he collates them with those of other people who are on the same track. At least she doesn't get paid for her efforts, however, that's something.'

Sir Nicholas compressed his lips. 'I shall get all this from Geoffrey, of course, but it's a pity your enquiries brought you to no conclusion.'

'Said there was more to come,' Vera reminded him. Antony took the opportunity to add about three drops of cognac to the snifter at his uncle's side. The spirit was so far almost untouched, and hardly needed freshening, but he hoped that this time the will might be taken for the deed and have a mellowing effect.

'Yes, there is more, Uncle Nick,' he said then. 'Would you consider altering your defence, on the grounds that Mrs Walpole didn't commit suicide after all, but was murdered?'

'Now, what on earth – ?'

'It's just an idea,' Antony told him. 'A bit of a long shot really.'

'What have I done to deserve this?' enquired Sir Nicholas faintly. He had been trying for years to discourage the use of colloquialisms in his household, though his efforts had suffered a bad set-back with Vera's arrival, from whom, however, he seemed to tolerate them well enough.

'Cheer up, Uncle Nick,' said Antony, deliberately misunderstanding him. 'It gets worse as it goes on.'

'What are you trying to tell me?'

'Sally Walpole came to see me. She and her young man. They were the couple you saw crossing the hall, Vera. She's a nice child, with a strong sense of abstract justice.'

'It hardly becomes you to speak cynically of abstract justice,' Sir Nicholas observed. And then, curiosity overcoming his desire to deliver a setdown, 'What does *she* know of the matter, anyway?'

'She knew Clare,' said Jenny, matter-of-factly.

'No!' Sir Nicholas's exclamation was almost a groan, and he sat upright as he spoke. 'If you're going to tell me, Antony, that she told you some tale or other, and you believed her implicitly just because she invoked Clare Canning's name – '

'I think that's perhaps why I listened to her,' Antony admitted. 'It wasn't what made me think there might be a case for investigation though.'

'The whole thing is perfectly obvious. In any event, the verdict at the inquest – '

'Might have been given on a mistaken premise. Will you let me tell you, Uncle Nick?'

'Would certainly be a good defence,' said Vera.

'There would still remain the charge of fraud, even if the claim for damages could no longer be pressed,' said Sir Nicholas.

'Think of the psychological effect on the jury.' Vera was becoming for her almost animated. 'We decided when we discussed this before – didn't we? – that their verdict would be influenced by the fact that Emily Walpole had been driven to suicide by the message, whether it was genuine, or believed to be genuine by the medium, or not. If that were removed from the equation, they'd be unlikely to convict. In any case, Mr Walpole would most likely be willing to drop the action. He's almost certainly motivated by spite . . . not that I blame him, if what Mrs Selden says about his attitude to his wife's visits to her is correct.'

Sir Nicholas was smiling now, but all the same he seemed to feel it was time to apply the brake. 'You're going altogether too fast, my dear,' he told her. 'We'd better hear what Antony has to tell us about his talk with this girl, Sally, before we jump to any conclusions.'

'That's all I want to do,' said Antony meekly. 'Tell you, I mean,' But he exchanged a Heaven Help Us look with Jenny, because he doubted if the recital was going to make him particularly popular. His uncle surprised him by sitting in silence until he had finished, and even then Sir Nicholas made no immediate comment, only turned to his wife and said noncommittally,

'What do you think of that, my dear?'

'Nothing like proof,' said Vera promptly. 'All the same – '

'You're about to remind me that nothing can be lost by giving him his head,' Sir Nicholas told her. 'Let's see, Antony, your recommendation is based on three facts: Miss Walpole's assessment of her mother's character; the assertion that Mrs Walpole was a most impractical woman and consequently unlikely to employ such means of ending her own life; and the further assertion that certain of the family's friends knew about the message and would have realised that this could be a good time to kill her in such a way as to suggest suicide. And this despite certain contrary indications that you have outlined to me.'

'Forgive me, sir, it wasn't exactly a recommendation,' said Antony.

'What do you propose, then?'

'I think we should talk to Geoffrey about it.'

'That, of course. But you must have had something else in mind. You admit that none of these people had any shred of motive.'

'Walpole might have done it himself, and brought the case as a cover-up,' said Vera. 'No, you said he was in Birmingham, didn't you?'

'I did, but that's one of the things I thought Geoffrey might find out. He can get Cobbolds on to it – I think they're the firm of enquiry agents he still uses – confirm that Daniel Walpole was actually out of town (it's a good point, Vera) and also go into this question of motive, which at the moment is absolutely in the air.'

Sir Nicholas gazed at him for a long moment. 'You're really serious,' he said at last, and picked up his brandy and sipped before continuing. 'I think I should point out to you however, my dear boy, that as none of these people you are talking about, people who know about the supposed message, are involved in Daniel Walpole's case as witnesses, there is nothing to prevent *you* from going to talk to them yourself.'

'I walked right into that one, didn't I?' said Antony ruefully. 'The thing is, I'm not involved in the case either, Uncle Nick.'

'Then we must ask Geoffrey to remedy that fact. Though I'm afraid your brief will have to be marked for some nominal fee, there really isn't enough evidence to justify anything else.'

'I've plenty of work on hand.'

'If you want to, you can make the time,' said Sir Nicholas flatly.

'That's all very well. Look, Uncle Nick, what I really want to do is to lay any ghosts that are haunting Sally Walpole. She's tried her ideas on her father, and he disagrees with them rather violently, I gather. There's this chap, Paul Bryan, that she's engaged to, he's a good type, but out of his depth in this sort of thing. I don't know whether he believes as she does or not, he was pretty noncommittal about it. But she's positive in her own mind that murder was done, and is intelligent enough to realise that if she's right it must have been somebody known to the family, though it hadn't occurred to her it was most probably one of the people present at the dinner-party on the Wednesday evening. That's what she can't bear the idea of, that a friend did this and she doesn't know who it was. I think she believes she'll come to hate them all, wondering.'

'And you think you can set her mind at rest?'

'If there's nothing in it, perhaps I can persuade her of that. Oh, I don't know, Uncle Nick. It's just a chance, but I should like to try. The thing is though, I'd rather have kept it unofficial.'

'Might that not make it rather more difficult?'

'In a way, but if it's unofficial I needn't take Geoffrey with me.'

'Don't tell me you've quarrelled with him. You seemed good enough friends the last time we were together.'

'Nothing like that. It's just that he doesn't always approve of my methods,' Maitland explained.

'Who in his senses would?' Vera started to say something. 'Yes, I know you're about to remind me, my dear, that what he does in this connection may have results beneficial to my client. But it's the way he gets those results,' Sir Nicholas complained.

Jenny caught her breath, and coughed, and it was a moment before she could say in a rather strangled voice, 'I was just as impressed as Antony was with Sally Walpole, Uncle Nick.'

'I'm willing to take your word for her sincerity,' said Sir Nicholas. 'I'm even willing to take Antony's word for that,' he added, with a certain gentle malice. 'What I am doubting is the facts she offers, and your conclusions from them.'

'Then I can go and see these people?' asked Antony, not quite sure whether he was getting his own way or whether his uncle had cleverly manoeuvred him into this position.

'Who am I to stop you?' the older man enquired rhetorically. Vera and Jenny exchanged a grin. 'I will even take it upon myself to advise Geoffrey of what you are doing,' Sir Nicholas went on magnanimously. 'Naturally, everything must be reported to him in full.'

'Naturally,' Antony agreed. And if he spared a thought for the briefs that might be refused, and the others on which work would have to be postponed, who should blame him? There were only twenty-four hours in the day.

FRIDAY, 17th MARCH, 1972

I

Verlaine and Walpole had their premises in one of a rabbit warren of side streets not far from Kempenfeldt Square. Their presence was announced by a discreet brass plate, and Antony, arriving on foot, noticed that Emily Walpole's name had not yet been removed. Inside the gallery opened out into greater splendour, though even here a certain discretion could be noted in the arrangement of the exhibits. Not too many to confuse the prospective purchaser, and in some subtle way the attention was focused immediately upon a magnificent jade horse, reigning in solitary splendour in the very centre of the big room. Maitland's request to see Mr Verlaine was received politely, though without the over-enthusiasm that might have discouraged a prospective buyer. A few minutes later he had passed through another gallery, this one displaying some modernistic paintings, and was facing his quarry across a highly polished desk in an office where comfort rather than display was evidently the criterion.

Julian Verlaine, getting up to greet him, surprised him by not looking at all how he considered a man called Julian should look. Something noble and lion-like, Antony had considered vaguely, whereas this man was rather on the small side, and dark, and certainly not noble. He was however, dressed with extreme propriety, and his manner as he greeted the visitor was – like his smile – welcoming but not over-effusive. 'I'm not a customer,' said Maitland, anxious to get that clear from the outset. 'I'm a lawyer.'

'Even lawyers are sometimes interested in art,' said Verlaine with a smile. 'However, sit down and we'll see how I can help you.'

'It's to do with Mrs Selden's defence. You know, I'm sure, of the case Mr Walpole is bringing against her. I'm collaborating with Sir Nicholas Harding – '

'That Maitland! I've heard of you, of course.' Antony wasn't sure, but he thought he saw now a distinctly wary look in the other man's eye. 'But isn't it more usual for any enquiries of this nature to be made by Mrs Selden's solicitor?'

'If you've heard of me,' said Maitland, trying to keep any trace of bitterness out of his tone, for his relations with the press had not always been entirely amicable, 'you'll know that my methods are not always completely orthodox. However, in this case, any help I can give my uncle is purely informal. So we felt there was no objection to my conducting one or two interviews alone.'

'That sounds very specious, Mr Maitland, but there's something else you'll have to explain to me. You say your visit concerns Mrs Selden's defence. What can I have to do with that?'

'As one of the people who were in Mrs Walpole's confidence about what happened at the last seance she attended – '

'Now, how in the world did you know that? Oh, Sally, of course,' Julian Verlaine answered himself. 'But I still don't see – '

'She spoke to a number of friends assembled for dinner at the Walpole's house the evening before she died, of a message from her son, which is alleged to be the motive for her suicide. I thought it was important to see you first, because you must have known Mrs Walpole better than the others . . . perhaps even better than her husband did.'

Verlaine thought about that for a moment. 'Yes, I think you're right,' he said. 'I suppose you want evidence about Emily's state of mind on Wednesday evening, and of course

I'm quite willing to tell you what I can. But if Mrs Selden's defence is going to be based on the suggestion of another motive for Emily killing herself, I think you're going to be unlucky.'

'We shall have to worry about that point when we come to it,' said Maitland. 'In the meantime, will you tell me about the dinner-party on Wednesday evening? And why did you assume that Sally Walpole had been to see me?'

'Because Daniel told me she's got an idea into her head about murder. I'm afraid he's rather angry with her.' Antony suspected that this was an understatement.

'You don't think there might be something in it?' he asked.

'No, and quite frankly I shouldn't have thought a man of your intelligence would have listened to her,' said Verlaine, 'though I can quite see it may have set your mind working on other possible motives for Emily's suicide.'

Maitland made no direct comment on this. 'That brings us back to what you were going to tell me about the events of the Wednesday evening before her death,' he said.

'You know who was present?'

'Yes, as you surmised, Sally told me.'

'And you want to know – ?'

'First, why you think Mrs Walpole chose that moment for confidences? And then, what you thought of the message that purported to come from her son?'

'As to the first, we were all old friends, intimate friends I suppose you might say, and in my case there was the business association too.'

'Yet she hadn't confided in you before that evening. After all, the sitting had been on the previous Monday.'

'No, but I was very well aware that she had something on her mind.'

'And you think it was that?'

'Of course I do. What else could it thave been?'

'I don't know,' Antony admitted. 'To go on to my second

98

point, then: what did you think of Michael's message?'

'Well, to begin with, I didn't think it came from Michael, but Emily was obviously quite convinced of it. That Selden woman had really got a grip on her. But personally I thought it was a wicked thing to upset her so much, it can only have been done with an eye to future profit.'

'When did Mrs Walpole speak of it? At the dinner table, or later?'

'After dinner, when we were sitting over our coffee and liqueurs.'

'Did she speak calmly?'

'Calmly, but emotionally, if that isn't too contradictory for a lawyer to understand,' said Verlaine. 'I knew her very well, as you said, and I knew how Michael's death had affected her. So she didn't cry or have hysterics that evening, but she was shaken.'

'Did she comment herself upon what had happened?'

'Yes, she said she felt better about it now she had thought it over.'

'Did you think that was true?'

'For the moment, perhaps. The very fact of talking about it may have helped her. But obviously her great distress at Michael's death, and at the message she believed she had received, overcame her later.'

'You would have said her life was a happy one.'

'Except for this one great grief. She had a devoted husband, a daughter who can have caused her no anxiety, and work in which she was completely absorbed. I have to admit though, and this is something I know you don't want to hear, Mr Maitland, that her feeling for Michael was something quite above and beyond all these things.'

'I see. You aren't giving me very much comfort, are you, Mr Verlaine?' said Antony, smiling.

'I think perhaps you didn't expect me to,' said Verlaine shrewdly.

'No, but hope's cheap, as they say. Now, I understand

that you shared with Mrs Walpole a common interest in the literature of crime.'

'So I did.' It was Verlaine's turn to smile. 'My wife considers it a morbid interest, Mr Maitland, I hope you don't share her view.'

'By no means. I also understood from Miss Walpole that her mother was a very impractical person.'

'That's true enough. Are you jumping from subject to subject, or do those two things tie together in your mind?'

'Most stories about crime, either factual ones or fiction, are mainly concerned with murder. I understand it was Mrs Walpole's knowledgeability on the subject that was cited at the inquest as explaining the rather unlikely way she chose of taking her own life.'

'Unlikely, perhaps, but not altogether unprecedented.'

'No, I agree with you there. But unlikely, surely, for an impractical woman to have chosen, be she never so knowledgeable about the possibility. I should like your comments on that.'

Again there was a silence while Verlaine pondered. 'It's not so easy a question,' he said at last. 'You're thinking, I suppose, that it would have been easier for her to take an overdose of sleeping tablets, for instance. Well, I can only tell you that there was nothing like that in the house. Daniel was positively rabid on the subject, and I think Emily shared his view. She thought sleep should be natural, and as for tranquillisers – '

'You haven't mentioned Sally or Michael.'

'No, but they're normal, healthy young people and could have no need for anything of the kind. Unless you're suggesting they're part of the modern drug culture, which I assure you isn't the case. And I keep on talking about Michael as though he was still alive,' he added. 'I only wish he was.'

'There are always aspirins,' said Maitland, sticking to his point.

'A very uncertain method,' said Verlaine positively. 'Many people recover, even after taking a whole bottle.'

'Yes, but in the circumstances, Mr Walpole being away, she wouldn't be discovered for many hours. I think she might have taken that into consideration.'

'Well, the fact remains that she didn't,' said Verlaine, showing the first sign of impatience. 'And she certainly knew all about carbon-monoxide poisoning from the exhaust of a car in theory. I admit it never occurred to me that she might employ such a method on herself, but then I never thought of her committing suicide at all.'

'You don't feel the practical application of the theory would have been beyond her?' Maitland insisted.

'How can I feel that, when that's obviously what she did?'

There was clearly nothing more to be got from that subject, and Maitland abandoned it. 'Will you tell me what her immediate reaction was when she heard of Michael's death?' he asked.

'Michael was killed on New Year's Day, which was a Saturday, Canada is behind us in time,' said Verlaine unnecessarily, 'and that meant the Walpoles didn't receive the news until some time on the Sunday. Daniel telephoned us, and my wife and I went round right away. When he phoned he said Emily was inclined to be hysterical, but by the time we got there she'd calmed down. In fact, we couldn't get a word out of her, she just sat and stared into space. I really feared for her reason.'

'And later?'

'She didn't come into the gallery at all that week, but Harriet and I visited them several times in the evenings. Then when we went to tea on the following Sunday, Daniel said she had made up her mind to come back to work. I don't know whether it was Emily's idea in the first place, but she agreed quite readily. I don't mean to imply that her grief was any the less, but she'd got hold of herself again. It wasn't until I saw her on Monday morning that I understood why.

She said she had remembered about this marvellous medium, who could answer your questions about your loved ones who passed over – I'm quoting her own words, Mr Maitland – and who might even be able to put her in touch with Michael. She was going to see her that very afternoon. Of course I asked her how Daniel felt about that, and she said I mustn't say anything to him about it. He knew, but that would just make him angry all over again.'

'And after she had been to see Mrs Selden?'

'She was enormously heartened. There hadn't been any direct message the first time she went, I understand that was a group sitting, but she said Mrs Selden's control had been trying to put her in touch with Michael. I don't know whether that was her imagination or not.'

'I thought you believed the whole thing was her imagination.'

'Yes, you're quite right about that. I think I meant, I didn't know whether that was the impression she had been intended to get. She told me she'd have gone to Hampstead every day if she could, but Mrs Selden wouldn't consider it. But I must say after she began to get messages, or believed she did, she seemed much more calm and much more like herself.'

'Then tell me something about Mrs Walpole,' Maitland invited.

'What have you yourself gathered about her?'

'She was obviously a very intelligent woman, I can't imagine you entering into a partnership with her if that hadn't been the case. But she was also emotional, and perhaps a little over-devoted to her son. I'm sure you can tell me more.'

'Intelligence and instability often go together,' said Verlaine. 'I think that was so in Emily's case, though she was completely normal except where Michael was concerned.'

'Wait a bit! That raises a question in my mind, Mr Verlaine, which is completely due to my curiosity, not at all to my real reason for being here. How did Michael feel about that?'

'He was young, away from home for the greater part of the year. I think, to tell you the truth, he enjoyed a certain amount of fussing over his welfare, but I'm quite sure he wouldn't have allowed consideration for his mother to have interfered with anything he seriously wanted to do.'

'I see. You were going to tell me your views of Mrs Walpole.'

'Did Sally tell you that our interests in artistic matters didn't altogether coincide? Not that I'm completely ignorant on the subject of paintings, or that Emily didn't know a lot about all the beautiful things that I love so much. But we each had our own sphere of greater interest, and more or less stuck to that. All the same, we naturally saw a great deal of each other.'

'Would you agree that if anything could have distracted Mrs Walpole from her grief about Michael's death it would have been her profession?'

'Yes.' He sounded a little doubtful. 'I suppose you could say to some extent that it did distract her, but unfortunately not enough.'

'Sally said she had something on her mind the last week of her life. Can you think what that could have been?'

'I've already answered that, I think. Naturally she was worried still about Michael. And about that awful message.'

'You don't think it could have been the disagreement with her husband about attending the seances? Or perhaps she was worried about Sally's engagement?'

'I don't think she cared about Sally's engagement one way or the other,' said Verlaine. 'As for the disagreement with Daniel, she was sorry about it, of course, but quite determined to go her own way.'

'How was her story received that Wednesday evening while you were all sitting over your coffee?'

'I've never discussed it with anybody since, except with

Harriet, of course. Nobody said much, but I wouldn't be surprised if the others were thinking the same as I was. It might have been more tactful to sympathise with her, but that might have caused an open row with Daniel, he was so very determined that the spiritualism business was a bad thing. On the other hand we couldn't argue with her, not in the state she was in. So nobody said anything much, except sort of murmurs of commiseration. I can't put it any better than that.'

'Sally also said that her mother was, above all, honest.'

'Oh yes! I don't quite understand what that has to do with anything, but it's very true. I told you she was an expert in her line, and if you want my opinion I'd have backed her judgement against anyone's. But she felt that her knowledge gave her a certain responsibility, that it was up to her to be completely open with anyone who asked her advice. I try to live up to that myself,' he added with a smile, 'but I may find it more difficult now that Emily's gone.' He paused there, his eyes fixed reflectively on Maitland's face. 'I have a feeling you're not being completely honest with me yourself,' he said after a while. 'You led me to believe that you were looking for another possible motive for her suicide, but there's more than that on your mind, isn't there?'

'As a matter of fact, there is, but it's a very nebulous idea so far.'

'You're thinking of murder,' Verlaine stated. 'That's altogether too far fetched.'

'The sort of thing that only happens to other people?' Antony enquired. 'The trouble is, it happens in real life too.'

'Have you any reason for that belief?'

'I think we'd better leave my reasons out of it for the moment.'

'In case you want to use them in court?' asked Verlaine knowledgeably.

'Something like that. But you could oblige me by answering one or two more questions.'

Afterwards he was certain that it was Verlaine's interest in crime that inclined him to agree, but even then the matter was obviously weighed in the balance, he didn't answer immediately. Then he said, 'Anything you like, within reason.' But there was again a shade of uneasiness in his tone.

'Nothing very difficult,' Maitland assured him. 'Just assume for the moment that this theory, which you categorise as too improbable, actually turns out to be true. Who could have had a motive?'

'Not I,' said Verlaine, 'she was much too valuable to me as a partner. Not Harriet, her interests are mine, and she had certainly no cause for jealousy. For the members of the Walpole household, Nan I suppose had a legacy, but I'm sure she preferred things as they were, rather than the prospect of retiring to a lonely old age. Michael and Sally would both have benefited from her will, she told me once she was leaving what she had to them, as Daniel had plenty. I suppose Sally will get everything now, Michael predeceased his mother, so that might be regarded as giving that young man of hers a motive, if you're really determined on finding one. Daniel had nothing to gain financially, and though he was sometimes impatient with her, I think he was also extremely fond of her. He wouldn't have been so angry about the seances if that hadn't been the case. As for the Hazlitts and the Chorleys, they were close friends, but not close enough to have any possible interest in her death.'

'I see you're assuming, as I have done,' said Maitland, 'that it was someone who knew that a motive existed for her to commit suicide.'

'If we are to assume murder – which I certainly don't – that seems to be obvious,' Verlaine retorted. He broke off as he saw Antony getting to his feet. 'No more questions?' he asked quizzically.

'Only one, and that again to satisfy my own curiosity. I

passed through one of the galleries on my way here. Was Mrs Walpole mainly interested in modern art?'

'On the contrary, I have to admit that I took the opportunity of her absence to put on that display. I hope that doesn't sound too callous. Her knowledge was wide, as I have said, but her interest lay mainly in the Renaissance period. And what good can that bit of information do you?' he was concluding, when the telephone rang. Antony hesitated while he answered it, feeling that he owed his host at least some expression of gratitude for the information he had received. 'That was my wife,' said Verlaine, putting down the phone a moment later. 'She's here to take me to lunch, do you want to see her first?'

'I doubt if she can add anything to what you've told me,' said Antony politely, 'but I should like to see her if I may.'

'That's all right then, I asked her to come straight in. I wish I could persuade you this notion of yours is all nonsense,' Verlaine added as they waited. 'There's nothing to back it up, and I can see one or two points against it, as I'm sure you've realised for yourself.'

'It can hardly be dignified with the word "notion" yet,' Antony assured him. 'And I'm just as aware as you are of the difficulties. However – ' He broke off as the door opened and Harriet Verlaine came in.

She was a tall woman, at least three inches taller than her husband if Maitland was any judge, and heavily built into the bargain. There was no denying that she was handsome, and looking at her Antony wondered immediately whether she herself chose her clothes or whether her husband did for her, they were of that studied perfection that generally goes unnoticed. 'I didn't mean to interrupt you, Julian, if you have a business appointment,' she said, as soon as she saw Antony standing by the desk.

'This isn't business,' said Verlaine, 'not in the sense you mean at least.' He explained Maitland's presence briefly, but without mentioning the word murder. 'I think Mr Maitland would like you to tell him your impressions of Emily's state of mind, immediately after she heard of Michael's death. And then later on, and particularly on the night we all dined there just before she killed herself.'

'It was a dreadful time,' said Harriet, turning large, rather cow-like eyes in Antony's direction. 'You can't imagine how we felt when we heard that Michael was dead, and of course we went round to the Walpoles' straight away. Emily had completely gone to pieces, I can't put it any other way. And when I say that I don't mean she had broken down, though Daniel told us when he phoned that she was hysterical, but she was sitting completely passive, as if no one was there. She wouldn't speak to me, or anything.'

'And later on?' Antony asked her.

'Julian can tell you more about that than I can, after the first week he saw her every day. But, of course, even during that first week she was gradually coming out of the state of shock. Not that she was in any way reconciled to Michael's death, but I think the idea had occurred to her that she might get in touch with him through a medium, and that was beginning to excite her.'

'What did you think of the message that purported to come from Michael, Mrs Verlaine?'

'Julian says it was nonsense, but I'm not so sure. Some of those people really have really extraordinary powers. And it was all so believable as Emily told it, how Michael tried to get in touch with her and couldn't, and then there were just brief messages, perhaps broken off in the middle, and then finally a much more intimate communication.'

'But you have no knowledge yourself of Mrs Selden?'

'No, I certainly haven't. Our children are all safe and well, thank heaven, I might feel differently if that weren't the case.'

'And on the Wednesday evening before Mrs Walpole died – ?'

'She told us about the message. And I know Daniel is blaming the medium, saying it was heartless to say such a thing, but knowing the relationship between Emily and Michael I can quite believe he might have said something like that.'

'Come now, my dear,' said Verlaine, 'you're idealising their relationship. Emily might have wished him to say such a thing, but Michael was not quite as devoted to her as she was to him.'

'Anyway, Mrs Verlaine,' said Antony, seeing her looking a little taken aback by this, 'whether genuine or not, Mrs Walpole believed there had been a message. Do you think it would have prompted her to kill herself?'

'What other reason could there have been? No, knowing Emily, I don't see any difficulty at all about that.'

'Do you think, in the last week of her life, Mrs Walpole might have had anything else on her mind besides Michael's death?'

'That was quite enough wasn't it? Enough for any one person to bear.'

'When she spoke to you on the Wednesday evening, had you any notion what she intended to do?' It was obvious that Verlaine didn't want the word murder mentioned, and in view of his helpfulness Antony felt he should do what he could to oblige him.

'How could I have thought of such a terrible thing?' She glanced at her husband with the first sign of uncertainty that she had shown. 'Emily said she was feeling better about things now that she'd thought it over, that it was comforting to be assured that Michael had only gone on before her, and that he loved and needed her just as much as ever. She said when her time came that would be the greatest consolation to her. I didn't dare sympathise with her openly because Daniel was looking daggers, and at that point he changed the conversation rather pointedly.'

'Thank you, Mrs Verlaine, I'm very much obliged to you and your husband. Will you add to your kindness by telling me what you think of Sally Walpole?'

'She's a nice girl,' said Harriet, 'and as a matter of fact the children – our two older ones, I mean – think she's a bit old-fashioned. I think Daniel would have liked her to marry someone with better prospects, as far as I know Paul doesn't intend to specialise. But I'm quite sure they'll be happy.'

There didn't seem to be anything else that could usefully be discussed, and as Maitland left he was rather blessing the fact that Harriet Verlaine had interrupted his conversation with her husband. Julian might have had a few more questions for him that he didn't want to answer. So he went back home to lunch, over which he dawdled a little, and when he arrived in chambers Sir Nicholas greeted him coldly.

'You've been talking to Geoffrey Horton,' said Antony, reading the signs easily enough.

'I have,' said his uncle grimly. 'I've been endeavouring to explain to him this latest aberration of yours.'

'I hope you didn't tell him that I believed in it implicitly,' said Maitland. 'After all, all I said was that there was a case for investigation.'

His uncle gave an exclamation, eloquent of extreme contempt. 'I've got a little to add to what I told you last night,' said Antony, and recounted briefly his talks with the Verlaines. 'Not helpful on the larger issue,' he concluded, 'but they both back up Sally's story of her mother's attitude at the dinner party. That might be helpful to you.'

'Facts,' said Sir Nicholas, stabbing at the blotting paper so that his pencil point was broken. 'Facts are what I need, and it's up to you to supply them.'

Antony thought of reminding his uncle that he was only doing what he could to oblige, and would be glad to lay down the burden of responsibility at any time, but on the whole he judged this to be inadvisable. 'I'll see the other two couples,' he promised, 'but I don't know what else I can do.'

'When?' asked Sir Nicholas uncompromisingly.

'Some time over the weekend. There are things I must

deal with this afternoon. Mallory's not at all sure when that malicious wounding case will come on.'

'Then don't let me keep you,' said his uncle. 'I've no doubt, though,' he added, as Antony turned thankfully towards the door, 'that by the time you have conducted these other interviews some other crazy idea will have struck you.'

II

For the rest of the afternoon Maitland was completely lost in his work, and found when he came to leave chambers that Sir Nicholas had already gone and that the clerks' office was empty, except for Willett who was waiting to lock up. From Willett at least he need fear no censure, but he wasn't surprised when he got back to Kempenfeldt Square to find Gibbs hovering in his usual place in the back of the hall and wearing his Inconsiderate-coming-home-at-all-hours expression. But that wasn't all that was on the old man's mind. 'There's a person here to see you, Mr Maitland,' he said disdainfully.

'Don't be a snob, Gibbs.' Maitland had had a long day, he was feeling tired, and his shoulder was aching. 'What sort of a person, anyway?'

'A police officer,' said Gibbs, and unbent sufficiently to add, 'Chief Inspector Sykes, he has been here before.'

'Sykes isn't a person, he's a friend of ours,' Antony protested. 'I hope you took him upstairs, and didn't immure him somewhere down here by himself.'

'Naturally, I acquainted Mrs Maitland with his arrival,' said Gibbs precisely. 'She asked me to send him up.'

'Thank you, then I'd better follow suit.' He was wondering vaguely as he went up the stairs what the detective could want; most likely, though, it was just a friendly visit, Sykes was particularly fond of Jenny, and he himself had nothing on his list at the moment that could possibly concern a member of the Murder Squad.

Jenny met him in the hall, closing the living-room door carefully behind her. 'I know,' said Antony, as he bent to kiss her. 'Sykes is here. Gibbs met me with the news in the hall. What does he want?'

'I haven't the faintest idea. In fact, he's been making small talk so hard I'd think it was a friendly visit, only there's something strange about him. I'd almost think he was embarrassed if I didn't know it was so unlikely.'

Antony grinned at her. 'That'll be the day,' he agreed. 'But you needn't look so anxious, love. I'm not involved in anything that could possibly concern him.'

'No, you aren't, are you?' said Jenny, relieved. 'I asked him if he would stay to supper,' she added as she preceded him into the living-room, 'but he said he had to get home.'

Detective Chief Inspector Sykes of the Criminal Investigation Department at Scotland Yard was an old friend of the Maitlands, a friendship that persisted, though sometimes he and Antony were allies and sometimes adversaries. He was a square-built, fresh-faced man, who looked more like a farmer than a detective, though perhaps his expression might be considered too cheerful for that. Now as he greeted Antony and enquired solicitously about his health – presumably he had already made the same enquiries about the rest of the family, for he was punctilious in these matters – he had a grave look, and it was obvious that Jenny had been right in her assessment of his state of mind. 'Out with it, Chief Inspector,' said Antony when greetings had been exchanged, and he had supplied Sykes with whisky and himself and Jenny with sherry. 'There's something on your mind.'

Sykes raised his glass, and contemplated the scotch as if admiring its colour. 'If I'm in the way, Inspector,' said Jenny, who could never remember to give Sykes his proper title since he had been promoted, 'I'll leave you alone together.'

'No need for that, Mrs Maitland. This is quite an unofficial matter.' He paused again, and then raised his eyes to scan Maitland's face. 'I understand you're interesting yourself in the civil suit of Walpole *versus* Selden,' he said.

Antony was still standing, and took time to retrieve his sherry and sip it before replying. 'I hope you won't misunderstand me,' he said carefully at last, 'if I say that I don't see what business that is of yours.'

'None ... at present.'

'In any case, how did you hear of it ?'

'You're admitting I'm right ?'

'Oh yes, you're right,' said Antony, impatiently. 'I still want to know how it came to your ears.'

'You know, I suppose, that in the police force the different departments aren't kept in completely separate boxes. What's known to one, is likely to be known to the rest. It can be a disadvantage, but at times it may also be a source of considerable strength.'

'I'll have to take your word for that. How does it concern me ?'

'It won't surprise you to hear that the local police have been keeping an eye on the Selden *ménage*. If there's any question of fraud, the public must be protected, and if Mr Walpole wins his case criminal action might follow.'

'So you saw me visiting Maurice Selden, in company with Geoffrey Horton. Why should that interest you ? You know my uncle is representing Mrs Dorothy Selden.'

'Where you go, Mr Maitland, trouble has a habit of following.'

'Well, in this case I only went there to oblige Uncle Nick. I don't think I'm betraying any secrets, Chief Inspector, if I tell you that the matter of Mrs Selden's sincerity or otherwise has troubled him. He wanted my opinion, that's all there was to it.'

Perhaps it was his choice of words that alerted the detective to the fact that there might be some prevarication involved. 'Can you assure me, Mr Maitland, that the matter rests there, as far as you're concerned? That you don't propose to take any further action in the matter?'

That was an awkward one. Maitland had recourse to his glass again before he attempted to answer. 'No, I can't give you that assurance,' he said at last evenly. 'And I don't think I can discuss one of my uncle's cases with you.'

'There's no need for that, I'll do the talking,' Sykes offered. Which would have surprised Antony if he'd taken time to think about it, the detective was not normally a talkative man. 'There are three lines of defence that Mrs Selden's lawyers can follow, as far as I can see. First that her mediumship is perfectly genuine –'

'I don't think there is such a word as mediumship,' Maitland interjected.

' – that the message was a genuine spirit message,' Sykes went on, ignoring him, 'for which she cannot be held responsible. Or it could be held that there was some other reason for Mrs Walpole's suicide, and that therefore Mr Walpole's claim for damages could not apply. Or – and this is where I think you come in, Mr Maitland – that Emily Walpole did not commit suicide at all, but was murdered.'

Jenny gave a gasp. Antony said nothing, but remained staring rather stonily at the detective. 'I'm not asking you to either confirm or deny it,' Sykes told him, 'but you must admit it fits in perfectly with what I know of you.'

'So this visit of mine came to your ears through the constabulary grapevine,' said Antony, 'and you drew certain conclusions from it. What then?'

'I've two reasons for coming here. You must realise, Mr Maitland, that if murder was done it is very much my affair.'

'Yes, I suppose Bruton Mews is within your bailiwick.'

'So what I want you to tell me is, what do you know?'

'Nothing,' said Antony, simply and with perfect truth.

'I'm not prepared to accept that. You've admitted – '

'Now, Chief Inspector, you know I hate that word. I'm telling you the truth when I say I don't know anything, but if

I did I couldn't tell you if it would prejudice my uncle's case.'

There was a pause while Sykes digested this. 'You said two reasons, Chief Inspector,' Antony prompted him after a while.

'The second reason is that the matter of your involvement has come to Chief Superintendent Briggs's ears,' Sykes told him. 'There's no use looking like a thundercloud, Mr Maitland, you know the superintendent as well as I do. He doesn't like the situation at all.'

'Much I care for that!'

'All the same, I'd like you to listen to me. Perhaps you can persuade him to take me seriously, Mrs Maitland.' Jenny just shook her head at him, but her eyes were anxious. 'This is awkward,' the detective went on. 'You've done me some favours in the past, and I don't want to see you get into difficulties.'

'What difficulties, for heaven's sake?'

'Briggs has been through the records of the inquest very carefully,' said Sykes. He seemed to be choosing his words with some care. 'There's nothing at all to suggest murder. But he says, if you've made up your mind on that third line of defence I mentioned, some evidence pointing to it is likely to turn up.'

'Oh, come now, Chief Inspector! You're talking about s-subornation of p-perjury. Or aren't you?'

'*I*'m not, Mr Maitland.'

'Well then, Briggs is.' He threw out his hands in a helpless gesture. 'I know he's always been w-willing to think the worst of me, but this is really a b-bit much.'

Even now there was no hint of apology in Sykes' manner, he remained completely impassive. 'This isn't a pleasant errand, Mr Maitland,' he said, 'but I felt I owed it to you to tell you.'

'And I'm g-grateful to you.'

Suddenly the detective smiled. 'As grateful as you can be

when you're blazingly angry,' he agreed. 'Don't you think it's better to be forewarned, though?'

'Of course I d-do.' He flung himself into the chair at the other side of the hearth. 'Whether I've lost my temper or not, I'm g-grateful to you, Chief Inspector. But you can't expect me to w-welcome the news.' He paused a moment, and when he went on seemed to have himself under control again. 'However, while you're here will you do something for me? I mean, absolutely in confidence, without repeating the rest of our conversation to Briggs tomorrow.'

'That's rather a difficult promise you're asking me to make.'

'No, I'll guarantee you won't find it so. Will you do that for me?'

'Ask your questions and we'll see.'

'It involves making the assumption for the moment that Mrs Walpole was murdered. I was telling you the truth when I said I've no evidence of that. But supposing she was, the question of motive would arise. And that's a bit of a facer.'

'I can imagine it would be. But we had nothing to do with the investigation into her death.'

'No, but you hear things, you've just admitted that. If I suggest certain possibilities, will you tell me whether they really are possibilities or not?'

Sykes thought that out in his slow way. ' 'appen I will, and 'appen I won't,' he said at last, lapsing into his boyhood dialect as he sometimes did in times of stress. But then he glanced at Jenny and saw her worried look. 'Try me,' he offered.

Instead of answering immediately Antony got up to freshen their drinks. 'I'm thinking about Daniel Walpole,' he said, coming back to his place by the fire.

'A financial man,' said Sykes.

'Yes, I know that, the chairman of Bramley's Bank. I understand he had no expectations from his wife's estate, but where families are concerned, I believe the police always consider it policy to suspect the husband.' He looked at Jenny and smiled. 'Even in the best regulated families,' he added.

'You may suspect the man on principle if you like,' said Sykes. 'I know nowt of it.'

'Come now, Chief Inspector, you just told us that things get about in the police force. Even if they were positive that Mrs Walpole's death was suicide, the local police must have made some enquiries about the family. I get the impression of rather an irascible man, very opinionated, intolerant of any ideas but his own.'

'Yes, naturally, at the time Emily Walpole died I heard this and that,' Sykes admitted. 'And I wouldn't say your picture was too much out of focus. All the same, there was no hint of any serious friction between them.'

'Not even the fact that she was much more concerned with her son's welfare than with her husband's?'

'I know nothing of that,' said Sykes flatly.

'I've been told it was a fact,' said Antony. 'Of course, my informant might have been lying, or mistaken, but Emily Walpole's actions after Michael's death seem to confirm it. And I think it's something her husband might well have resented.'

'I can't help you, I'm afraid, Mr Maitland.'

'Then let's consider Paul Bryan, who's engaged to Sally Walpole. If my information is correct she scoops the pool now that her brother is dead. He's going to be a doctor – Bryan, I mean – and wants to go into general practice, which doesn't argue a particularly mercenary nature. All the same, a wife with money of her own might not be unwelcome to him.'

Sykes shook his head sadly, rather as though he were regretting all the sins of mankind. 'What about Sally Walpole herself?' he asked.

'I won't even consider her,' said Antony.

'You've met her then? Perhaps she was the informant you speak of,' said Sykes shrewdly.

'Not about her mother's will.'

'Then you have been asking questions. You really are taking this matter seriously.'

'I've been trying to convey to you, Chief Inspector, that at the moment I don't know what to think. But there can be no objection to my doing some devilling for my uncle. All these people were to some degree in Emily Walpole's confidence, and if we take your second line of defence, that Mrs Walpole didn't kill herself because of the message she received through Mrs Selden, their evidence may be material.'

'Yes, Mr Maitland.' Sykes sounded almost indulgent. 'You always could put up a good argument for doing exactly as you pleased, but that doesn't make it any less likely that I'm right about what started you on this enquiry. You know something I don't.'

'I'm g-getting tired of telling you –'

'All right then, we'll leave it here. Who else are you curious about?'

'The only other member of the household is the old nurse, I don't know her by any other name than Nan. It sounds very unlikely to me that she murdered her mistress, particularly not in the way it was done.'

'The whole thing is unlikely,' said Sykes, with more frankness than Maitland appreciated.

'Bear with me a moment longer. The other people to whom Mrs Walpole talked about Michael's message were a Mr and Mrs Hazlitt – Theodore and Alfreda. She's a dress designer and he's a chartered accountant and owns three cars.'

'Are you telling me there's some significance in that?'

'I'm not telling you anything, Chief Inspector, because I'm sure you wouldn't listen. I'm just trying to get a little information. The other couple are called Chorley, and their names are David and Louise. I believe he runs an advertising agency and she writes poems for one of the evening papers.'

'I've never heard of any of them. Unless . . . did you say sentimental verse?'

'I didn't say so, but I believe it is. Don't tell me you're an addict, Chief Inspector.'

'No, I've never succeeded in getting through one of them,' said Sykes seriously. 'But my wife always stocks up at Christmas with a whole pile of the latest collection. They put them out as a sort of little booklet, and she uses them as Christmas cards.'

'Then there are the Verlaines, Julian and Harriet. She's a wife and mother, and a good one I dare say. He was Emily Walpole's partner in the firm Verlaine and Walpole, so naturally I'm more interested in him than in any of the others. From all I've learned the business is flourishing, Verlaine didn't seem to have a care in the world except regret for his partner's death. But he did confirm a fact I heard elsewhere, that Mrs Walpole had something on her mind during the last week of her life. He put it down to Michael's message when he heard about that, but supposing it was something else.'

'Suppose it was.'

'What I'm trying to say, Chief Inspector, is that it might have been (a) an alternative motive for suicide, or (b) something she'd discovered that led to her murder. You promised to suspend disbelief for a moment,' he added quickly, seeing Sykes's sceptical look. 'And if there was something else on her mind, it seems most likely that it concerned her work.'

'Let's see, she was an art expert, wasn't she?'

'She was, and I gather very well thought of. Her own particular passion was for the Renaissance period.'

'Well, I don't think I can do anything for you, except to confirm that the affairs of Verlaine and Walpole were looked into by the local people at the time of her death, and everything was in order. She couldn't have been worried about business matters in the ordinary way.' His voice trailed off as he spoke, and Antony took him up eagerly.

'You've thought of something, Chief Inspector. What is it?'

'The trouble is, Mr Maitland,' said Sykes heavily, 'when I talk to you for half an hour I finish up by being as daft as you are yourself.' Antony grinned at this, he was used to the detective's ways. 'This talk about art put me in mind of something that has been happening recently. A series of art thefts, very well organised, very well planned.'

'Now we're getting somewhere! When you say art – ?'

'I mean famous paintings, not antiques in general. The sort of thing Emily Walpole specialised in.'

'Any particular period?'

'No, but – this will interest you, Mr Maitland – not a trace of any of the stolen articles has ever been found afterwards.'

'You mean they are sold to – to venal collectors?'

'That must be the case, it's the only explanation. I don't have to tell you, Mr Maitland, what someone who has got the collecting bug will pay for something he really covets. But that's all beside the point, it can't have anything to do with this Walpole affair.'

'Can't it though? Have there been any other deaths?'

'You mean, in the course of the robberies. No, there haven't, though violence has been used on several occasions, fortunately not fatal. That couldn't apply here, Mr Maitland. You're talking nonsense. Emily Walpole was at her home, and died in their own garage just across the mews.'

'And you know an extraordinary amount about it,' said Antony accusingly. 'That makes me think you aren't quite so uninterested as you try to make out.'

'I came here –'

'To pick my brains,' Antony suggested.

Sykes smiled in his sedate way. 'Yes, perhaps. You must admit I haven't been very successful. But I also had your own interests in mind.'

'Yes, Briggs's crystal gazing. Not that I'm not grateful, Chief Inspector. I am . . . really! But aren't you beginning to wonder a little? I'm not suggesting a theft from the gallery, but supposing with her expert knowledge she stumbled on something incriminating. That Julian Verlaine was the brains behind all this, perhaps.'

'Mr Maitland, you can't be serious about this.'

'I'm serious about anything that may lead to a miscarriage of justice,' said Antony. 'But you've got me wrong, Chief Inspector, as I told you before. So far I'm only looking around.'

'Wasting your time, lad.' Sykes came to his feet slowly. 'Well, if I can't talk any sense into you I'd best be getting along.' He made his farewells to Jenny with the punctiliousness that was usual to him, but even then he paused in the doorway. 'There's just one thing, Mr Maitland.'

'Well?' Antony was losing his patience, always inclined to be fragile in the face of questions and the necessity of answering them. Or avoiding answering them, as the case might be.

'If you should by any chance be right, I wouldn't tangle with these people if I were you. The people responsible for the art thefts,' he explained, seeing Maitland's blank look. 'They might be even more dangerous than Chief Superintendent Briggs is when he's annoyed.'

III

When Antony got upstairs again after seeing the detective out, he found Jenny wandering rather distractedly around the living-room, picking up glasses and putting them down again. 'Don't clear them away yet,' he told her. 'I think we may both need another.'

'Did he say anything else?' asked Jenny, making immediately for the writing-table where the tray of drinks was set out.

'Not a thing. I think on the whole he'd said enough, don't you?'

'Don't you remember what that woman said to you?' said Jenny tragically. 'It's all coming true!'

'Come off it, love! Have you been taking lessons in play-acting from Meg? You know as well as I do that what Mrs Selden says doesn't mean a thing.'

'You said yourself she was telepathic.'

'Yes, but that wasn't because of what she said about a tall bald man, or whatever it was. That might have been anybody.'

'Or it might have been Superintendent Briggs,' said Jenny stubbornly. 'Now there's going to be trouble with the police again, and Uncle Nick will be furious.'

'If he ever hears of it.'

'Gibbs will tell him the inspector was here, of course he'll want to know why. Antony, you've got to tell him.'

'All he needs to know is that Sykes was curious.' He took his glass, and this time sat down on the sofa beside her. 'I know I lost my temper over Briggs's ideas,' he admitted, 'but they can't do any real harm. I've no intention of procuring false witness, so there's nothing he can do. I'm not even obstructing the police in their inquiries, because they aren't making any.'

'Oh dear!' said Jenny. 'You always make things sound so reasonable. But I can't help feeling –'

'Superstition,' Antony told her. 'Uncle Nick has been warning me against it, but I think it's you he should have been talking to.'

'No, it isn't that.' Jenny's lie was not altogether convincing, and perhaps she realised it because she added, 'At least not altogether. You see I'm wondering . . . there've been so many times you've come up against Superintendent Briggs before, once he even suspected you of murder. Things have always turned out all right in the past, but now I wonder whether he ever really believed you were innocent of the things he accused you of. Everybody else did, but he may just have let the matters drop for want of proof. That would make him angrier than ever.'

'I should think,' said Antony thoughtfully, 'it's a hundred to one you're right. But, Jenny love, it's nothing for you to worry about.'

'Nothing!' said Jenny, still on a note of high tragedy. 'There are these art thefts too,' she added.

'That's the wildest of wild ideas, I can't think why Sykes brought it up at all.'

'He did it to help you. Well I suppose you're determined to go on with it, Antony, but I don't know why you always care so much,' said Jenny.

'If you stop caring, you might as well be dead,' said Antony positively.

'But you don't really like the Selden's, and if they are frauds they shouldn't be allowed to prey on the public,' said Jenny. The unlikely phrase seemed to have a cheering effect on her.

'I don't like Maurice,' Antony corrected her. 'I did like Mrs Selden. Her powers may or may not be genuine, but I think she believes in them. I admit though, her husband may influence her more than she knows.'

'Have you told Uncle Nick that?'

'No, but I'm going to. But I thought you understood, love, my main reason for wanting to know the truth –'

'Which may have already been discovered.'

'You're right, it may. But I'd like to set young Sally's mind at rest, one way or the other.'

'I should like that too,' said Jenny, sighing. 'And I don't know why I'm arguing,' she added, 'because you know I only want you to do what you think is right.'

'Don't worry then,' he told her. 'All these fears of yours, they're probably quite groundless. In any case, who lives may learn.'

IV

They had dinner after that, and Roger arrived, having left Meg at the theatre, and was regaled in a rather disjointed way by Jenny with the story of Mrs Selden's affairs. But Antony's prophesy was proved to be only too true before the evening was out. At about half past nine the phone rang, and when he answered it a girl's voice said breathlessly, 'Is that you, Mr Maitland. It's Sally Walpole.'

'Hello, Sally.'

'Am I disturbing you? I'm really sorry, but this won't wait,' she went on without giving him time to reply.

'My time is yours,' said Antony, trying his best not to sound resigned. He pulled up a chair with his foot and sat down, because he had a feeling this might take some time. He also had a feeling, even more strongly, that whatever Sally had to say he didn't want to hear. 'Carry on,' he prompted.

'You haven't forgotten what we were talking about last night?'

'Well, hardly.' He ought to have found some amusement in the suggestion, a barrister's memory being one of the largest parts of his stock-in-trade, but just for the moment he was much too tired to see the humour of it.

'You wanted proof, and now I can give it to you. Well, I don't know if you'll regard it as proof exactly, but at least it's suggestive,' said Sally with belated honesty. 'Paul says I should leave it to you to decide on its evidential value.' That was evidently a quotation, and Antony took a moment to wonder where Paul Bryan had come across the phrase, before he remembered having used it himself the evening before.

'Sally,' he protested, 'I asked you to leave this to me.'

'I didn't do anything. At least, not until . . . well, I'll tell you. A neighbour of ours, a Mr Mottram, has just got back from South America.'

'I hope he enjoyed himself there,' said Maitland bitterly.

'I *am* being a nuisance.' But again she didn't wait for reassurance. 'This is important, Mr Maitland, really it is! You'll see!'

'Well, what has this Mr Mottram been doing in South America, if that's material to your story?'

'It doesn't matter. The point is he went away on the morning of the 18th of January, and didn't get back till this afternoon.'

'Wait a bit! The 18th was the morning your mother was found?'

'Yes. Mr Mottram left really early, before all the commotion of ambulances and things. Don't you see how important it is, Mr Maitland, he didn't know a thing about it until today.'

'I suppose this story has a point, Sally, but you're getting there very slowly.'

'Are you cross with me? But even Paul agreed this was important. Mr Mottram came across this evening before dinner to offer his condolences. Of course, he doesn't know a thing about the case Father is bringing against Mrs Selden or anything like that. But he said, "I saw Emily, just to say good night to, the evening before I went away." That's the 17th, Mr Maitland, the evening she's supposed to have killed herself. "She was crossing the mews to the garage." ' Her voice had changed again, subtly, so that he gathered this was another quotation. "Which of your friends was it who was with her? He must have been able to tell you something about her frame of mind." '

Antony closed his eyes for a moment. If Briggs was also to be counted among the prophets . . . Then he pulled himself together. 'What time was this?' he asked sharply.

'About ten-thirty, he said.' A faint shade of resentment coloured Sally's tone. 'I thought you'd be pleased, Mr Maitland.'

'I dare say my uncle will be,' said Antony, which was as

near as he could bring himself to come to reassurance. 'This Mr Mottram, was he quite positive that it was your mother he saw?'

'Yes, he'd just been putting his car away, and she was passing under the light between the two garages.'

'Then he must have got a good look at the man too. Was it anyone he knew?'

'No, he didn't recognise him, but he said he couldn't have done so anyway. He was in the shadows, beyond the circle of light.'

'Then is Mr Mottram sure they were together?'

'Quite sure. But Father was getting cross, I couldn't ask him a terrible lot of questions. Couldn't you see him yourself?'

'I suppose I could,' said Maitland grudgingly. 'Or Mr Horton could, it's his job really. Can you think of any conceivable reason, Sally, why your mother should have been going to the garage at that time of night, if it wasn't for the reason that was given at the inquest?'

'No, I can't. But she wouldn't set out to commit suicide with a companion,' Sally protested. 'Surely you can see that it makes nonsense of the whole thing.'

'Unless . . . well, we shall have to try to find the man, I suppose. At the very least he might be able to throw some light on her state of mind, as your Mr Mottram suggests.'

'Then that's all right,' said Sally with satisfaction. 'I can leave it all to you. But there is one other thing, Mr Maitland – '

'What is it?' asked Antony. For some reason the fact that she broke off there renewed his uneasiness.

'There's another bit of evidence too,' said Sally. 'I was talking to Soper.' Antony groaned, and she answered his unspoken comment. 'There's no reason why I shouldn't, he's been with us for years and I can't exactly cut him dead when I see him, just because he's giving evidence for Father.'

'I rather suspect, though, that your conversation took the

form of a question and answer,' Antony explained. 'Am I right?'

'Yes,' said Sally hesitantly. 'You know you said it was a funny way for Mother to have killed herself, if that's what she did. So I began to think about it, and I asked him where the tubing came from.'

'I see.' Just for moment any further comment was beyond him. 'And could he tell you?' he asked after a pregnant pause.

'No, and that's what seems so funny, Mr Maitland. He'd been wondering about it himself, and he talked to Nan. She knows everything that goes on at home. She swore there was nothing of the kind in the house and never had been, and Soper says there was never any tubing in the garage either. So Mother would have to have bought it herself, and kept it hidden too, so that Nan wouldn't see it. Only I don't believe she did. If she really killed herself, she couldn't have plotted it so far ahead. And don't you really think the man Mr Mottram saw must have killed her '

'It's a possibility,' said Antony, and then chided himself for his grudging tone. 'I'm sorry Sally, things seem to be coming rather thick and fast this evening, that's all.'

'You found out something else,' she asked eagerly.

'No, I didn't mean that.' He didn't attempt to explain. 'I'll take it from here, and may I implore you again, Sally, not to do any more investigating yourself. Somebody will go and see Mr Mottram. You said he's a neighbour. Where does he live?'

'Next door to us, Number three. And what about Soper?'

'It wouldn't be etiquette for any of the defence team to approach him, but I'll see that my uncle is primed what questions to ask him and Nan in court.'

'Thank you.' Sally sounded subdued now. 'I'm being a nuisance, Mr Maitland, and I'm sorry for it, but I can't get it out of my mind that that man might have been someone we know. Must have been in fact. And I can't go through the rest of my life suspecting all our friends.'

'Let's hope you won't have to. Is Paul with you?'

'Yes, do you want to talk to him?'

'No, nothing like that. I just didn't want you to be alone.'

'I couldn't telephone till he came, that gave me an excuse to leave Father by himself in the study. I don't like to go behind his back, but you do see I've got to?'

'I see you feel you have to. Good night, Sally, try not to worry about this and I'll be in touch.'

He turned from the phone in time to catch the quick flare of anxiety in Jenny's eyes. She knew as well as he did when his shoulder was paining him, though she had never commented on it and probably never would. But talking over something that was worrying him was a different matter. 'I don't think you like whatever it was Sally had to tell you,' she said tentatively.

'No, I didn't.' He gave her the gist of their conversation. 'Coming so hard on the heels of Sykes's visit –'

'We shall have you believing in ESP before you're much older,' said Roger in a rallying tone. No more than Antony, did he like to see Jenny worried. 'But he can't really hold you responsible for what this man Mottram says, particularly as he only just got back home.'

'No, that's true,' said Jenny eagerly.

'The thing is,' Roger went on, 'will it help Uncle Nick's case?'

'I can't possibly tell that until Geoffrey or I have talked to him. He may fall apart completely under questioning. The trouble is, Sally's altogether too eager.'

'There's also what the chauffeur says, and apparently the old lady will back him up.'

'So there is. That's something I ought to have thought of before, the size of piping needed. It might not have been easy to obtain on the spur of the moment.'

'But not impossible, with a bit of shopping around,' Roger suggested.

'No, but it's another line of enquiry to suggest to Geoffrey. Yes, love,' he went on quickly, forestalling Jenny, 'I know what you're going to say. I'd better go down and make a clean breast of everything to Uncle Nick.'

'Antony, I'm sorry, but I do think you should go. He hates your being mixed up with the police. I said that before, didn't I? But he hates it still more if you try to keep him in the dark about what's going on.'

'I know. Will you keep Jenny company while I go downstairs for a few minutes, Roger? It shouldn't take very long.'

Roger privately had his doubts about that, but he agreed amiably enough; though at the same time formed the intention of phoning Meg to tell her he couldn't call for her if the time came for her to leave the theatre before Antony came back. Roger, whom Clare Canning, now Clare Charlton, had once sketched with a bandana round his head and one gold earring, had, as she had endeavoured to convey, a distinctly piratical look. But he had an odd streak of sensitivity as well (any but his closest friends would have argued about that) and he realised now that Jenny was far more upset by what was happening than she wanted her husband to know. 'Get along with it, Antony,' he recommended. 'Uncle Nick won't eat you.'

Antony, smiling over the idea as he went downstairs, realised suddenly that he was distinctly unsure of his reception. He found his uncle and Vera in the study, Sir Nicholas's favourite room, and heard the murmur of their voices in companionable converse before he went in. 'It's a shame to interrupt you,' he started abruptly, 'but things have been happening.'

'Since I saw you this afternoon?' Sir Nicholas raised his eyebrows, and his calm tone deprecated to some extent his nephew's urgency. 'I thought you were going to work in chambers for the rest of the day.'

'Yes, so I did. I mean, since I came home.'

'Chief Inspector Sykes's visit,' said Vera in her grim way. 'Told you about it, Nicholas.'

'So you did, my dear. I hoped it was merely a social call. Was I wrong about that, Antony?'

'Just about as wrong as you could possibly be, Uncle Nick. It was about the Selden case.'

'Don't tell me the police are coming round to the idea that Mrs Walpole was murdered after all,' said Sir Nicholas languidly.

'No, nothing like that.'

'In any case, how did they know you were concerned?'

'They'd been keeping an eye on the Seldens – not Sykes's lot, of course – I think they've got the idea something fishy may be going on.' Sir Nicholas closed his eyes as if in pain. 'So they made a note of my visit there with Geoffrey, and Central heard about it through the grapevine.'

'There seems to be no reason why you should not have visited the Hampstead house,' said Sir Nicholas, opening his eyes again.

'It gave them ideas. And . . . well, you know, I couldn't lie to Sykes directly, Uncle Nick. He asked me straight out if that was the end of my participation in the affair.'

'And when you admitted it wasn't, jumped immediately to the conclusion that you were trying to prove murder?'

'Well, he outlined the three possible defences to me.'

'Did he, indeed?'

'Yes, and he came to the conclusion that the most likely one for me to be trying for was murder. I couldn't persuade him that I didn't know a thing to back up that idea, and then he told me that Briggs didn't like my interference.'

'Briggs?' Sir Nicholas, forgetting his languid air, sat up straight in his chair. 'What the devil has Briggs got to do with it,' he demanded.

'Nothing directly. But he's been trying his hand at a spot of clairvoyance too.'

'Better tell us what you mean,' Vera recommended.

'Only that he's apparently been saying that if I wanted to prove Mrs Walpole was murdered, he wouldn't be surprised if some evidence turned up to confirm the theory.'

'Slander!' said Sir Nicholas and Vera with one voice.

'Yes, but can you see me going to court about it? Every newspaper in the country would eat the story alive,' said Antony ruefully. 'But I haven't told you the real punch line, Uncle Nick. Some evidence *has* turned up.'

'You've been at home all the evening.'

'Sally telephoned. I'd better tell you exactly what she said.'

He paused there, and didn't continue until his uncle said, 'Well, go on!' impatiently. Then he repeated the conversation he had had with the girl, word for word as far as he could remember it. By the time he had finished Sir Nicholas was glaring at him. 'Fool of a girl!' he said.

'Nice girl, according to Antony,' Vera put in. 'Can't expect her to understand the situation.'

'No, but you do, my dear, and so do I. And so, I imagine, does Antony. This wouldn't have happened if you'd left things alone,' he added turning on his nephew.

'Obliging you,' said Vera gruffly. 'Know as well as I do, Nicholas, that you asked him to see the medium.'

'But not to continue with this – this wild-goose chase,' said Sir Nicholas scathingly. 'And he's never told me, after all, what he thinks of the woman, which is all I wanted to know.'

Antony was getting a little tired of being talked across as though he wasn't there. 'I can tell you that if it will make you any happier, Uncle Nick,' he said. 'Dorothy Selden's powers may or may not be genuine, I don't feel I'm competent to judge that, but I think it's all the same to her either way, she thinks they are.'

'Could anyone delude themselves about a thing like that?' asked Vera curiously.

'Yes, I think so. I think it's possible that's what she has

been doing all these years. But I wouldn't give tuppence for her husband's honesty, and I think he may be able to influence her, help her in many ways, perhaps without her realising it.'

'I suppose you think that's helpful,' Sir Nicholas growled. 'Do you think this Sally Walpole of yours reported their neighbour's conversation correctly?'

'I don't know.'

'Well, you'd better add him to your list, hadn't you? Only in this case you'll take Geoffrey with you, if you please. No good giving Chief Superintendent Briggs any more of a handle against you than he has already.'

'Jenny and I were wondering –'

'What were you wondering,' asked Sir Nicholas, after the pause had lengthened a little.

'I've had dealings with Briggs in the past on a number of occasions – '

'Indeed you have.' Sir Nicholas might have been mimicking his wife's habitual grim tone.

'Well, as I say, we were wondering . . . he's got ideas into his head about me before now, but do you think he has ever believed I was really in the clear?'

'Since you ask me, I think – as I have always thought – that it's very unlikely. But if Mrs Walpole's death really was murder and not suicide, we can't leave things where they are. It wouldn't be fair to my client.'

'I should like to see Mrs Selden off the hook,' Antony agreed. Sir Nicholas flung himself back into his chair.

'This passion for colloquialisms,' he protested. 'I was about to add, it wouldn't even be fair to this girl of yours. And as you're so concerned about her, you'd better do what you can to find out the truth.'

'Will you phone Geoffrey in the morning or shall I?'

'I'll phone him, and let you know the result. I think he'd better go with you to see the two other couples as well, to see fair play. What I can't make up my mind about, and should like to sleep on, is whether he should give you that brief I spoke of. Would that make things better or worse?'

'Couldn't make them worse,' said Vera gruffly.

Sir Nicholas smiled at her. 'I'm glad that you at least appreciate the situation, Vera,' he said unfairly. 'I'll speak to Geoffrey, anyway, and see what he can arrange. Seeing the neighbour is the most important thing, of course.'

'The most important thing for the defence, but perhaps not the most important from Sally's point of view,' said Antony, feeling that the time had come to assert himself a little. 'Sykes let one thing drop, Uncle Nick, he says there's a – a ring I suppose you'd call it, of art thieves operating. I wondered whether Emily Walpole, being an expert, might have stumbled on something incriminating.'

'And I wonder what other gems of information you'll come up with if we talk long enough,' said Sir Nicholas. 'I suppose you're thinking of Mrs Walpole's partner, Julian Verlaine?'

'The thought had crossed my mind.'

'Forget it until you hear what Mottram has to say. And until you have seen the others, of course. Or did Mr Verlaine strike you as a shifty sort of character, only too likely to be a murderer?'

'Anything but. I'll leave you to it then, Uncle Nick, and I'm sorry to have spoiled your quiet evening, Vera.' He got up as he spoke and made his way towards the door.

'Would you like a nightcap before you go?' asked his uncle, suddenly amiable again.

'No, thank you, Roger is upstairs with Jenny.'

'Good night then.' But Sir Nicholas spoke again, when his nephew's hand was already on the doorknob. 'Don't refine too much on Mrs Selden's prognostications,' he advised. 'What she told you won't help the situation, certainly, but it won't make it any worse.'

SATURDAY, 18th MARCH, 1972

I

Sir Nicholas duly telephoned Geoffrey Horton the next morning, which resulted in the solicitor presenting himself for luncheon, which the Maitlands habitually took on Saturday with their uncle and aunt. Geoffrey, it must be admitted, was a little out of temper, though in Vera's presence he tried to disguise the fact. He was not yet quite at ease with the new Lady Harding. But this didn't prevent him speaking his mind to Antony, whom he cornered before they went into the dining-room. 'It means beginning all over again,' he said, 'and all the work I've done already wasted.'

'I'm sorry about that.'

'As for this idea of Sir Nicholas's of briefing you – '

'You don't think it's a good one,' said Maitland hopefully.

'As a matter of fact, I do. It may keep you out of mischief, by placing the responsibility exactly where it ought to be.' Then suddenly Geoffrey smiled. 'No, seriously, Antony,' he said. 'If you think the wretched woman was murdered, that's a good defence. I'll be very glad of your help.'

'You do understand, I hope, that the operative word there is "think",' Antony pointed out.

'Yes, you can be as cautious as you like, but I know you when you've got an idea into your head. The aggravating part about it is that you're generally right,' Geoffrey admitted.

'I know I'm a trial to you,' Maitland said meekly. 'But you do realise we're treading on what may be a quagmire at the moment. Sally Walpole's opinion is one thing, she may or

133

may not be right. But unless this man Mottram comes up with any definite evidence – '

'Sir Nicholas explained all that to me. We've an appointment with Mottram at three o'clock. I don't suppose it will take us more than five minutes to walk round to the mews.'

'Did Uncle Nick also tell you what Sykes had to say?'

'He did.'

'And about Briggs's prediction that new evidence might turn up?'

'That too. I really don't think you've anything to worry about though, Antony.'

'In spite of what's happened in the past? Do you remember what happened seven years ago for instance? Almost exactly seven years ago.'

'Am I likely to forget? There have been occasions since then, too, when you haven't seen eye to eye,' Geoffrey pointed out. 'But he can't accuse you of being anything but unorthodox, Antony, a thing even your best friends will admit. As your solicitor I'm perfectly well aware that you've never done anything contrary to either the letter or the spirit of the law.'

'That's making rather a mouthful of it. Still, I thank you for these kind words.' Maitland's humorous look was for the moment very marked, as he recalled the one occasion, unknown to Horton, when a purist might have held that he stepped out of line. 'I don't seem to remember though,' he went on, 'that you've ever had much success in convincing Briggs of that.'

'Not in convincing him perhaps, but pretty successful in getting you off the hook,' said Geoffrey stoutly. And broke off when he saw Maitland put his finger to his lips.

'Don't let's destroy the harmony of this luncheon party by letting Uncle Nick hear you using slang,' Antony said. 'One way and another, he's a little touchy at the moment.'

'I'll be careful,' Geoffrey promised, and glanced across to where Jenny was keeping Sir Nicholas and Vera in conversation. 'I never expected, as a matter of fact, that he would accept the brief in the first case, considering who the client is.'

'He was intrigued I think, as I am. Do you still think Mrs Selden is a fraud?'

'You know my opinion about all this fortune-telling business.'

'Now you're running the risk of getting up against Uncle Nick again. He'll tell you to be more exact in your terminology. Dorothy Selden is a trance medium and a clairvoyant, not a fortune-teller.'

'I stand corrected. Anyway, Antony, you know perfectly well what I mean.'

'Perhaps I do. But *you* tell *me*, Geoffrey, allowing it's all humbug for a moment – and I'm not at all sure about that – what do you think about her?'

'I think her husband –'

'Yes, we've already discussed that and I agree with you. It's Mrs Selden I'm talking about.'

'She seems a good sort of woman,' said Geoffrey a little grudgingly. 'And since you press me, I can't see her deliberately setting out to deceive people.'

'Then aren't you a little sorry for her? Think what losing this case would mean, even leaving the financial considerations aside.'

'Ruin!' said Geoffrey in a hollow tone. 'No, I'm not taking it lightly,' he added in response to Antony's reproachful look. 'I only think you've been side-tracked by sympathy for Sally Walpole. If it leads to an acquittal, I'm grateful of course. But I don't see much point in arguing about it until we've seen this man Mottram.'

'Tell me at least about the medical evidence.'

'That's the last thing I expected you to be interested in,' said Geoffrey, who knew his friend very well.

'I shall have to be interested in it when we got into court,' Antony pointed out.

'Carbon-monoxide poisoning.'

'Yes, I know that. At this juncture I only want to know whether the time Mottram said he saw Mrs Walpole going across the mews towards the garage with a male companion, fitted in with the time of death according to the doctors.'

'When I spoke to him, he wouldn't give the time to a minute or two, but it was about ten-thirty. But then, the doctors aren't exact either. However,' – seeing Maitland's downcast look – 'they say the whole messy process might have been started earlier than that, but hardly any later. So if Mottram comes up to proof, that will be a big point in favour of murder. Though I must remind you, we've only heard from him at second-hand so far, plus the few words I exchanged with him over the phone.'

'When is the case likely to come on, by the way?'

'Didn't Sir Nicholas tell you? It's been put forward in the list. Easter is early this year, so we may be in court about the middle of April, or a little later.'

'I suppose that's all to the good,' said Maitland reflectively, 'considering there's very little we can do in preparation.' He broke off there as he caught Vera's eye. 'I didn't see Gibbs come in, did you? But I think we're being summoned to lunch.'

II

By common consent, the subject was avoided while the meal was in progress, but afterwards they lingered over their coffee until it was time for Antony and Geoffrey to leave for Bruton Mews. They went on foot, leaving Geoffrey's car parked in the square, and the only words that passed between them on the way were Antony's invitation to tea afterwards, and Geoffrey's acceptance.

It occurred to Antony as they turned into the mews, that they might not know much about Mr Mottram – not even his first name or his profession yet – but that he was obviously a man of means. It had taken money in the first place to do the renovations that Sally Walpole had spoken of, and at today's prices it must take almost as much money to keep everything ship-shape. That was his first impression, of a perfection that is rare today, and when the door at Number Three was opened there was nothing in the tiny hall within to make him change his view. It was a smaller house than its neighbour, the renovations must have been done, as Sally had said, to the individual requirements of the purchasers, and this impression was confirmed when the door at the right of the hall opened and a little gnome of a man peered out. He was very small, perhaps not more than five foot, and he had a fringe of brown hair round a brown shiny pate. 'Mr Horton,' he said. 'And Mr Maitland! I'm very pleased to see you. That will be all, Mrs Marlow, thank you. My housekeeper,' he added, leading the way to the room from which he had emerged. 'An invaluable woman, if only she wouldn't fuss.'

His voice was high and thin, to Antony's ears more like a bat's squeak than anything else, though his appearance certainly didn't suggest one.

The room was very masculine, though everything about it was as perfect as what they had seen already. 'I wonder,' said Antony, smiling and looking about him, 'whether you were not, perhaps a customer of Verlaine and Walpole?'

'Poor Emily! But sit down, sit down do. To be away all that time and never hear a word! And then, when I came home, to find that she had gone. But you're quite right, Mr Maitland, I think perhaps I was one of their best – certainly one of their oldest – customers. They are an excellent firm you know, absolutely reliable.'

'Pardon me, Mr Mottram,' said Geoffrey, seating himself upon his host's invitation, 'you know why we're here?'

'Certainly I do. You explained it all to me very fully on the telephone. I'm curious, though, as to how you knew I had what you chose to call evidence.'

'It may or may not turn out that way.' Horton set himself

to explain, as fully as he felt was politic, the ramifications of the case against Mrs Selden.

'And you heard of me through Sally Walpole, eh?' said Mottram shrewdly when he had finished.

'Yes we did,' said Geoffrey. And,

'How did you guess that?' Antony asked, almost simultaneously.

'I went round to see Daniel as soon as I could, after hearing the tragic news. I don't suppose it will surprise you to know it was the first thing Mrs Marlow told me. Sally was with him. They are not in agreement about this very sad business, but I dare say you know that yourself, Mr Maitland.'

'Yes,' Antony admitted, but did not attempt to amplify the statement. After a moment Mottram went on.

'She . . . well, I can only say she pounced on the information I gave them. Daniel was clearly angry with her about it. I had known, of course, before I went away, that he was very bitter that Emily should consult such a person after poor Michael's death. I don't quite understand Sally's attitude, I'm afraid.'

'An innate sense of justice,' said Antony solemnly. The other man smiled at him suddenly, an extraordinarily charming smile.

'She thinks her mother was murdered,' he asserted. 'And you think that if you can prove that, or even suggest it very strongly to the jury, it will clear your Mrs Selden of the accusation Daniel is making against her. And of her possible liability for damages,' he added thoughtfully.

'You're perfectly right, of course. And that's why we want some details from you. May I ask you first – Mr Horton is a stickler for getting things in the right order – what your full name is, and what is your profession?'

'Charles Mottram. I'm a bookseller.'

'Then it couldn't have been business that kept you abroad for so long.'

'That would depend on my destination. I should have said,

I'm an antiquarian bookseller. But in this instance, my trip to South America, I went to see my niece and her family. My business is more or less a hobby really, it wouldn't suffer in my absence, and in any event my assistants are perfectly capable.'

'And nobody here corresponded with you while you were away?'

'No, why should they? I suppose the Walpoles were my closest friends, and Daniel certainly had other things on his mind. But I mustn't mislead you, Mr Maitland, I'm something of a recluse, and it was only the interest I had in common with Emily that brought us together. I'm sure from the Walpoles' point of view I was really no more than an acquaintance, they have a very wide circle of friends.'

'Your friendship – your acquaintance, if you prefer the word – was more with Mrs Walpole than with her husband, then?'

'I have a regard for Daniel, but our values are not at all the same. In a way I think you could say his world is bounded by financial considerations.'

'Do you think that's why he's suing Mrs Selden?'

'No, I think I indicated that. It was a very deep revulsion from his wife having had anything to do with something he disapproved of so thoroughly.'

'But with Mrs Walpole you felt more at home?'

'Oh yes, indeed. We are neither of us very knowledgeable about each other's affairs, of course, but you'd only to see her handle a book to know how much she loved beautiful things. As for me, I had an interest, but very little knowledge, in all the lines where her expertise was acknowledged. You see that painting.' Both Antony and Geoffrey turned to look. 'She sold it to me years ago, I had to refurnish the whole room when I hung it. You must admit it's a beautiful thing, and deserves nothing less than a perfect setting.'

'Yes, very beautiful. Then I take it you can confirm that Emily Walpole was happy in her work.'

'As happy as anyone can be. I shouldn't say she had a worry in the world until Michael was killed.'

'Tell me about that. How did you hear?'

'Sally came round to tell me. She's a very thoughtful girl, you know, and was afraid I might meet her mother and talk to her, not knowing what had happened. That way I could easily have said something to hurt her more.'

'When did you see her?'

'Emily? Not for a day or two. Sally said she was too upset. So I just sent flowers, and then went round about tea time . . . I should think it was the Thursday, I can't be sure about that. She was alone and we had an hour's talk together. Michael was . . . very dear to her, you know.' He paused there and looked from one of his companions to the other. 'I don't want to deceive you,' he said, 'and even taking what you call my evidence into consideration I think you may be all wrong about Emily's death. The verdict of suicide seems such a very likely one.'

'Why is that, Mr Mottram?'

'Because, just on that one subject, she wasn't really normal. This is not for publication, but I think you are both serious in wanting to know the truth, and I don't want you to be misled by what I have to say and by Sally's enthusiasm. There was something not quite healthy in Emily's devotion to her son.'

'Don't distress yourself, Mr Mottram, we already had some inkling of that. Tell me what you talked about that day. The day you took tea together.'

'About Michael, about her grief, at that stage I hardly said a word. But then she began to talk of this Mrs Selden she had heard of, a wonderful person, she said, and I had to remind her that she had heard of her through me.'

'Is that so? Nobody could tell me who had put them in touch.'

'Well, I have to claim that distinction. I've never been to one of Mrs Selden's seances, but I have heard of her from friends, and I think there's no doubt she's an extraordinary woman. When I mentioned her to Emily, of course, it was months before Michael's death, and I never had the faintest idea she would ever consult her.'

'But now she thought she might?'

'It was the obvious thing to do, wasn't it, when she missed Michael so badly and wanted to get in touch with him again?'

'You didn't try to discourage her.'

'Do you think I should have done? No, I thought no harm could come of it, and that at the very least she would gain a little comfort.'

'I gather you are a believer yourself, Mr Mottram?'

'Oh yes, indeed, I've attended the spiritualist church close by here for many years. But in Emily's case, when she mentioned Mrs Selden, I could see that it would be more appropriate. Another woman – ' He didn't attempt to finish the sentence.

'And after you heard of Michael's message?'

'I never did hear of it, not until Daniel told me when I went to see him yesterday. It horrified me of course, but you must understand, Mr Maitland, that a trance medium has no control over what the spirits may say through her. But I do really think you should forget this nonsense about murder, and concentrate on proving that she isn't a fraud. I have heard of cases where a medium's powers were demonstrated in court.'

'It may come to that,' said Geoffrey with a sidelong look at his friend.

'Well, let's not anticipate trouble.' Maitland was brisk again. 'You saw her again later, I suppose, from time to time. Was she comforted by her visits to Mrs Selden?'

'Oh, certainly. Very much comforted.'

'And during the last few days of her life, that is between the Monday and the Thursday, did you see her at all?'

'I saw her once. I think it was on the Monday morning, I walked round to the gallery to tell her of my plans. You see she was in the habit of letting me know if anything came in that might interest me, I didn't want her to be worried by my absence.'

'The Monday morning. Before the seance at which she got Michael's last message then?'

'She didn't mention it. I'm sure it was the Monday,' he added in rather a worried way. 'Absolutely certain,' he went on with more conviction. 'But if it weren't for that I'd have said she had already heard that Michael said he needed her. She already seemed *distrait*, hardly as if she was taking in what I was telling her at all.'

'Now that *is* interesting.'

'Is it?' said Mottram, inclined to be nervous now. 'I'm afraid you're getting some very strange ideas into your heads,' he added doubtfully.

Antony took no notice of that. 'What do you know of Julian Verlaine?' he asked.

'A pleasant man,' said Mottram vaguely.

'That wasn't quite what I meant. As a business-man, for instance. You said the firm had the highest reputation.'

'Indeed they had, and Verlaine no less than Emily. I saw him many times at the gallery, of course, but it was because of living next door that I was more intimate with Emily.'

'At those visits of yours to her, did you meet any of her other friends?'

'There was a Mrs Hazlitt, who must have been a frequent visitor at the Walpoles. I say that because I met her many times, even though I went there so rarely.'

'Had she any other friends who were interested in art or antiques as you were, and whom you might have met at the gallery?'

'That I can't tell you. I remember her mentioning once that someone called David had been worrying her with a continuous series of questions about art. Who were the great collectors? What were their preferences? Things like that.'

'They were natural questions in the circumstances, I should have thought.'

142

'No, because Emily said he had no interest in the subject himself. She thought he was trying to get round her, making a pass at her I believe you young people would call it.'

'I see.' It might be considered flattering, of course, to be relegated to the same age group as Sally Walpole, but he didn't feel particularly elated. 'Then that brings us, I'm afraid, Mr Mottram, to this story of yours that you are so reluctant to call evidence.'

'You mean what I saw the night before I left England? It's easily told, and not particularly informative. I'd been out to dinner. Mrs Marlow hates waste so – she says it's a relic of the war years, but I think it is an ingrained habit with her – that she'd quite run us out of food, so I had no alternative. I don't like to dine early, and I've nothing to get home for, so it must have been half past ten or very nearly when I ran my car into the garage. When I came out and pulled down the door Emily was just coming across the mews towards the garages.'

'You saw her quite clearly?'

'Oh yes, there's no question about that at all. There's a lamp on a bracket jutting out from the wall between our two garages, well you must have seen it for yourself as you came in. The light was falling full on her face.'

'How did she look?'

'Now that's a question I've been asking myself ever since I heard of the tragedy. The answer is that she looked just as usual, I mean just as she usually did since Michael's death. Not happy. I sometimes wonder if what happened wasn't the best thing, if she would ever have been happy again. And perhaps she was a little flustered, but I may be imagining that.'

'Thank you, Mr Mottram, that's very clear indeed. Now, about the man who was with her.'

'Daniel doubts his existence,' Mottram told him. 'I didn't get a very good look at him, you know. He was walking behind and a little to the left of her, the lamplight didn't fall so far.'

'You're sure however, that it was a man.'

'Oh yes, quite sure. I know so many women wear trousers nowadays, very foolish of them I think it, not the thing that suits them best. But they walk differently, I'm sure you've seen that for yourself. The figure I saw was certainly male.'

'Can you give us any description at all?'

'A tall man, though nowhere near your height, Mr Maitland. Perhaps Mr Horton would form a better comparison. He had on a dark overcoat, and I have the impression that what I could see of his suit – just the legs of his trousers – was dark too.'

'Was he wearing a hat?'

'No, I'm quite sure about that.'

'Isn't there anything else you can tell us? Had he a moustache for instance, or did he wear glasses?'

'I couldn't be sure about either of those things.'

'I suppose then you wouldn't recognise him again.'

'I might if I saw him under the same conditions. No, I'm not being exact, Mr Maitland. I could do no more than tell you that it *might be* the same man.'

'Isn't it rather odd, if he was really with Mrs Walpole, that you didn't see him follow her into the circle of light?'

'I . . . that is rather odd now you mention it.'

'You're quite sure he stayed in the shadow?'

'Yes. Yes, I am.'

'But are you equally sure that he really was with Mrs Walpole?'

'Quite positive. She spoke to him, you see.'

'Not to you?'

'Oh yes, of course. She said good evening, and paused a moment to wish me a safe trip. Which you are going to say, Mr Maitland, makes it all the odder that her companion didn't catch up with her. But what she said to him was quite different. She was speaking over her shoulder and she said, "Soper will be eternally grateful to you if you can fix it." '

'Soper,' said Geoffrey, accustomed to keeping counsel in line, 'is the Walpoles' chauffeur.'

'I haven't forgotten it. Have I covered all the ground, Geoffrey, or is there anything else you want to ask?'

'You've been pretty thorough,' said Horton smiling. 'We're grateful to you, Mr Mottram.'

'Does this mean I shall be called as a witness?'

'I'm afraid it does. Does that worry you?'

'No, not in the slightest. Daniel will be angry with me. But then, now that Emily is gone, there's really no reason why we should see much of each other. And Sally, I think, will bless me.'

'I expect she will,' said Antony, when they got out into the mews again. 'What do you think now about the chances of Mrs Walpole having been murdered?'

'Mr Mottram is a very important witness,' said Horton slowly. 'He can't make a positive identification, but –'

'This man he saw,' Antony interrupted eagerly, 'who seems to have tried to avoid being seen clearly, must have known something about cars. Surely that fact should be of some help to us.'

'Yes, I think it should.'

'That's one more question for Uncle Nick to ask Soper when we get him into court,' Antony persisted. 'Was something wrong with the car?'

'And supposing he says no?'

'If Mottram is telling the truth – and I don't see why he should be lying – there must have been something wrong with it. And I don't see why Soper should lie either,' he added slowly. 'Unless he's bright enough, and has sufficient knowledge of the law, to see where the questions are tending. In that case I suppose he might answer as he felt his employer would like him to do. Anyway,' Antony added buoyantly, 'we're miles ahead of where we were. What's the next move?'

'I haven't made any arrangements with the other two

couples,' said Geoffrey. 'I thought we'd better see what Mr Mottram had to say first. If we're going back to Kempenfeldt Square for tea, perhaps I can use your phone.'

'Good idea. And if I know anything of Uncle Nick and Vera, they'll be with Jenny when we get there.'

He was right about that. He was probably also right in his private conviction that Vera was just as interested in the matter as his uncle was. In any event, nobody tried to start any other topic of conversation, though they did not wait until the tea was poured before all the questions started. Antony said, 'You have the floor Geoffrey,' and left it to Horton to recount their interview with Mr Mottram. When the solicitor had finished, Sir Nicholas's eyes were fixed meditatively on his nephew's face.

'Do you think he'll make a good witness?' he said.

'He's very sure of himself, and not at all put out by the prospect of appearing in court.'

'And if the police try to suggest he's being . . . shall we say prompted to tell the story?'

'Why should they? He's a respectable man –'

'So far as we know,' said Geoffrey, *sotto voce.*

' – and obviously a wealthy one. No, I don't think we need worry about Briggs, Uncle Nick. And Mottram's evidence opens up a whole new line of questioning for the chauffeur, in addition to the things you were going to ask him already.'

'Do you think you can find Emily Walpole's mysterious companion?'

'We're going to have a damned good try.'

'Are you working on the theory that he's one of the people you had already in mind to question, one of the guests at the dinner-party?'

'Yes I am. If he really killed Mrs Walpole, and rigged it to look like suicide – '

'I think I agree with you. But you must also bear in mind, Antony, that you have adopted this theory because it is the only one open to you, you can hardly question the entire circle of the Walpoles' friends and relations.'

'No, that's true. But don't damp my hopes altogether, Uncle Nick. I want to talk to Sally again, she may be able to help me in the light of this new knowledge. And also I'd like to talk to Mrs Selden.'

'I thought we had covered everything pretty exhaustively with her.'

'In a way.' The idea that was in his mind was too tenuous for explanation, but he couldn't resist adding, with intent to annoy, 'Geoffrey's talking of holding a seance in the court-room, to convince the judge and jury that she's genuine.'

Sir Nicholas – seeming to forget for the moment that the idea had been put forward before – sat up suddenly very straight and spilled his tea. 'Is this true?' he asked, scowling at his instructing solicitor.

'It was a suggestion of Mr Mottram's,' said Geoffrey hastily. 'But it's been done before, you know. If we were surer of her – '

'All the same,' said Antony, 'it might be illuminating to make the suggestion. I think the thing we have to decide now is whether the police should be told about this new evidence, or whether we should wait and spring it on them at the trial.'

'What do you think, Geoffrey?' asked Sir Nicholas, relaxing again.

Horton didn't get time to reply to that. 'Should be told,' said Vera positively, and glanced at Jenny curled up in her own corner on the sofa. 'Agree with me?' she said.

'Yes, of course I do,' said Jenny, more definitely than she was accustomed to speak.

'This is obviously a joint decision,' said Sir Nicholas, interested. 'Are you going to explain it to me, my dear?'

'All the circumstances,' said Vera, at her most elliptical. 'Better for Antony that way.'

'You mean in view of the suggestions that have been made?' Vera nodded violently, and, as so often happened, the pins began to slip from her hair. 'Hear it officially from Geoffrey, put a different light on everything.'

'I think you're right. The question is, whom should he approach?'

'Local police, try to get them to reopen the investigation. If it's murder it's within Central's jurisdiction, Briggs will be bound to hear about it.'

'So he will. And that seems to have been decided, Geoffrey. Will you proceed along those lines?'

'Yes, of course. I have to say, I agree with Lady Harding.'

'The only thing is,' said Antony, 'are we prejudicing our client's case by doing that?'

'Not in the slightest, as far as I can see,' Sir Nicholas told him. 'In this particular case I don't think it matters whether we spring the evidence on the prosecution or not. The only thing is' – he looked round his audience deliberately before he went on – 'I don't think any of you should get your hopes up too high. This man Mottram may prove a broken reed.'

'You mean he may not stand up to cross-examination?'

'That's exactly what I mean, Antony.'

'I'm more worried about what the jury will make of him. Another spiritualist – '

'That just underlines what I was going to say. Our safest plan is to prove murder, not just suggest it. And I don't see how we can do that without identifying the murderer.'

'You're right of course. Besides,' he added smiling, 'there's Sally to consider.'

'She didn't sound to me like a vengeful young lady.'

'No, not at all. I mean that isn't the reason she wants the person found. She realises it must be a friend of the family, and feels she can't face the uncertainty of going through the rest of her life not knowing. Uncle Julian for instance – that's what she calls Mr Verlaine, although he isn't really her uncle. If she were talking to him, and suddenly began to wonder whether *he* was the one . . . you can see it isn't a nice position to be in.'

'Well, as her interests seem to run parallel with our client's, there seems to be no reason not to try to oblige her,' said Sir Nicholas. 'I think Vera was right in what she said the other night: if an arrest were made Daniel Walpole might be willing to drop his charges against Mrs Selden.'

At that point Vera wrenched the conversation forcibly into other channels. The matter was returned to again briefly after tea when Geoffrey did his telephoning, and came back to report that both the Chorleys and the Hazlitts would be at home the following afternoon, and would be pleased to see him. 'I'll call for you about two o'clock, Antony, shall I?' he asked.

'Yes, that would do splendidly. In the meantime I'll phone Sally — '

'I think,' said Geoffrey seriously, 'we'd better see her together too.'

'Just as you like,' said Maitland, but not without certain mental reservations. 'When will you get in touch with the police?'

'If it's to be done at all, I suppose I'd better do it straight away,' said Geoffrey, showing some signs of reluctance, now that the time for action had come. 'The question is,' he added as he and Antony went downstairs together, 'will it have the desired effect on Briggs?'

'I should think so. He may suspect *me* of some double dealing, but he can't possibly suspect Mr Mottram.' At that moment, though he would have died rather than say so, Sykes's warning about the organised art thefts was more clearly in his mind. Which goes to show that nobody can be right all the time.

I

The next afternoon Geoffrey Horton called for Maitland as promised, and as it was Sunday and he felt there was some hope of getting parking space they took the car with them, instead of looking for a taxi. The Chorleys' flat, which was really what the estate agents rather revoltingly called an Upper Maisonette, was more conveniently situated, so they went there first. It was an old, rather shabby building in need of a lick of paint, but conveniently central and probably fabulously expensive. (Since his encounter with Sally Walpole, Antony found himself automatically thinking in superlatives.) Inside, however, the rooms were large and airy, and if the furnishing had been done with a regard for comfort rather than for taste, neither of the visitors felt inclined to cavil about that.

David Chorley let them in, and led them into the drawing-room, where his wife was awaiting them. He was a man of medium height, squarely built, with a red, good-humoured face and dark hair that waved irrepressibly. Looking at him, Antony realised for the first time that Charles Mottram's estimate of the height of the man he had seen in the mews was likely to be just about as much use to them as a sick headache. To a man as short as that, pretty well everyone must seem tall. Louise Chorley remained seated, but even so he thought she probably had an inch or two's advantage over her husband. She was a thin, rather droopy-looking woman – or was that impression caused by the way she dressed? – with a rather intense look in her eye that didn't seem in keeping with the rest of her appearance. Geoffrey in his meticulous way was performing the introductions, explaining that they were anxious to get as many opinions as possible as to Mrs Walpole's state of mind immediately before the tragedy, and it was obvious that Chorley had difficulty in hearing him out in silence.

'I've never seen one of you fellows before,' he burst out as soon as he decently could, his eyes now on Antony's face. 'Not you, Mr Horton, of course. You fellows are ten a penny if you don't mind my saying so. I've read about some of your cases, though, Mr Maitland, but I've never actually met a barrister before.'

'Haven't you?' said Antony. The gentleness of his tone made Geoffrey glance at him in alarm.

David Chorley was quite unabashed. 'Interesting line of business,' he said, 'but I've always thought . . . I'm an advertising man myself – '

'Then that explains why you've never encountered any of my colleagues. We don't go in for advertising.'

'I know that. Silly, I call it. Do you the world of good professionally to have a good PR man.'

What Antony's reaction to this ingenious suggestion might have been, if he hadn't seen the funny side of the situation, is uncertain. As it was he smiled with something that at least approximated amusement and said, 'I'm afraid it wouldn't go down well with the Bar Council.'

'There you are you see,' said Chorley, as if he had just proved his point. 'But what's all this about Emily Walpole now? *We* can't tell you anything.'

'Such a tragedy,' said Louise Chorley in a fading voice.

Antony turned to her. 'Yes,' he agreed, rather too readily, Geoffrey thought. 'But you see, we need help badly in preparing our case, and the opinion of someone as sensitive as yourself would obviously be invaluable.'

'Anything I can do, of course.'

'You can answer a few questions for us. Quite simple questions, nothing to be alarmed about. For instance, when did you last see Mrs Walpole?'

'The Walpoles had a dinner-party on the Wednesday evening, the day before she – she killed herself.'

'I didn't mean that evening. Did you see her during the previous week?'

'Yes, she came in here on the Sunday afternoon, quite unexpectedly. I was resting as it happened and David was a little annoyed because Carmelita showed her straight into the study, which he considers very much his own private domain.' She paused and smiled at her husband, the indulgent sort of look she might have bestowed on a loved, but tiresome child, and turned her attention to Maitland again. 'I think as a matter of fact that he was having forty winks himself,' she explained, 'though he said he was doing *The Times* crossword puzzle.'

'You didn't see her at all yourself, then?'

'No, not that day.'

'Then we shall have to rely on Mr Chorley's impressions. How did she seem?'

Chorley took up the tale. 'She was a very sad woman,' he said. He seemed to be making a real effort to tone down his natural exuberance, in face of the tragedy that had followed. 'She wasn't any different that day than she had been in the half a dozen times we'd seen her since Michael died.'

'She did her best,' said Louise, 'but the wound ran very deep. I wrote her a little poem about it, if I'd seen her that day I would have given it to her, but David didn't want to disturb me. I don't always sleep well at night.'

'What was her reason for coming?'

'To see me.'

'Did she tell you that, Mr Chorley?'

'No, I gather Louise only knows it because of something Emily said the following Wednesday.'

'That brings us to that evening then, two days after the

152

seance where Michael is supposed to have spoken to her. What did you think when you heard the story?'

'I thought the Seldens were on to a good thing, and had got Emily properly hooked,' said Chorley bluntly.

'What about you, Mrs Chorley?'

'It's so difficult to know. There could be something in it, Harriet Verlaine says there is, and we can't deny Emily was finding some consolation in her visits. That's what she wanted to talk to me about on Sunday, you know, only David being a complete sceptic she didn't mention it to him. And I don't know that I'm any more a believer myself, but at least I wouldn't say anything that might hurt her or disturb her faith.'

'This last message from Michael, how did she take it?'

'I thought it did her good to tell us about it,' said Louise. 'Anything is better than keeping things bottled up inside you. She seemed to have got over the worst of the shock, and to be taking some consolation in the fact that he said he still needed her. That's a very real necessity for a woman you know, Mr Maitland, to be needed. And there was also the fact that he would be waiting for her.'

'Well, I don't agree with you at all, my dear.' Chorley was at his bluntest again. 'I think the whole thing had upset her very badly, talking about it only made it worse, and though it never occurred to me at the time that she might do anything drastic I wasn't a bit surprised when I heard what had happened.'

'You think then, Mr Chorley, that the message was a complete fake? Why should Mrs Selden have done such a thing?'

'It's as I said, they'd got their hooks into her. That message was just meant to make her more dependent on them.'

'Yes, that may be so. There are two things that puzzle me though. Don't you think it was a little odd that she didn't leave a suicide note?'

This time it was Louise who answered more quickly, saying definitely, 'Yes, I thought that at the time. Emily had a passion for explaining herself. But I suppose David's right, she was too upset to think what she was doing.'

'Well, I don't think it's strange,' said Chorley. 'You've got to admit, Louise, that she was more interested in Michael, even after he was dead, than she was in anything else in this world. If she was going to join him – I mean, of course, if she thought she was – why should she bother about Daniel? Or even about Sally.'

Louise just shook her head doubtfully. 'The other thing – an even smaller point really – is why a woman like her, an artistic woman I suppose you could describe her, should choose just that way of killing herself?' said Maitland carefully. He had to admit that in Mrs Chorley's company he felt very much as though he were walking on eggshells.

'But nothing could be more simple,' said David, getting in first this time. 'If anyone would understand how it could be done it would be Emily, she always had her nose in some book or other about crime.'

'Unwomanly,' said Louise, and shuddered. 'Though I shouldn't say that now she's dead. And now I think about it I can only suppose you're right, David, she was too upset to know what she was doing.'

'Then that seems to cover everything. Unless you can think of anything else, Geoffrey. Do you think,' said Antony, getting to his feet, 'that Mrs Walpole's profession was of any comfort to her during those weeks after Michael was killed?'

'Comfort is too big a word, Mr Maitland,' said Louise. 'Perhaps you could say it was a distraction for her.'

'I understand you have some interest in art yourself, Mr Chorley.' He was moving towards the door now.

'I? No. What made you think that?'

'Something I heard,' said Antony vaguely.

'From Sally Walpole, I bet. Do you know Sally?'

'I'm hoping to see her this evening if she's at home,' said Maitland evasively.

For all her woebegone appearance Louise produced unexpectedly quite a jolly laugh. 'It was a game he used to play,
Mr Maitland,' she told him, 'asking Emily questions, pretend-
ing an interest to make her interested in him. She was a very
attractive woman, you know, and David can't resist a pretty
face.' It was obvious that this was a fact she had accepted
years ago, and that it no longer caused her any distress.

'That's right,' said David Chorley a little uncomfortably.
'Give away all my secrets. Got to do the polite thing, but it's
not always all that easy to find a subject of conversation with
the ladies.'

'Not if you assume that they're all nitwits, or incapable of
grasping more than one subject at a time,' Louise retorted,
without apparent resentment. And this time it was she who
came into the hall with her visitors, while her husband remained in the drawing-room. 'He went so far as to buy a
painting from Emily once,' she confided, her hand already on
the knob of the front door.

'When was that Mrs Chorley?'

'Not long before she died. He's a kinder person than you
might think, just meeting him casually, and I expect he
thought it might distract her. But it was a dark, gloomy thing,
I couldn't stand it. So I was glad he had sense enough not to
keep it, we aren't furnished to provide a background for that
sort of thing.'

'Did he send it back to the gallery?'

'I suppose so, it was the obvious thing to do. It wasn't,'
she said, droopy again and looking very much as if she were
going to burst into tears, 'as though Emily could be hurt by
anything any more.'

But Antony had already lost interest. 'Mrs Chorley, do you
really think Emily Walpole would have chosen that way
out?'

'I think she was the type who might often have considered
suicide,' said Louise, to his discomfort. 'But, of course, I didn't
expect anything of the kind, and I was surprised at the way

she had chosen. But then, her interest in crime surprised me too, it just shows you never can tell about other people?'

'Satisfied?' asked Geoffrey as they walked back to the car.

'We shan't be calling them,' said Maitland positively.

'You're talking now about our ostensible reason for going there. Obviously his mind is made up, and hers isn't much better. But you're looking for a murderer . . . remember? What was all that business about art?'

'So are you,' said Antony. 'Looking for a murderer, I mean. And I told you what Sykes said about the art thefts, it's obviously something we have to consider. But I can't say I'm much interested in a friendly transaction that was called off as soon as one of the parties was dead. There's obviously no lack of money, and Chorley is just the type to do anything to make himself popular. Even to saddling himself with a Picasso I shouldn't wonder.'

'It didn't sound like a Picasso,' said Geoffrey.

'No, just a figure of speech. The only other thing that struck me was that I don't think Louise Chorley is a particularly good judge of character, do you?'

'That sounds like a *non sequitur*.'

'Perhaps it is. Here we are, Geoffrey, let's see if the Hazlitts can be any more helpful. Sally Walpole told me he owns three cars,' he added, as Geoffrey unlocked the door and he got into the Humber.

Geoffrey made no reply to that, he was already engaged in the tricky manoeuvre of extricating himself from a parking space that was really six inches too short.

II

Their way to the Hazlitt's house led them a short distance through the park, where the signs of spring were even more evident. Antony's thoughts were idle, and concerned mainly with the feeling that it would be nice to get out of town, and that it was pleasant that Easter came early this year. And then there popped into his mind an odd thought about Dorothy Selden, who had showed no signs of anxiety at all over her forthcoming ordeal. He thought she had a naturally placid disposition, but was that all it was?

It would seem the Hazlitts occupied the whole of one of the tall narrow houses in Eastholm Court. It couldn't possibly be kept up without help of some kind, but again it was the husband who answered the door. Theodore Hazlitt was very thin, very round-shouldered, very dark, with a sprouting black moustache – not neat like Angus Fyleman's – and heavy eyebrows. He had rather a sad air, as though the troubles of the world weighed heavily upon him, but he greeted them pleasantly enough and led the way into the drawing-room. Again the promise made to Geoffrey Horton had been kept to the letter, and Mrs Hazlitt was waiting for them. Antony took a moment or two to study her, while Geoffrey went into what Maitland had been known to call irreverently his song and dance act. Was she a beauty, or did she create an illusion of beauty by the elegance and the perfection of her turnout? She had short dark hair, which looked as if it had been cut by a master and then forgotten, eyes that looked green (perhaps that was due to a heavy application of eye shadow), and a rather thick-lipped sulky mouth, the kind that spells trouble in any language. That, at least, was Antony's conclusion, even before her attitude confirmed the diagnosis. Hearing Geoffrey nearing his conclusion, he called his mind to order again, and found that his hostess was eyeing him with equal curiosity.

'That's all very well,' she said, when Horton had finished. 'I don't see why we should try to help this Selden woman.'

'We don't know yet whether what you have to say will help her,' Antony pointed out.

'Well, Alfreda, I think we should do what we can,' said Theodore. (Had Sally really said that most people called him Ted? It seemed very unlikely.) 'We can certainly tell these gentlemen something of Emily's state of mind during the last week of her life, you perhaps better than I.'

'Oh, very well! It seems to be a lot of fuss about nothing. All these people are charlatans, and I don't suppose she's any different.'

This was obviously as near to agreement as they were going to get from her. 'The Walpoles had a dinner-party the night before Mrs Walpole died,' said Antony, 'and I believe you were both present. Had you seen her before that, say during the week before?'

'No, we hadn't.' Hazlitt took it upon himself to answer, looking very much as though he was about to burst into tears. 'Unless, Alfreda, you went to the house to see her as you sometimes do.'

'I did, as a matter of fact. What of it?'

'Nothing, except that I should like you to tell me when it was, and how Mrs Walpole seemed to you.'

'I remember it very well because it was at teatime on the Thursday.'

'The day she died?'

'That's what I mean.' She condescended to explain a little. 'My salon isn't far from where the Walpoles live, and if I can get away I often go – I mean, I often used to go – to have tea with Emily.' She paused there, still eyeing him speculatively, and then added in an abrupt way, 'You're the man the newspapers say never loses a case, aren't you? How interesting to meet you!' The sarcasm in her tone cut like a knife.

Her obvious hostility had, however, the effect of distracting Antony from his perennial grievance against the newspapers. 'I'm glad you think so,' he said lightly. 'But we were talking about Mrs Walpole's state of mind that Thursday afternoon.'

'She was . . . just as usual. That is, she'd never been exactly a cheerful companion since Michael died. Considering how wrapped up in him she was, I suppose one couldn't expect anything else.'

'Did she behave like a woman with suicide on her mind?'

'I don't know. I've never known anybody who killed themselves before.'

'Let's go back to Wednesday evening then.' He turned slightly to include Hazlitt in the conversation. 'She told you, I believe, about the message she had had from Michael.'

'She did,' said Theodore Hazlitt, 'and I think she felt the better for it. She was taking what comfort she could in the fact that he said he needed her still, and that meant a great deal to her. Wouldn't you agree with that, Alfreda?'

'I suppose I should,' she said negligently. 'It's certainly what she said.'

'What did you think about the message?'

'I agree with Daniel,' said Hazlitt, 'she should never have gone anywhere near these people. But, of course, I couldn't say so, that would have been to hurt her more than ever.'

'What about you, Mrs Hazlitt?'

'I don't know, there might be a thrill in it I suppose. But I think if I went to a medium I'd need a good deal of convincing that he or she was genuine.'

'On that Thursday, Mrs Hazlitt, did Mrs Walpole say anything about expecting a visitor in the evening?'

'Not a word. She did say Daniel was going away overnight to Birmingham, or somewhere outlandish like that. Are you thinking she might have been planning to entertain a lover? I can tell you at least one person who wouldn't have minded playing that part.'

'Now, Alfreda!' said her husband feebly, and looked more distressed than ever.

'Well, I can! Mr Maitland is interested, even if you aren't, and I expect Mr Horton is too.'

'Very interested,' said Antony, and left it there. Geoffrey murmured something which his friend interpreted as a rather outraged agreement.

'Then I'll tell you! You shouldn't be so persuasive, Ted, it was you who said we should help if we could. And you know perfectly well that David Chorley has been mooning after Emily for at least two years now. She was an extremely attractive woman, you know.'

'So Mrs Chorley told us.'

'Yes, but Louise! She always thinks the best of everybody,' said Alfreda rather scornfully. 'See no evil, hear no evil, all that sort of thing. I'm different – aren't I, Ted? – I watch every move my husband makes.'

It seemed at that point extremely unlikely to Maitland that Alfreda Hazlitt contented herself with one man's love. Even allowing for her scornful manner, the signals she sent out were unmistakable. The puzzle was why she had married the rather ineffectual Theodore in the first place. Presumably, thought Antony uncharitably, at that time he'd been the one with the money. He didn't know much about dress-designing, but if you had a faithful clientele it was probably extremely profitable, and he wouldn't be surprised if she was her husband's equal financially by now. But all this passed through his mind in the rather awkward silence that followed Afreda's last remark. It couldn't be allowed to lengthen any further, or they might find themselves out in the street before they were ready, so he hurried on with his next question. 'From what you know of Mrs Walpole,' he said, 'don't you think it would have been more in character for her to leave a letter for her husband before she killed herself?'

Theodore answered that. 'Yes, I do,' he said, quite firmly. Perhaps he was wondering what his wife might come out with next. 'But the fact remains she didn't, so there's really nothing more to be said.'

'What do you think about it, Mrs Hazlitt?'

'Oh, I agree with my husband. I don't see its relevance really, unless there's more to these enquiries of yours than you've told us.'

'Mr Horton told you the exact truth. I'm associated with my uncle in Mrs Selden's defence, and he is our instructing solicitor.'

'It's your being mixed up in it that makes me wonder.'

'That's a pity. But you'd better forget that nonsense about my never losing a case, for instance. Mr Horton can confirm that it's quite ridiculous.'

'Is it indeed?' She sounded sceptical. 'Well, are there any more questions for us or is that the lot?'

'One or two things.' Maitland was vague again. 'About Mrs Walpole, for instance. I've been told she was a very impractical person, so it seems that she chose a very strange way of killing herself.'

'Not if you knew Emily. I always said if I wanted to kill anyone I'd go to her for advice. Crime stories, you know, they were a sort of hobby of hers. So I suppose it wasn't too surprising that she applied her knowledge when she wanted to end it all.' She stopped there, and added in quite a different tone, 'You're laughing at me, Mr Maitland.'

'I was only thinking that that rather trite phrase sounded unlikely, coming from you,' said Antony, and hoped she would take it as a compliment. 'But I still think that for a woman, and particularly for an impractical woman – '

'Nothing easier!' For the first time Theodore Hazlitt spoke with authority. 'If you have a length of tubing, the whole thing can be rigged up in less than a minute.'

'I understand you're something of an expert on cars yourself, Mr Hazlitt.'

'I own three, if that makes me an expert. And yes, I do take a good deal of interest in their inner workings. Comes of my war service, I suppose, in REME. But I'm trying to explain to you that even someone as ignorant as Emily could have done what was done quite easily.'

'I don't think that's what Mr Maitland wants to hear, Ted,' said Alfreda Hazlitt consideringly. 'Don't you realise where his questions are tending? He thinks somebody murdered Emily.'

'Yes, I've realised that for some time. Perhaps that's something we should all feel more comfortable if we didn't discuss, however.'

'Well, there's no reason why *we* should worry. And I can't say I'm very much concerned about Mr Maitland's or Mr Horton's state of mind.'

'No reason why you should be.' Maitland's tone was suddenly cheerful, and Horton gave him a look in which suspicion and anxiety were nicely blended. 'Do you both know the Walpoles' neighbour, Mr Mottram?'

'I've met him,' said Theodore Hazlitt. 'I couldn't say I know him, though.'

'And you, Mrs Hazlitt?'

'Oh yes, I was forever bumping into him when I went to have tea with Emily, as I told you. Dreary little man, forever wanting to talk shop.'

'Shop?'

'Well, I mean, his line was books, and hers was art. But they seemed to find a good deal in common. I wasn't particularly interested.'

Antony glanced round the room. 'I'm a complete ignoramus about paintings myself,' he admitted, 'but aren't some of the things you've got on your walls here rather good examples of their kind?'

'I suppose so, we paid enough for them.'

'From Emily Walpole?'

'Yes, of course. But I must tell you, Mr Maitland, all we wanted really was something to go with the rest of the decoration in this room. You'll have gathered we like things to be up-to-date. Neither of us is a connoisseur.'

'What do you think of Mr Mottram?'

'I haven't thought of him at all for ages,' said Alfreda. 'In fact, that reminds me, I haven't seen him either since Emily died.'

'He's been away.'

'And now you've been interviewing him too? Well I'll tell you one thing, Mr Maitland, and I think this is a point on which Ted will corroborate what I say, he's a bit of an oddity. For instance, he encouraged Emily in this foolishness of hers, going to see the medium. I dare say he believes implicitly in the whole thing himself.'

'Would you agree with that, Mr Hazlitt?' Antony asked.

'For what little I've seen of him, yes, I would. But I think,' he added, 'you may rely on the accuracy of what my wife tells you. She's a very good judge of people.'

'I'm sure she is. Anything else, Geoffrey?' he asked, turning to Horton.

'Not a thing, except to thank Mr and Mrs Hazlitt for their helpfulness,' said Geoffrey. That might have been said tongue-in-cheek, but he sounded sincere enough. They made their farewells, and Theodore Hazlitt saw them to the door. Alfreda remained seated, Antony had the distinct impression – rather contradicting his earlier thoughts – that she was glad to see them go.

III

So again they went back to Kempenfeldt Square for tea, and this time found the whole clan gathered together, Roger and Meg Farrell as well as Sir Nicholas and Vera. Jenny went to make more tea, and Roger, displaying the streak of domesticity which still surprised Antony, went with her to replenish the stock of sandwiches. Meg turned her most seraphic smile on Geoffrey. 'He's overworking you, isn't he?' she said. 'What a shame!'

'The boot's on the other leg,' said Antony. 'He's overworking me.'

'I don't believe a word of that. I know you, darling, once you get your teeth into a thing –'

'I was co-opted completely against my will,' Antony maintained. 'The idea of wasting a good Sunday afternoon –'

'Was it wasted?' asked Vera. Antony turned to her and smiled.

'Not altogether,' he admitted. 'I've got a sort of idea – '

Sir Nicholas, who was eating the last of the buttered toast, looked up sharply. 'I seem to have heard something like that before,' he said, not very enthusiastically. 'But if it's true, you'd better tell us.'

'Too nebulous,' said Antony, and waved a languid hand in imitation of a gesture his uncle was fond of making. 'I'll tell you one thing though, I'm beginning to believe Sally when she says it's murder.'

'Thought you believed that all along,' said Vera gruffly.

'I believed it was a possibility, that's a very different thing. And now,' he added as Roger pulled the door open and Jenny preceded him into the room, 'I want my tea!'

'You shall have it,' Jenny promised him. 'But *we* want to know what's been happening.'

'Nothing much. Tell them, Geoffrey,' he commanded.

'There's nothing that I found particularly illuminating,' said Horton obediently, 'except perhaps the characters of the people concerned. We saw the Chorleys first. David Chorley is an extrovert, an advertising man, and would certainly like to do a public relations job on both you and Antony, Sir Nicholas.' Sir Nicholas shuddered visibly and closed his eyes. 'His wife is the one who writes poetry. She'd written a poem for Emily Walpole after Michael's death, but thank heavens she didn't read it to us. She is a droopy sort of female, and her clothes match what I suppose her character to be. How those two ever got together in the first place I can't imagine.'

'There was another couple you were going to visit.'

'Yes, the Hazlitts. The husband is Theodore, who seems to be called Ted for short, though judging from his appearance it's a most unlikely diminutive. In fact, he and Louise Chorley would make a good pair.'

'He reminded me of Lamb,' said Antony, mentioning a barrister of particularly melancholy disposition. 'I thought any moment he might burst into tears.'

'Yes, that's quite a good description,' Geoffrey agreed. 'He's a car buff, you may find that interesting.'

'And Mrs Hazlitt?'

'Alfreda. Another inappropriate name. She's a man-eater, I should say.'

'In the usual sense in which that phrase is used?' asked Sir Nicholas interestedly.

'That, and in any other way you can think of. Any man alone with her would be subjected to an intense dose of sex appeal, don't you agree, Antony?'

Antony grinned. 'Yes, I think I do.'

'There being three men present, one of them her husband,' Geoffrey went on, 'it cramped her style a bit. So she contented herself with a few snide remarks, but luckily Antony kept his temper.'

'I'm relieved to hear it.' That was Sir Nicholas at his driest. 'And is that, may I ask, the sum total of your researches?'

'You're forgetting the most important thing,' said Antony. 'Alfreda Hazlitt says that David Chorley was sweet on Mrs Walpole.'

Sir Nicholas put down his plate and wiped the butter from his fingers carefully on his napkin. 'If by that revolting phrase you mean that he was in love with her,' he remarked austerely, 'why not say so?'

'I thought I'd put it both clearly and briefly,' Antony protested. 'He carried his infatuation far enough to buy a painting from her, at any rate, which his unfortunate wife hated. It was returned after Emily's death.'

'And the Hazlitts, have they any interest in art?'

'Everything of the most modern. According to them, they're only interested in paintings so far as they fit in with their general scheme of decoration. I've no means of knowing whether that's true or not. What is interesting – you forgot this too, Geoffrey – is that Mrs Hazlitt had tea with Emily Walpole on the afternoon of her death.'

'The Thursday?'

'Exactly. It didn't occur to her that Mrs Walpole was contemplating suicide, but then why should it?'

'Why indeed? We'll all of us have a talk tomorrow, Geoffrey, and see which of these people you feel we should call. What time would suit you?'

'I think Antony has ideas for the morning. Say after lunch?'

'No, we'll all lunch together, that will be the best thing,' said Sir Nichoas decisively. 'And meanwhile' – he looked round at the assembled company – 'let's forget about the whole unsavoury business.'

'You're so right, darling,' said Meg soulfully. 'I can't think where Antony gets these dismal ideas of his, but there's no reason why we should allow them to spoil our whole evening.'

IV

Sir Nicholas and Vera went down to their own quarters about half an hour later – they had tickets for a concert at the Royal Albert Hall – and Geoffrey left at about the same time. 'On the face of it,' said Meg stretching herself luxuriously, 'it all sounds a very simple matter.' She seemed to have forgotten her earlier strictures on Maitland's activities.

'I'm glad you think so,' said Antony a little grumpily.

'Well, I do. Interesting of course, but not complicated. So why is Uncle Nick so worried?'

'Is he?' said Antony, stalling for time.

'Darling, you know he is. And I expect you've told Roger all about it while I've been slaving away in the theatre these last evenings, but he hasn't said a word to me.'

'Slaving away!' said Roger bitterly. 'If only I could get you to retire.'

'Yes, well, let's not talk about that now. What *is* biting Uncle Nick? From what I've heard, the case for the defence has been considerably strengthened in the last few days.'

'But the trouble is you see, Chief Superintendent Briggs has raised his ugly head again.'

'Good heavens, I thought he must be retired by now.'

'Not a hope. And you know how it is with the police, if one of them knows a thing, everybody knows it.'

'What has that got to do with anything?'

'Only that observation was being kept on the Seldens, in case the charge of fraud against them could be sustained. My visit was observed, and it wasn't very long before Briggs and Sykes and company all knew about it.'

'I don't see why that should matter.'

'Only that Briggs, emulating Mrs Selden perhaps, was suddenly given the gift of prophecy. He said some evidence would turn up that made the case for suicide doubtful, and the one for murder more likely, and it did.'

'You mean this Mr Mottram?'

'So Roger hasn't kept you entirely in the dark, *darling*,' said Antony. 'Yes, I do mean Mr Mottram, and some incidental evidence from the chauffeur too, though we can't approach him, of course, as he's one of Daniel Walpole's witnesses.'

'Yes, but –'

'In case I haven't made myself completely clear, the implication is that I procured this evidence,' Antony explained. 'That's what's worrying Uncle Nick, and Vera too, I shouldn't wonder.'

'And me,' said Jenny. But when he looked at her more intently for a moment, Antony realised that wasn't all that was on her mind. Her first thought was always for his physical safety, it was only when that was assured that she had time to worry about his reputation.

Maitland left for Bruton Mews almost as soon as they had finished dinner, having telephoned first to ascertain that Sally would be at home. 'And Father's out,' she told him encouragingly, 'so we shan't be disturbed. Paul's with me, of course, but you don't mind that, do you?'

He didn't mind, indeed for one reason and another he would be glad to see that young man again. It was a short walk, and they had obviously been looking out for him. Paul pulled the door open, when Antony's finger was still on the bell-push. 'I'd like you to know I'm grateful to you, Mr Maitland,' he said, ushering the visitor in. 'If we can only succeed in setting Sally's mind at rest . . . at the moment I can't get her to think of anything else.'

'You realise, of course, that setting her mind at rest might not be in exactly the way she wants,' said Antony, following him.

'Yes, of course, Mrs Walpole may have committed suicide after all. Even so it would be better to know. It's suspecting people, people she's known all her life, perhaps, that's getting her down.'

'I can understand that. All the same,' he added, as Sally appeared in the doorway at the left of the hall, 'I'm much more inclined to agree with her view of things now than I was.'

'I'm so glad about that, Mr Maitland, and so glad to see you,' said Sally enthusiastically. 'Come in here, it's my very own room, we can be comfortable and nobody will disturb us.'

'It's nice to be made to feel welcome,' said Maitland appreciatively, following her in and taking the chair she had indicated. Somehow the room was very like Sally, an honest place with no pretensions, but with a certain attraction of its own. 'I've been busy since I saw you,' he added, 'and even more busy since we spoke on the telephone.'

'Nobody's been horrid to you, have they?' asked Sally anxiously, taking his first remark more seriously than he had intended. 'They're really all quite nice people, but I suppose if they thought you were accusing one of them of murder that would make a difference.'

168

'I didn't go about it quite like that,' Antony assured her. 'All I wanted to know, ostensibly, was their impressions of your mother's state of mind that Wednesday evening.'

'Did they agree with me?'

'Most of them did. When you came to see me, Sally, you told me Mr Hazlitt owned three cars. He admits to being a pretty good mechanic. That isn't how he put it, but I think it's what he meant.'

'You're telling me he would have known how to . . . to do what was done?'

'I suppose that's true, but I'm not trying to imply that he did anything of the sort. Only it's a point that has to be considered, and I did wonder about Mr Chorley and Mr Verlaine.'

'Uncle Julian is hopeless. I don't think he could change a light bulb without help.' (Which was hardly material. If Emily Walpole's researches into the subject of murder could be supposed to qualify her to rig up the rather simple apparatus that caused her death, the same must be held to apply to her partner.) 'But Mr Chorley rather prides himself on being able to take care of small repairs about the house, and I dare say that includes the car too.'

'Were either of them in the forces?'

'During the war? That seems so long ago,' said Sally, immediately making him feel his age.

'The trouble is,' Maitland told her, 'it's a thing that may have a permanent effect on a man.' That was only too true, but he hoped as he spoke that she would only take his remarks in a general way.

'Uncle Julian could never get accepted,' said Sally. 'Medical reasons, but I don't know what they were. And – honestly, Mr Maitland, it's too silly – Mr Chorley has told me so many stories, cloak-and-dagger stuff mostly – that I just don't know what the truth about him is. But you've met him, that's absolutely typical.'

'Absolutely,' Antony agreed.

All this time Paul Bryan had been standing with his hands

in his pockets, turning his head from one to the other of them as they spoke in turn. Now he said, rather abruptly, 'I can't help but realise, Mr Maitland, that if you're serious now in thinking it was murder you must be considering me as a possible suspect.'

'Why on earth should he do that?' asked Sally indignantly. 'Of course he doesn't think any such thing.'

'I was one of the people who knew about Michael's message, and that seems to be an important point,' said Paul stubbornly. 'Besides, there's the question of motive.'

'Don't be silly! You know perfectly well, Paul, that Mother didn't really care who I married. She'd never have put any difficuties in our way.'

'I didn't mean that, I was thinking of the money you'll inherit from her. I don't want a rich wife. I mean, I want you, but I don't care whether you have any money or not. But I can't expect Mr Maitland to understand that. And I certainly know about carbon-monoxide poisoning, and could have rigged up the very simple appliance that was needed.'

Sally turned a stricken look on Antony. 'You don't believe that,' she said.

'I think,' said Maitland cautiously, 'that I'm glad Mr Bryan brought the subject up. It helps to clear the air.'

'Then you did consider it?' she said accusingly.

'How could I help it? But only, I assure you, in passing. I think . . . well, I've got a few ideas on the subject, but they're too vague to explain them to you now.'

'One of those three – ?' Sally sounded horrified.

'There were six people present on Wednesday evening besides the two of you and your father and mother,' Antony pointed out.

'Yes, but there's what Mr Mottram saw. He said it was certainly a man.'

'What do you think about Mr Mottram?'

'He's a little odd, I suppose,' said Sally slowly, 'but I'm sure if he says he saw someone he did see them. He wouldn't lie about a thing like that, why should he?'

'Has it occurred to you that Mrs Verlaine is at least three inches taller than her husband?'

'Well, so is Mrs Chorley. Taller, I mean.'

'Yes, but your Aunt Harriet is also what used to be known as "a fine figure of a woman". And though I saw no signs of it, there might be some jealousy involved over her husband's close business relationship with a woman.'

'Oh no!' said Sally, distressed. 'I won't believe that.'

'Let's get back to Mr Mottram, then. If we accept his evidence, it raises certain other problems. Your mother's words to the stranger implied that there was something wrong with the car, that he thought he knew what it was and could offer assistance, or at least a diagnosis that would help in dealing with the problem. Have you talked to Soper about that?'

'Yes of course I have. And I ought to tell you, Mr Maitland, he's an excellent driver, and always keeps the car beautifully clean. But he isn't really much of a mechanic. He said that on Thursday morning he had difficulty in starting the car, nothing he could put his finger on, and the same thing made him late in taking Father to catch the train. He mentioned it to Mother when he came back from the station, because he was afraid she might want the car on Friday, and he thought he ought to take it to be seen to as soon as he'd met the Birmingham train.'

'That was the first time he had noticed the trouble?'

'Yes, on Thursday morning.'

'Is the garage always kept locked?'

'Father thinks it is, but I'm sure Soper doesn't think very much of the garage door as a safety measure. He'd take great care about seeing the car was locked, but that was all. Of course, the spare keys are in the house, but nobody but family would know where they are, and in any case there's nothing there of value except the Daimler. Are you suggesting someone might have deliberately put it out of order?'

171

'It's an idea. But whether that happened or not, what you've told me reinforces your idea about the possibility of murder.'

'Why is that?'

'If Soper, who is used to the car, found it difficult to start, don't you think your mother would have found it even more so? And can you imagine a woman bent on suicide, spending five or ten minutes over that without her resolution ebbing? Long before the engine caught she'd have thought better of the idea.'

'That does seem likely, doesn't it, Paul?'

'I'd say it was a good psychology,' said Paul Bryan seriously.

'And it leads to another question,' said Maitland. 'What was the matter with the car anyway? I take it it has been fixed by now.'

'Nothing. I mean, there was just no more trouble with it. Does that . . . do you think that means the man repaired it that night?' She stretched out a hand to Paul who went to sit on the arm of her chair. 'I'm beginning not to like this very much,' she admitted. 'I know what I said when we came to see you, Mr Maitland, but I can see it all so vividly now. A deliberate, cold-blooded plot. Do you think you'll be able to find out who did it?'

'Nothing is certain yet.'

'Well at least,' said Sally with determined cheerfulness, 'this will mean that your Mrs Selden will be acquitted, won't it? And that's all to the good, because it obviously wouldn't be fair to blame her.'

He didn't point out the difficulties in the way of that, the imputation that might be made that the evidence had somehow been rigged. Instead, 'Did you know that Mrs Hazlitt had tea with your mother the day she died?' he asked.

'No, I don't think Mother mentioned it.'

'That phone call you made to me, Sally –'

'Yes, why were you so annoyed with me about that? You were, weren't you?'

'That's too long a story. I was going to ask you, have you spoken to your father about Mr Mottram's evidence and Soper's?'

'Well, you know he was there when Mr Mottram came to see us. He didn't like me asking him questions, but all he said afterwards was silly old fool! And I'm afraid I didn't say anything to him about what Soper had told me, Father is hurt too, Mr Maitland, and I don't want to make things worse for him. In a way I think being angry with Mrs Selden makes him feel better, but I can't let something so unfair as her being blamed happen just for that.'

It was on the tip of his tongue to tell her that the police might bring charges, even if Daniel Walpole dropped his case. But he was tired suddenly, and they were getting nowhere. Call it a day, then. 'I'd better be getting home,' he said. Neither of them made any move to escort him, and when he turned in the doorway Paul's arm was around Sally, and she had buried her face against his shoulder.

'I'm sorry if I've upset you, Sally,' he said gently.

'It isn't your fault.' Sally's voice was muffled. '*I* came to *you* after all. Only please, please, Mr Maitand, try and find out who did it.'

He raised a hand in salute and left them. Outside it was a bright starlit night, though cooler than it had been for several days. He hesitated a moment on the doorstep, pulled up his coat collar rather fumblingly with his left hand, and wondered if there was any point in walking across to the garage at Number Three, and trying to decide how much Mr Mottram could actually have seen. And as he hesitated he sensed rather than saw a movement in the shadows away to his left, and realised for the first time that, except on the side where the garages were, the mews was ill-lit. It was certainly not reason that caused him to fling himself to the ground, but rather that the instinct for danger, long buried, took hold of him. Even so he could have sworn he felt the breath of the bullet's passing, certainly he heard the crack of a shot, and ludicrously his first thought was that at least he hadn't made a fool of himself by the rather ignominious evasive action he had taken.

V

When he climbed the stairs of the Kempenfeldt Square house an hour later – fortunately it was past Gibbs's bedtime – he found Meg and Roger just on the point of leaving. Roger took one look at his friend and swept Meg back into the living-room again. 'What's up?' he enquired abruptly.

'I'm sorry I was so long,' said Antony, only too obviously prevaricating. He didn't like the stricken look in Jenny's eyes.

'Sit down,' Meg commanded, 'and Roger will get you a drink. And you sit here, Jenny. That's better,' she added, after they had obeyed her, and gave Antony what in a lighter mood he would have called a Lady Bracknell look. 'Tell!' she ordered.

Perhaps Antony was remembering Paul Bryan's comforting arm around Sally Walpole's shoulders. In any event, un-usually for him, he had taken his place beside Jenny on the sofa and taken possession of her hand. 'No harm done,' he said. 'Nothing to worry about. I'll tell you exactly what happened.'

'You'd better!' said Meg. Her anxiety, he knew, was as much for Jenny as for himself. 'But you can drink some of that first,' she added, as her husband came across the room with a glass in his hand.

Antony sipped the whisky, which was very nearly neat, and after a moment said thoughtfully, 'It occurs to me to wonder why you all jumped to the conclusion the moment you set eyes on me that something had happened.'

They all answered him at once. 'If you come in here look-

174

ing like a cat with its fur rubbed up the wrong way – ' said Meg, and didn't try to complete the sentence.

'You're obviously excited about something,' said Roger, less whimsically. And,

'You've hurt yourself,' said Jenny. 'Have you seen the doctor?' That was as near as she would ever come to referring to his injured shoulder.

'On my way in,' Antony assured her. 'That's one of the advantages of his being a neighbour. He read me a lecture, which I seem to have heard before, and strapped me up pretty tightly. But there's nothing to worry about, love,' he said again.

'I think we should perhaps all feel better,' said Roger, who was nearly as sensitive to Jenny's feelings as Antony was, 'if you told us exactly what it is we are not to worry about.'

'Very true. All right then, someone shot at me as I left the Walpoles' house. As you see, he missed me.'

'Because he was a bad shot?'

'He may or may not have been. I was flat on the ground, because I saw a movement out of the corner of my eye that alerted me. So you see, love – ' he added, turning to Jenny, but the explanation stopped there. The sentence should have been completed by the words, 'I strained my shoulder in falling, that's absolutely all that's wrong.' But that, in the Maitland household, was one of the forbidden subjects.

'You can't leave it there,' Roger insisted.

'This passion for details!' He was rapidly adjusting to the situation now. 'The first thing I did – but it took me a moment or two to realise what was happening – was to go and look for the marksman.'

'Damn fool thing to do,' growled Roger.

'Perhaps it was, but what would *you* have done? I thought Bruton Mews was a dead end, but when I'd gone the length of it, moving from doorway to doorway in a way that any onlooker would have found most sinister, I discovered there was a passageway leading through into the next street, what

Sykes would call a ginnel. The chap with the gun must have escaped that way. I went back to the spot where I thought I'd seen him, the light wasn't good, you know, on that side of the road, so I think he might quite well have missed me anyway, even though the Walpoles' house is the centre one, so that it wasn't a particularly long shot. Afterwards I knocked up Sally Walpole and her young man – they hadn't heard a thing, Sally's room being at the back of the house – and used their telephone to call the police. Of course, all sorts of people were milling about by then, but that seemed the most advisable thing to do.'

'Well, as no harm seems to have been done,' said Roger, deliberately refraining from pressing the panic button, 'the important thing seems to be what the police had to say about it.'

'It was the local chaps, of course, they were all solicitude. They seemed to take it quite for granted that someone might be gunning for me, a disgruntled client perhaps. The thing is,' – he paused and looked round his audience – 'as I'm sure has occurred to all of you, there'll be a report about the incident on Sykes's desk in the morning, and Sykes will show it to Briggs.'

'If you're going to say,' said Meg indignantly, 'that that horrible man will think you invented the whole thing, I really can't see why you should have done.'

'He'll suggest it was an attempt to back up my theory that Mrs Walpole was murdered. Somebody objected to my questions, and took rather a drastic way of trying to stop them. The trouble is, that's exactly what I think has happened.'

'Did they find the bullet?' Roger asked pertinently.

'Yes, it looked like a .45. It was embedded in one of the gateposts at the end of the mews. The gates have gone long since, of course, they may have been taken for scrap during the war, or just because it was inconvenient having them there. But the posts are wood, pretty rotten as a matter of fact, and as they stand right against the wall of the end

176

houses they hardly interfere with the cars going in and out at all.'

'In that case – ' Roger began, but Antony interrupted him.

'I could quite well have fired the shot myself,' he said, 'or rather, as it would have been difficult disposing of the weapon, I might have got someone to fire it for me, while I was standing safely by his side. You know, and I know, that my acquaintance in the underworld is not exactly restricted.'

'Did you tell Uncle Nick all this?'

'No, I think they were dining out after the concert. Anyway, there's no sign of life downstairs. They've a favourite place they go, after a concert at the Royal Albert, Jenny and I have been there with them. You walk through all those jolly little streets, past the pubs with red curtains in the windows, and when you get there it's a homely sort of place with the most marvellous strawberry tart.'

'Strawberry tart in March?' said Meg censoriously, her Presbyterian blood for the moment in the ascendant.

'Why not, if you can afford it? Anyway – '

'Antony, you're burbling,' said Meg accusingly. 'Just because you don't want to talk about what happened.'

'But I've told you everything.'

'As briefly as you decently could, but I meant, talk about the implications.'

Antony gave Jenny's hand a squeeze, and got up restlessly. 'It's too late to discuss the implications,' he said. 'Anyway, we've nothing to go on. It all depends on how far Briggs is prepared to go.'

'I think he hates you,' said Jenny quietly.

'Well, he isn't exactly my favourite person either,' Antony admitted. 'But I can't say it occurred to me until I talked to Sykes the other day that he still harbours suspicions of my – of my probity.'

'The question is, what effect will those suspicions have?'

'If you mean in the case of Walpole *versus* Selden, nothing,

I suppose, unless the jury consider that fraud has been proved.'

'Can they reasonably do that, in view of all the things you've found out that point to murder?'

'The two things have nothing to do with one another, if you think about it for a moment. If they find for Mr Walpole it will mean they reject the murder theory outright, and in effect they'd be rejecting Mr Mottram's evidence too, not to mention the chauffeur's second thoughts. That would leave Briggs firmly convinced I prompted their testimony. It's no good looking like that, Meg, it happens to be true. I can't say I like the idea, but it doesn't really matter.' He said that firmly enough, but Roger noticed that he was avoiding Jenny's eye.

'And in the future?' Roger asked.

'I don't see that it will make the slightest difference. Whatever I do Briggs will suspect my motives, but apparently he's been doing that for years and it hasn't had much effect. And now let's drop the subject for tonight, shall we? I'm heartily sick of it.' He did not speak of the deeper fear that was in his mind.

'We ought to be going in any case,' said Roger. 'How long do you think this business will take to clear up?'

'I think by tomorrow I shall probably have done all I can in the matter until the trial comes on,' Antony told him. 'But if you're thinking of the question of my safety' – he glanced at Jenny and smiled at her – 'you needn't worry about that. Forewarned is forearmed, and I shall take the greatest care.'

If Roger thought he'd heard that story before, he made no comment. 'You'll let me know if there's anything I can do,' he said in parting.

Antony promised, this time quite sincerely, though he realised (and thought Roger probably did too) that in the circumstances that had arisen Geoffrey Horton's company was probably more useful to him. For once he didn't escort the visitors to the front door, but left them to find their own way, which they knew well enough. 'You'll talk to Uncle

Nick in the morning,' said Jenny, as he went back into the living-room.

'Not first thing, I think, but as soon as I get the chance. I want to talk to Julian Verlaine first, and then to the Seldens.'

'And then you'll have done all you can?'

'I can't think of anything else for the moment. I know this is beastly for you, Jenny, but it doesn't really matter that Briggs is ill-disposed towards me, you know.'

'Perhaps not,' said Jenny doubtfully. 'But if you think I like your being shot at – '

'Look on the bright side, love. If I had ideas before – '

'You always have ideas,' Jenny agreed.

'Well, they're bubbling twice as busily now. And there's this much gained too. I no longer have the slightest doubt that Sally's theory is the correct one.'

'You said the police thought . . . Antony, you must have made some enemies in your time.'

'Yes, but don't you think the place where the attack took place is suggestive? Anyway, love, I shall work on that assumption. And now I'm quite sure it's time we were in bed.'

Jenny agreed docilely enough, though she didn't expect to sleep herself, and recognised her husband's mood well enough to know that for him too rest would be impossible. When morning came they were both heavy-eyed, and disinclined for conversation.

MONDAY, 20th MARCH, 1972

I

Maitland was on the phone to his instructing solicitor soon after seven o'clock. 'I want to see Julian Verlaine again as soon as possible,' he said, 'and I think you'd better come with me.'

'Well, you needn't have called me at dawn to arrange that.' Geoffrey was inclined to be grumpy. 'I don't suppose that gallery, or whatever they call it, is open before ten o'clock. Unless you want to interrogate him over the breakfast table.'

'No, when he gets to the gallery will do. I don't think there would be any point in seeing Mrs Verlaine again at this juncture. Things have been happening since I saw you, Geoffrey.'

'I knew you were going to see Sally Walpole,' said Horton disapprovingly. 'Don't tell me she had any more evidence for us.'

'Unfortunately, no. Or perhaps fortunately, I'm so confused by now I don't know what will be best.' He went on to describe his conversation with the two young people, and then to recount what happened after he left the house. Geoffrey was suitably horrified.

'I ought to have foreseen something like that happening,' he said.

'I don't see why you should, especially as you didn't altogether believe that Mrs Walpole had been murdered. It reinforces my opinion that that was the case, but it doesn't have any evidential value.'

'Surely even a jury could see its relevance.' Horton, in

common with a good many of his profession, had no great opinion of the collective intelligence of the general public.

'And how do you propose to get it into the record? This is officially a trial for fraud, you know, and even if Uncle Nick made the attempt . . . well, I can tell you, I don't fancy hearing what Walpole's side, prompted by the police, would have to say about it.'

Geoffrey thought about that for a moment. 'You're quite right, of course,' he said. 'But it's always the same when I get involved with you. I don't know whether to be more worried about what Briggs is thinking, or about what may happen to you before the trial comes on.'

'In that case, why worry about either? Will you phone Verlaine, Geoffrey, and see what you can arrange?'

'When it gets to a less ungodly hour, yes, I will. I'll ring you back. Will you be at home?'

'I'll wait for your call here,' Antony agreed. There were things he could be doing in chambers, as well he knew, but he also knew that he couldn't possibly concentrate on them. So he went into the kitchen to start preparations for morning coffee, and sat at the table there waiting for it to drip, and wrestled with temptation. There had been a thought at the back of his mind for several days, and now he might as well take it out and look at it squarely. What do you care about the Seldens, anyway? You don't like Maurice, for all you know Dorothy may be as crooked as you suspect he is. So why not withdraw from the case, let it take its course, surely if you did that you couldn't be blamed for anything Charles Mottram or the chauffeur might have to say? That would be the common-sense decision, but as soon as he formulated it clearly in his mind he knew it wasn't for him. The habit of responsibility for a client's affairs was too deeply ingrained, and still applied even though in this case the client had originally been his uncle's. Besides, there was Sally Walpole, who had asked his help, who had said – almost unforgiveably – that she trusted him. For all he knew she might even suspect that young man of hers, that would be a fine thought to take to the altar when the time came. He could have marshalled other arguments, his duty as an officer of the court, for instance, but those two were sufficient for him without thinking the matter through any further. 'And damn the consequences!' he said aloud, and looked round to see that Jenny had emerged from her bath and was standing, wrapped warmly in her dressing-gown, in the doorway.

'Is coffee all you want, Antony?' she asked anxiously.

'Yes, and it's nearly ready. Why don't you get dressed, love, and I'll get the fire going and we can have it in comfort. I'm waiting for a phone call from Geoffrey, so I don't know what time I'll be going out.'

The call came through at about ten to nine. Julian Verlaine would see them when the gallery opened at ten o'clock. 'Don't bother to call for me, Geoffrey, it's so near I may as well walk round there,' Antony told him. And turned from the phone to acquaint Jenny with his plans.

He arrived at the gallery exactly on the stroke of ten, and found Horton there before him. 'Park early and avoid the rush,' said Geoffrey by way of explanation, and when Antony asked where the car was added gloomily, 'About a mile away.'

They found Julian Verlaine in the first gallery, fondling an intricately carved piece of jade. He replaced it carefully when he saw them, and closed and locked the door of the cabinet. 'Come into the office,' he invited hospitably enough, but added over his shoulder as he led the way, 'I can't think why you want to see me again.'

'There have been a few developments,' said Antony vaguely.

'Developments? What developments?' There was a sharpness in Verlaine's tone, but he didn't forget to wave them both to chairs before taking his own behind the desk.

'You said, if I remember rightly,' said Antony, seating himself, 'that Sally had a bee in her bonnet about murder. Well, that bee is buzzing rather more loudly now.'

'The coroner's verdict – '

'Forget about the coroner. I thought perhaps Mr Walpole might have told you, a neighbour has come forward who saw Mrs Walpole crossing the mews at about ten-thirty the night she died, in the company of a man.'

'A neighbour?' Verlaine seemed to have got a parrot complex badly that morning. 'Who was it? And why didn't he come forward before?'

'A Mr Mottram, he'd been abroad. Do you know him?'

'Not to say know, I've met him,' said Verlaine a trifle grudgingly. 'Could he recognise the man he saw?'

'No, he couldn't.' Was he mistaken, or was the denial received with some relief? 'To anticipate your next question,' Antony went on, 'he's quite certain the two were together, as Mrs Walpole spoke to her companion. The time element fits in with the estimated time of death well enough.'

'Not conclusive evidence,' Julian decided.

'Some doubt has also arisen as to the provenance of the tubing that was used. So you see I've a little better basis for my enquiries than I had before.'

'And you've been making these enquiries of the other people who attended the dinner-party you were so interested in? If you marched in accusing them of murder, I don't imagine you got a very good reception.'

'The word was never mentioned, I was enquiring about Mrs Walpole's state of mind. They hadn't your inside information, Mr Verlaine, so there was no need to say anything else. Besides,' he added, smiling, 'I'm far too cautious a man to lay myself open to a charge of slander.' And hoped Geoffrey wouldn't be moved by one of his fits of candour to deny this.

'I suppose that's the only thing that prevents you from accusing me,' Julian grumbled.

'No,' said Antony, growing weary of this fencing, 'it's simply a matter of one or two questions. I told you that.'

'What are they, then?'

'You told me that Mrs Walpole had something on her mind during the last few days of her life. I wonder if you've given any more thought as to what this something might have been?'

'There was no need for me to do so. Michael's death was quite sufficient to explain her mood, and I've had no reason to revise my opinion about that.'

'A piece of information has come to my knowledge that interests me a good deal. I think it will interest you too, unless you know it already.'

'What is that?'

'That the art community – and in this connection I'm not speaking of all the beautiful things you specialise in, Mr Verlaine, but specifically of paintings – has been suffering a series of thefts. The police, I understand, consider them to be carefully organised, and as that was Emily Walpole's line of country –'

'You're thinking, perhaps, that I was the organiser, and somehow Emily found out and had to be silenced,' said Verlaine harshly.

'Something of the sort had crossed my mind,' said Antony, forgetting for the moment the caution of which he had boasted. Geoffrey Horton made a sharp movement, and then was still again. 'But what I'm wondering at the moment is merely whether you've suffered any losses yourself.'

'No, we haven't. I pride myself that our security is pretty good. But I have heard about the matter, Mr Maitland, everybody in the art community must have done so. There have been thefts from private galleries like our own, from public galleries even. All valuable stuff.'

'Well-known paintings should be easily identified when they turn up again.'

'That's just it, none of them ever has.'

'I haven't got the collecting bug,' said Antony, and spared a moment's thought for the books that were always overflowing their shelves, and the collection of records for which they had really no room, 'but I understand there are people who are quite content to keep such things to themselves, to gloat over them in secret, to be completely satisfied just in their possession.'

'Oh yes, that's quite a familiar trait.' Verlaine paused a moment, perhaps to consider the vagaries of human nature. Then he asked, 'Am I right in thinking that all you know is the fact that there have been some thefts?'

'And that the police believe them to be carefully organised, yes.'

'Then I can tell you a little more. The first occurred about three years ago. We – I'm speaking now of all my colleagues in the same line of business – thought at first that one man was responsible, one of the rather eccentric collectors you mentioned, who had a passion for Dégas. That's because the first three paintings that were stolen were by him, though they came from widely different parts of the country. Later the scope widened, if it had been one man adding to his collection it must have been someone of extremely catholic taste. But there were too many of these thefts for a single person to have done them all, sometimes a gallery in the provinces might be robbed the same night as one here in London.'

'What does that suggest to you?'

'Like the police, we all came to believe in an organisation. If there was one man heading it, he must have been someone with wide acquaintance among the art lovers of the world, and enough of a psychologist to know which of these people would be willing to accept a picture they could never show to anyone else.'

'And working for this man there would be others, perhaps not knowledgeable at all, who actually carried out the thefts?'

'That was our conclusion.' Funnily enough, since Antony's indiscretion a few moments before, Verlaine seemed less defensive now.

'Have you spoken of this to anyone outside of your profession? I'm thinking particularly of the people who were present at the dinner-party at the Walpole's house.'

'Well, Emily and I spoke of it often enough, I think that was natural. And it's quite likely that Daniel was there on some of those occasions, in fact, now I think of it, I'm sure he was. Otherwise . . . no, I don't think I mentioned it to any of them. None of them has displayed much interest in art, though Alfreda Hazlitt bought some modern paintings from Emily. But I think that was at the suggestion, and following the advice, of her interior decorator.'

'Did Mr Walpole seem surprised when he heard what was happening?'

'As far as I remember he said it was a lot of nonsense, the theory, I mean. Nobody would be fool enough to pay good money for something he couldn't display.'

'How did he explain that the paintings never turned up again, then?'

'He said someone was making an investment. Sooner or later they would be marketed, perhaps in America to individual collectors, astute enough to know a good thing when they saw one, but not expert enough to realise at first that they had been stolen.'

'Did Mrs Walpole agree with him?'

'No, I think she agreed with me. After all, we were both familiar with the kind of people who are our customers, and some of them can have very odd ideas indeed. Not that I'm suggesting there's anything strange in having an interest in beautiful things, of course.'

'There's one slight sign of interest shown by one of your fellow guests at the Walpoles', that you haven't mentioned,' said Anthony. 'What about the painting that Mr Chorley pur-

186

chased from Mrs Walpole? His wife described it as something very dark and gloomy.'

'Now, that's odd.'

'What's odd about it?'

'David Chorley, who isn't lacking in self-confidence, as you may have noticed, was rather making the running with Emily in the last year of her life.'

'I've heard some suggestion of that, but Mrs Chorley didn't seem at all distressed by the possibility.'

'No, but she's a sentimental soul who believes marriages are made in heaven. You'd never get her to admit that anything might go wrong with hers. As for Emily, I think she was more amused than anything else. Until Michael died, you know, after that nothing had the power to amuse her. But David used to hang around her asking questions and trying to sound as if he knew something about her own particular interest, the Renaissance period. I wouldn't have been at all surprised if she'd sold him something in the end, as a sort of revenge for all the time of hers he'd wasted. But I don't remember anything of the sort happening.'

'According to Mrs Chorley, it was a week or so before Mrs Walpole's death, and Mr Chorley had the good sense (I'm still quoting his wife) to return the picture later.'

'Now that I can be sure about. No return of any kind was made. I know, because I was running both departments, as I have been ever since Emily died.'

'Could you look up the sale, just to make sure?'

'Certainly, but I'm sure Emily would have told me.' He picked up the telephone, dialled one number, and spoke briefly to the person who answered. There was a short period of waiting, during which Geoffrey gave Anthony a look which was nicely blended of admonition and enquiry, then Julian Verlaine put down the telephone again. 'No such sale was made,' he said. 'I thought I couldn't be wrong about that.'

'I wonder where Mrs Chorley got the idea.'

'I haven't the faintest idea. But if you're thinking of David as the kingpin of this organisation, forget it! He's far too much of a Philistine. Besides, Louise . . . you never know what idea she'll get into her head next. If he acquired a painting, something he wanted to use for advertising purposes perhaps, she might have jumped to the conclusion that it came from Emily.'

'That might mean she was perhaps a little more jealous than you believe,' said Antony tentatively.

'Yes, I see your point. But she isn't a reliable witness, you know. Fanciful,' said Julian Verlaine, as if that closed the matter.

As indeed it did, so far as Antony was concerned. 'There's just one more question,' he said, 'and then we'll leave you in peace. If there was something wrong with your car, what would you do about it? Deal with the matter yourself, or consult one of your friends?'

'I certainly shouldn't attempt to deal with it myself,' said Verlaine, and this time his smile seemed to have some genuine amusement in it. 'Mechanical matters are not my strong point. I should do what anybody else would do, take it to the garage.'

'Suppose this was a matter of diagnosis, something the mechanic there couldn't put his finger on. What then?'

'If you're still concentrating on the people who were present that Wednesday evening, to begin with I shouldn't consult Daniel. I don't know whether he is naturally incapable, but he's had things done for him for so long now that it amounts to the same thing. As for young Bryan, I know nothing about his capabilities in that line or any other. I take it you're not considering any of the women. Sally wouldn't have been the one to cry murder if she killed her mother; Harriet, as you may have gathered, is a thoroughly domesticated person; Louise would write a poem about my difficulties, and leave it at that; while as for Alfreda, she might be as competent as you please, but she wouldn't dream of dirtying her fingers over such a mundane matter.'

'There are still David Chorley and Theodore Hazlitt.'

'Yes, I wasn't forgetting them. David I'd call a practical man, inclined to do small repairs for himself rather than send for an expert. But the one I'd consult, of course, would be Ted Hazlitt. Cars are his hobby, he owns three, and won't let anybody else touch them. In fact I've known him diagnose a fault in our car when I didn't even know there was one, just by listening to the engine.'

'The question is, was he right?'

'Absolutely right. As a matter of fact I didn't take any notice of him, and was caught by a complete breakdown a few days later, at the most inconvenient moment, of course. It turned out that what he'd told me had been a hundred per cent accurate.'

Maitland got up. 'Then that's that,' he said, 'and we're both very much obliged to you.' But he paused unexpectedly on his way to the door, so that Geoffrey, who had delayed a moment to make his farewells, bumped into him. 'It seems only fair to warn you, Mr Verlaine,' said Antony turning, 'that ours may not be the only questions you'll have to answer.'

'What do you mean?'

'Mr Mottram's evidence has reopened the matter. However they regard it, the police are bound to take some notice, and as Emily Walpole's partner you're the obvious person for them to consult.'

'What about Daniel?'

'And Mr Walpole, of course. They won't be making the same assumptions that I started with, naturally. What they will be enquiring about is possible motives, they'll think you can help them there. And perhaps alibis for the Thursday evening.'

If he had hoped for some response to that he was disappointed. Julian Verlaine contented himself with saying, 'Daniel's out of it at least, he was out of town.'

When it became apparent he wasn't going to add anything

more, Maitland said, 'Good morning, Mr Verlaine,' again, and resumed his course to the door.

There were several assistants around in the gallery, all immaculately turned out, as their employer could never aspire to be. Antony paused to look at the jade horse that Verlaine had been handling when they arrived. 'A thing like that saved my life once,' he said. 'A statue of a person, though, not an animal. I've forgotten his name, but ironically enough he was the God of a Long Life.'

'I know all about that,' said Geoffrey. It was obvious it wasn't one of his more pleasant memories. 'Come along, Antony. They'll be selling you that thing if you're not careful.'

So they went out into the pale March sunshine and began to descend the steps. And there at the bottom, just as though Maitland's words to Julian Verlaine had conjured them up, were Detective Chief Superintendent Briggs and Detective Chief Inspector Sykes.

II

Seeing Antony and Geoffrey, the two detectives stopped and waited for them. Briggs was scowling. 'What are you doing here?' he demanded, disdaining a conventional greeting.

'I might put the same question to you,' said Antony, his hackles rising as they always did when he encountered the Chief Superintendent. 'As for Mr Horton and I, we've been talking to Julian Verlaine.'

'Some more of this nonsense about Emily Walpole's death, I suppose?'

'Is it nonsense? No, Chief Superintendent, the only thing that surprises me is to see a man of your rank making an enquiry like this. Or is your presence warranted because a mistake has been made, and has to be put right?'

'Nothing of the sort! The coroner's verdict –'

'People keep quoting the coroner's verdict to me,' Maitland complained. 'It won't stand up, you know, in view of the new evidence that has come to light.'

'If you mean this man Mottram,' Briggs snapped, 'he's obviously a nut and could be persuaded of anything.'

'P-persuaded?' said Antony in his gentlest tone. 'I don't think I l-like the implications of that Chief S-superintendent.'

'Like them or not, it's a true assessment of the situation,' said Briggs coldly. Sykes, who had been effacing himself in the background, took a step forward and said in his mild way,

'I think we should listen to what Mr Maitland has to say. I'm sure he could help us. And after all, as he has pointed out, in the circumstances that have arisen some enquiries must be made.'

'I don't think I'm very interested in what he may have to say,' said Briggs. 'You spoke of the circumstances –'

'He was the first person to suspect murder,' Sykes said. Briggs's colour heightened alarmingly at the interruption. 'I think we should at least hear his conclusions.'

Maitland glanced at his friend. 'Your decision, Geoffrey,' he said. 'Can it harm Mrs Selden's defence if I'm open with them about what we've dug up?'

'Nothing but good can come of it in the long run, if you can persuade them that there was no suicide.'

'It might result in Daniel Walpole's team being forewarned of the line we're taking.'

'It might also result in the case being withdrawn altogether. I think it was Lady Harding who pointed that out.'

'You think I should talk to them, then?' Geoffrey nodded.

'If you have anything to say –' remarked Briggs ominously.

'Quite a lot, as a matter of fact. If you don't frighten me to death first.'

That caused Sykes to smile in his sedate way. 'You still believe it was murder?' he asked.

'I not only believe it, I also know who did it,' said Antony deliberately.

'Tell us, then!' That was Briggs, as impatient as ever; a command, rather than an invitation.

'Not here.' He glanced around him. 'If there's somewhere we can get a cup of coffee, and talk without being overheard,' he suggested.

'Just round the corner,' said Sykes, whom Antony sometimes suspected of knowing every café in London where a cup of tea could be obtained. 'I really think it might be a good idea,' the detective added persuasively, speaking to his superior.

'I'll listen if I must,' said Briggs. 'But you know my opinion, I think, of Mr Maitland and his methods.' Still, he allowed himself to be shepherded away, and five minutes later they were all seated at a corner table, at the back of the café, with nobody within earshot. It was an attractive room, so Antony concluded that either the coffee was very bad, or it hadn't been opened long and no one knew of it. It must be the latter, he concluded when the beverage arrived. It was hot and strong, and he found it heartening.

Chief Superintendent Briggs had been waiting with ill-concealed impatience. 'Well?' he demanded, when they were alone again.

For a moment Antony watched Sykes stirring his coffee industriously; there was need for this, he never took less than five lumps of sugar. 'I think I should begin by reiterating what I told the Chief Inspector when he came to see me, that to begin with I was very doubtful that murder had been done. Still, it was a possibility, and I felt it should be investigated. As I haven't the facilities you gentlemen enjoy, that meant making certain assumptions in order to narrow the field a bit.'

'Guesswork,' said Geoffrey, rather as Sir Nicholas might have done. Antony, intent on his recital, smiled at him absently.

'It seemed to me that if Mrs Walpole had been murdered,' he went on, 'it was rather too much of a coincidence that it should have taken place just at the time when she had a very good motive for suicide, and in a way that suggested she had killed herself. So I tried to find out who knew of the message from Michael and concentrate my attention on them. Don't look so scornful, Chief Superintendent, I'm not passing any opinion on the genuineness or otherwise of what Mrs Walpole was told. But obviously, one way or another, it had an effect on her.'

'In the circumstances that seemed a fair enough starting point,' said Sykes rather hurriedly. 'And you would learn more as you went on.'

'Precisely. I learned from Mr Horton here that Mr Walpole himself would be giving evidence as to his wife's reaction to the message, and also a lady who had been Mrs Walpole's nurse, though I don't remember her name, I've heard her mostly referred to as Nan. So it was obvious that these two were aware that a motive for suicide existed, but being on the other side – though at that time unofficially – I couldn't approach them. Then I found that the night before Mrs Walpole died the Walpoles had given a dinner-party, eight people being present besides themselves. I didn't consider Sally Walpole very seriously, nor the young man she is engaged to, Paul Bryan. He's a medical student, and though I don't know much about their activities I felt sure he could have found some easier method of murder if he'd had a mind to. That left Julian and Harriet Verlaine; Verlaine was Emily Walpole's partner, and might be presumed to know her well. Also David and Louise Chorley and Theodore and Alfreda Hazlitt. So I set out to see them all in turn.'

'There are two things a policeman considers in an investigation of this sort,' said Briggs. 'One is motive and the other is opportunity. I suppose proceeding along those lines would be too obvious for you?'

'As I said, I haven't your facilities. I wasn't in a position, for instance, to go to any of those people and demand an alibi. The only thing I could conclude on that score was that the Thursday evening had been chosen because it was known that Daniel Walpole would be out of town. As to motive, I heard from several sources that Mrs Walpole had had something on her mind in the last few days before she died. Her daughter was certain it hadn't concerned the message from Michael, but could only suggest three other things that could have caused her to worry. Something to do with her husband, with her daughter, or with her profession, in which she was very interested. Sally also said that her mother was a very honest person, and somebody else – I think it was Julian Verlaine – supplied the information that she considered her expert knowledge of art as involving a certain responsibility towards people less well informed.'

Briggs stirred and glanced at his watch. 'I suppose all this rigmarole will get somewhere eventually,' he said.

'Wait for it!' Antony adjured him. 'Michael had obviously been very much his mother's favourite, and I got the impression, again from various sources, that nothing concerning her husband or daughter would have weighed very heavily on her mind. So we were left with some worry to do with her profession, or her professional knowledge. Yes, I know I was still in a state of uncertainty, but I hoped you understood me when I said there were certain assumptions I was bound to make in order to have a starting point at all. And this one seemed to get some backing when Julian Verlaine told me that there had been an outbreak of art thefts all over the country, which his colleagues in the profession put down to careful organisation.' He didn't glance at Sykes as he spoke, but heard something from the detective rather like a sigh, which he assumed betokened relief. After all, Maitland didn't know how much Briggs had heard of what had passed between himself and the Chief Inspector the other day.

'So now,' said Briggs, still heavily sarcastic, 'we have reached the conclusion that Emily Walpole was worried by something other than her son's message. Or are you suggesting that she was the brains behind these thefts?'

'Nothing like that. Quite simply, I thought she'd found out something about the thefts, so that it had been necessary to silence her. And quite naturally my first thoughts went to her partner, Verlaine.'

'And I suppose you told him so?' Sykes suggested.

'Not exactly. He made a guess at what I was thinking, and I didn't deny it.'

'Rash,' said Sykes, shaking his head dolefully at what he obviously regarded as a piece of folly. Antony took up his story.

'You must understand that it was only after the attack on me' – Briggs snorted his incredulity – 'that I was really wholeheartedly convinced that murder had been done, and that these organised art thefts were somehow involved. As I said, my mind went first to Julian Verlaine, whose knowledge must be considerable even though his speciality seems to be jade, but later I realised that the person concerned need not necessarily be the organiser, the kingpin, whatever you like to call him, but could be merely one of his operatives.'

'So you have come definitely to suspect one of these people. Are you going to tell us who it is?' Briggs asked him.

Antony took his time about answering, and drank some of his coffee. 'I think I'll just tell you what emerged from these interviews,' he said, 'and leave you to draw your own conclusions.'

'I'm glad you think us capable of doing so,' said Briggs disagreeably. 'But what I suppose you mean is that you have no proof to offer us.'

This was uncomfortably near the truth, and Maitland had to struggle for a moment with a feeling of helplessness. 'There's nothing we can present in court,' he admitted, 'except Mr Mottram's evidence, and what my uncle can get out of Soper in cross-examination. And a certain amount of confirmation, too, for Sally's opinion that her mother felt better for talking about the message that Wednesday evening at the dinner-party, and went so far as to say that she was comforted by the knowledge that Michael still needed her, and would be waiting for her.'

'Well, now you've gone so far you may as well tell us the rest,' Briggs told him, with the air of one conferring a favour.

'Very well. Of the three couples, only the Chorleys appeared not to know what I was getting at.'

'I don't suppose you went straight in and accused any of them of murder.'

'No, Chief Superintendent, of course I didn't, but it must have been obvious what I had in mind. As I say, the Chorleys asked no awkward questions, and while Mrs Chorley was obviously concerned to present an appearance of guilelessness, her husband is a different matter. Another interesting point is that only David Chorley contradicted Sally's story about the dinner-party, at least as far as interpreting what Emily Walpole said quite differently from the rest of them. Furthermore, and this to me is the clinching point, he was the only one who knew I would be visiting Sally on Sunday evening.'

'Wasn't Mrs Chorley aware of that fact too?'

'Yes, as it happens she was, but Mr Mottram was quite clear it was a man he saw, and though Louise Chorley is as tall as Harriet Verlaine, or nearly, she isn't built on ample enough lines to justify a mistake.'

'Let's leave Mottram's evidence out of it for the time being.'

'There's one more point about Chorley, but I admit this is an extremely tenuous one. If you haven't met him you won't understand what I mean, but that attack on me was an extremely hit-and-miss affair, just the kind of thing he would have thought up.'

'You seem to have forgotten that we were going to draw our own conclusions about these points of yours, Mr Maitland,' Briggs reminded him.

Antony smiled suddenly. 'Perhaps I thought I was asking too much of you,' he said. 'So what I think happened is this: Mrs Walpole called unexpectedly on the Chorleys the Sunday before she died. Mrs Chorley didn't see her, she was lying down, but Mr Chorley did, in his study. At that time, according to Mrs Chorley, he had in his possession a picture that she disliked intensely, that he said he had bought from Emily Walpole. Afterwards, after Emily was dead I mean, he resold the picture or returned it to the gallery. Julian Verlaine denies that there was any such transaction.'

'That much, at least, should be susceptible of proof,' said Sykes. 'Even if Mrs Chorley refuses to give evidence when she knows what's involved, some member of the household must surely have seen the picture during the few days it was in Chorley's possession.'

'That's what I think,' said Antony, relieved at getting even so much support. 'I admit I can't think of any reason why he should have had the thing on display, but I remember Louise Chorley saying he was annoyed that Emily Walpole had been shown into the study. Anyway, Emily saw the picture and went away, and perhaps it didn't strike her immediately, but then she realised that what she had seen was one of the stolen pictures.'

'You're into the realms of speculation again, Mr Maitland.'

'No, but look here, it all fits in. I don't think she was sure at first, but if the picture was familiar to her she may have remembered where it should have been, and perhaps looked it up in a catalogue. I don't know exactly how she would set about it. But say she found out that it should have been in a certain gallery, and remembered that that gallery had been the scene of a recent theft. Wouldn't she have wondered what her friend David Chorley was doing with it, particularly as I gathered from Verlaine she didn't have any confidence in his ostensible interest in art, but believed it was more an interest in her? Don't you think she'd be worried? They were close friends, remember, betraying him would have been unthinkable; but there was that sense of responsibility she had, and the honesty that Sally talked about. And I'll admit I'm guessing again, Chief Inspector,' – more and more he was addressing Sykes, as being the more sympathetic of the two detectives – 'but I think she took an opportunity of talking to Chorley at the dinner-party. Whether that's right or not, somehow he realised that she was dangerous to him, and so concocted his plot.'

'That sounds a little complicated.'

'Yes it was, but it was slapdash too, which again I think was typical of him. I keep on reminding you of this, but he was a close friend of the Walpoles, must have known the chauffeur or at least heard him talked of. Perhaps he knew the garage was usually left unlocked, perhaps he knew too that Soper wasn't too bright where repairs were concerned. (I got that from Sally, by the way.) In any case, he took a chance and found the door open. I haven't the faintest idea what he did to the car, if Jenny were here probably she could make a guess at that, but it was enough to give Soper some difficulty the next day – this is something else that can be checked – but not enough to incapacitate it altogether. So the next evening he called on Emily Walpole, and I'm sure he had some tale concocted to account for his possession of the painting. It had been given to him, or he had bought it, in either case without his knowing what it was, and of course he would see it was returned to its proper place. Something like that, enough to set her mind at rest for the moment, but he'd know when she had time to think it out she'd see the flaws in it. Then, with her for the moment at her ease, they talked of other things and I'm sure he took the opportunity of leading the talk round to the car. He may not even have needed to have done so, it was probably on her mind that Daniel Walpole had nearly missed his train, and Soper was baffled, and would have to take it to the garage the next day. Nothing easier than for him to offer to take a look at it. Theodore Hazlitt is a car buff, and that made me suspect him for a while, but there's nothing to stop David Chorley, a practical man by everyone's admission, from having sufficient knowledge to do whatever it was that was done.'

'He was a commando during the war.' Sykes' voice was expressionless.

'Well then! Sally told me that a spare set of the car keys were kept in the house, so once in the garage the natural thing would be for Mrs Walpole to sit in the driving-seat, to try the starter and make sure that all was in order after he had finished fiddling. Obviously he did put the car in order, because Soper had no difficulty with it the next day.'

'And she continued sitting there calmly, while he rigged up his boobytrap?' Briggs was sarcastic again.

'You know all about the carotid artery,' Antony told him. 'There would be nothing easier than to render her unconscious that way, and Sykes has just told us how Chorley might have come by the knowledge of how to do it.'

'Then why not finish her off? Why such a complicated method of murder?'

'To foster the illusion of suicide, I've been postulating that from the beginning. That, I hoped you understood, was what made me look at this particular group of people in the first place.'

'And that's all?'

'That's all. There are things that can be proved, as Chief Inspector Sykes has pointed out, if you care to take the matter a little further. Chorley's possession of a painting for instance, somebody must have seen it besides his wife, and I think Soper's evidence will establish a strong suspicion that the car was tampered with. And you can't get round Mr Mottram's evidence, Chief Superintendent, you really can't, however unbalanced you think he is.'

Briggs was breathing heavily, rather as though he had been running. He leaned forward now with his hands on the table, his face thrust forward so that Antony recoiled a little involuntarily.

'I'll tell you what I think, Mr Maitland. You've made a very good job of concocting a story, even if you have had to distort the facts a little. Mrs Selden will go on trial, and if you try to put on this particular defence with Mr Mottram as your only witness you'll be laughed out of court.'

'Do you really think so?' asked Antony politely, but he knew in his heart that what the Chief Superintendent said had elements of truth. None of the arguments he had used could be paraded before the jury, and Mr Mottram was undeniably an odd-looking little man.

'Yes, I do think so,' said Briggs. 'And after the fraud has been proved, and damages awarded, two things will happen. Your friend Charles Mottram will be charged with perjury – and perhaps Soper too, it depends on what kind of a showing he makes on the witness stand – and *you* will be charged with subornation of perjury.'

'And how do you p-propose to prove that, S-superintendent?' asked Maitland interestedly. He had himself pretty well in hand, but the slight stammer betrayed his rising anger.

'I don't think I shall have too much difficulty, you have a certain reputation, you know.'

'Let's leave my reputation out of this. What do you think you can prove?'

'Can you deny you had a talk with Miss Sally Walpole, and that following it she spoke to these people and then reported back to you?'

Antony leaned back. 'No, I can't d-deny it, I don't even w-want to. What is supposed to have h-happened then?'

'Mottram, if not a spiritualist himself, is at least sympathetic towards it. He might not take too much persuading that this story of his was assisting the course of justice. As for Soper, every man has his price.'

'And uncle has been k-known to call me c-cynical! What is *my* p-price supposed to have been, Superintendent?'

'That may be more difficult to discover.'

'Very d-difficult indeed, I should think. Mr Horton will t-tell you – ' He broke off there, noticing for the first time that Geoffrey had slipped away from the table. 'Anyway, it can be quite clearly d-demonstrated. My b-brief is marked for only a n-nominal sum.'

'I have no doubt about that,' Briggs sneered. 'An elementary precaution. Besides, I'm not so foolish as to think that Sir Nicholas, or even your friend Mr Horton, had any part in this.'

'I see. What *was* my p-price then?' Antony insisted.

'You have a record of successes in difficult cases, which you may be anxious not to see spoiled. In any case, I'm sure the Seldens would find it less difficult to pay you off than to pay the kind of damages that are likely to be assessed against them in the event that Mr Walpole proves his case.'

When Maitland lost his temper, he lost it completely. 'You asked me what I t-thought and I t-told you,' he said. 'You've accused me often enough of not c-co-operating, and I was t-trying to remedy that. But if you think I'm going to s-sit here and l-listen to these – these p-products of your d-diseased imagination, you're very much mistaken.' He was halfway to his feet when he felt Geoffrey's hand on his arm.

'I just telephoned Sir Nicholas,' said Horton. 'He's coming over here straight away.'

'Oh, is he?' said Antony deflated. As usual when his temper got away from him, it left him with an overpowering feeling of shame. But he stayed where he was, and it was Briggs who rose instead.

'I see no reason for prolonging this conversation,' he said. 'I've outlined my position to you, Mr Maitland, and you may be sure I meant every word I said.'

'Oh, go to hell!' said Maitland, and turned a shoulder on him. 'See if you can signal the waitress, Geoffrey, we may as well have some more coffee.'

Briggs spoke for a moment in a low voice to his subordinate, and then turned on his heel. But Sykes was still sitting there when the fresh supply of coffee arrived. 'You should try not to annoy the Chief Superintendent, Mr Maitland,' he said in his sedate way.

'*I* . . . annoy *him*? I meant what I said, Chief Inspector, I was genuinely trying to co-operate, which you've accused me often enough of not being willing to do. Do you agree with his estimate of our chances in court?'

'Yes, Mr Maitland, I do. None of what you've told us this morning – '

'I know that well enough. But the rest?'

'The jury are likely to regard Mrs Walpole's motive for suicide as overwhelming, and the evidence for murder just isn't good enough as it stands. Chief Superintendent Briggs is in the right of it, the best you can say of Mr Mottram is that he's an eccentric.'

They sat for some minutes in silence after that, sipping their coffee, but Sykes made no move to go. After a while he said, 'What do you mean to do, then, lad?'

The form of address was obviously an indirect expression of concern. Antony looked at him and smiled. 'If you mean about Mrs Selden's defence,' he said, 'what can I do? I won't suppress a witness in her favour, just because using him may get me into trouble.'

'I don't see how Briggs can prove anything against you,' said Geoffrey.

'He had one or two points,' Antony admitted. 'You weren't here the whole time we were talking, were you? But even so, I doubt if he could prove I tampered with the witnesses.'

'Of course he couldn't,' said Geoffrey stoutly. Sykes shook his head in rather a worried way.

'I dare say you're right about that,' he said. 'Both being legal gentlemen, of course you'd know. But there's one other thing I should remind you of, Mr Maitland. The fact that the charge is brought at all is going to mean that some people will believe it. That's why I wish you'd reconsider.'

'There's nothing to reconsider, you must see that.'

'Knowing you – ' said Sykes, and shook his head again sadly.

To this rather depressed group of people Sir Nicholas added himself a few minutes later. He stalked the length of the room, stood a moment looking all round him in a disparaging way, and then fixed his gaze on his nephew. 'What's all this about, Antony?' he enquired.

'It was Geoffrey's idea to send for you, so he may as well tell you,' said Maitland. 'You didn't bring Vera with you?'

Sir Nicholas looked outraged. 'Do you think I'd bring your aunt to a place like this?' he enquired awfully.

'It isn't so bad really, in fact the coffee is pretty good. Shall I order you some?'

'Don't try to change the subject, Antony. I'm waiting for an explanation. And if neither of you will give me one, perhaps Chief Inspector Sykes will oblige me.'

In the event they told him of the morning's events in chorus, which didn't serve to improve his disposition at all. 'And having bungled the whole affair between you,' he said, dividing his censure equally between his nephew and his instructing solicitor, 'I suppose you want me to find a way out.'

'Have we harmed your case?' asked Antony with unusual meekness.

'It's no better and no worse than it was before you embarked on this ridiculous conversation with the police,' said Sir Nicholas. 'And I suppose, to be fair to you, there's no harm in knowing exactly where you stand.'

'Briggs can't prove anything,' said Antony hopefully, and not altogether honestly, seeing that this question had already been thrashed out with Sykes. His uncle replied much as the detective had done.

'I dare say not, but the charge itself . . . well, we'll worry about that later. I won't insult you by asking what you want me to do.'

'Go ahead as planned,' said Antony, just as though the

203

question had in fact been asked. Then he grinned, but rather half-heartedly. 'Sykes did – er – insult me,' he said, 'but I told him the same thing.'

'And just what are you going to do, Chief Inspector?'

'I won't disguise from you, Sir Nicholas,' said Sykes slowly, 'that Mr Maitland has given me some food for thought. I'll making a few enquiries – unofficial they'll have to be – into the points that may be susceptible of proof. That may lead somewhere, or it may not. You see – I'd better be honest with you – I'm not at all sure it isn't just one of his flights of fancy.'

'I can appreciate your dilemma,' said Sir Nicholas dryly.

'However – ' He broke off as Antony interrupted him with sudden eagerness.

'There's just one other thing we might try.'

'Another one of your bright ideas!' said Sir Nicholas bitterly.

'No, Uncle Nick, this is a good one.' He whipped round on Sykes. 'Will you come with us to see the Seldens?' he asked.

'I've no objection, if you think it will do any good.'

'It's just a chance, and if it works it might convince you.' And if you *are* convinced, Chief Inspector, I can't help feeling those enquiries of yours may be rather more enthusiastic than would otherwise be the case.'

'I don't see how visiting the Seldens can convince me, one way or the other.'

'If you're worried about Mrs Selden's supernormal powers, my presence should be sufficient protection,' said Sir Nicholas blandly. Antony ignored the interruption, and responded directly to Sykes's objection.

'Listen then. Mrs Walpole trusted Dorothy Selden, would have visited her every day if she'd been allowed to do so. If something really was worrying her, as I believe, something about a stolen picture, might she not have asked about it when she went for that final seance? If you remember the timing, she could only have seen the picture on Sunday after-noon, the seance was on Monday evening, and she was dead

204

before the end of the week. You can ask the questions if you like, Chief Inspector, I'll promise to keep my mouth shut. But if anything is said to confirm my belief – '

'It's a big If,' said Sykes heavily, 'but I'm game, if you are.'

Sir Nicholas was already on his feet. 'Another of your wild goose chases,' he told his nephew, 'but I ought to be used to them by now. And I suppose,' he added, almost as gloomily as Sykes had done, 'we shan't be any worse off afterwards if the question is asked and receives a negative reply.'

III

Both Sir Nicholas and Sykes were in favour of telephoning ahead, before undertaking the journey to Hampstead; Antony, on the other hand, was adamant that the visit should be a surprise one, and when Geoffrey threw his weight in unexpectedly behind him, Sir Nicholas agreed, though with some reluctance. They all fitted easily enough into Geoffrey's car, which was large and luxurious, though showing signs of its years. On the whole, the journey was completed in silence, though Sykes said once, rather as though he were reassuring himself, 'This, of course, is quite unofficial.' By the time they arrived Antony was inclined to regret his veto on phoning ahead, but for once his luck held. The door was opened almost immediately by Maurice Selden. Understandably, he displayed signs of extreme surprise on seeing the four men on the doorstep, and took an involuntary step backwards, as though he were actually being threatened. And then, after looking rather wildly from one of them to the other, zeroed in on Geoffrey Horton, as being perhaps the more stable of the two members of the group with whom he was already acquainted.

'Mr Horton!' he said. 'What on earth does this mean?'

'If you'll let us in I'll explain,' said Geoffrey, who had no intention of doing so. 'This is Sir Nicholas Harding, Mrs

Selden's counsel,' he added, when they were once inside the hall. 'Detective Chief Inspector Sykes; and Mr Maitland you know.'

'Yes.' Selden still sounded doubtful. 'I can't see what the police are doing here. Not in your company, at any rate.'

'The Chief Inspector has nothing to do with the fraud squad. But there is a question he would like to ask Mrs Selden. I won't go into details at the moment, but I do assure you that it may be of the greatest help to her defence.'

'My wife has a seance this afternoon, she always rests before one. It isn't really convenient – '

'Come now, Mr Selden, it isn't lunchtime yet. Surely we could have five minutes with her.'

They were never to know what Maurice Selden might have replied. At that moment a door at the right of the hall opened and Mrs Selden appeared in the doorway. 'If Mr Horton say's it's important, I'm sure it is,' she said in her composed way. 'Good morning, Sir Nicholas; good morning, Mr Maitland. Did I hear you say,' she added to Geoffrey, 'that this other gentleman is from the police?'

Geoffrey repeated the introduction. 'Well, I must take your word for it that anything I can tell him will be helpful,' she said. 'But I have a feeling that he's an unbeliever.'

'Whether I believe or don't believe in spiritualism, Mrs Selden, is quite beside the point,' Sykes assured her. 'It's a very simple question I have to ask, and as I understand you were in trance during the last seance that Mrs Walpole had with you, perhaps we'd better ask your husband to be present also.'

'Very well. Please come in here.' She led the way into the room she had just left. At that hour the sun was shining straight in, and Antony had a momentary qualm as to whether she might pull the curtains, and immediately go into a trance. However, she did nothing of the sort, just sat down composedly, and waited for Sykes to begin.

'I'm sure you remember the last seance Mrs Walpole

attended, the Monday evening before she died,' said Sykes tentatively. In spite of the seriousness of the situation, Antony couldn't help a momentary twinge of amusement. The detective sounded as if he thought the whole situation might explode at any moment in his face.

'That isn't altogether true,' said Dorothy Selden carefully. Standing beside her chair her husband was visibly uneasy. 'These other gentlemen will recall that I told them I was in trance when the message from Michael Walpole came through.'

'It isn't about that I want to ask you,' Sykes assured her. 'Did you have some conversation with Mrs Walpole when she first arrived?'

'Oh yes, that's quite normal. It puts both of us in the mood, you see.'

'And that part of the sitting you would remember?'

'Certainly I should.'

'Then you can tell me what was said on that occasion? I should like you to listen very carefully, Mr Selden, and perhaps if your wife forgets anything you'll be kind enough to put her right.'

'Anything you say,' said Maurice Selden, still uneasy.

'Then let me think,' said Dorothy. 'Mrs Walpole had been getting a good deal calmer as the weeks went on, as she was in touch with her son more often, and was assured of his continued survival, and of his love for her. Now you must understand that is hearsay, things that I learned from my husband or from conversations with Mrs Walpole. But the part about her becoming more resigned is my own observation.'

'Yes, I understand what you mean.'

'Well, that evening she had what I suppose you could call a relapse. She seemed much more agitated.'

'This was before the message from Michael?'

'Oh yes. I only knew about that later. After she'd left, when Maurice told me about it.'

'I understand your clients sometimes consult you even when you aren't in trance. Business worries, love affairs, things like that,' said Sykes improvising freely.

'Yes, indeed they do. As Mrs Walpole did that evening.' If she noticed a sudden stillness among her hearers she took no notice, but went on directly. 'She said she had evidence that a very serious crime had been committed, and wanted to know what she should do about it.'

'Dorothy told her to go to the police,' Maurice Selden put in.

'Yes, of course, that was my first thought. She said it wasn't quite so simple. She had visited a friend's house the previous day, and been shown into his study through an error on the part of his servant. Her intention had been to see his wife, but the lady was resting, and while her husband went to see if she was awake Mrs Walpole noticed a framed painting leaning against the wall in one corner . . . actually facing the wall, she said. Naturally she was curious, art being her great interest, so she moved it into a better light and studied it carefully. While she was doing this, her friend returned, and she congratulated him on a wise purchase. It was a famous painting – she didn't go into any particulars, knowing my ignorance of the subject – and she recognised it as being genuine. It wasn't until after she had left the house that she realised she knew where this particular painting should have been, in a gallery in one of the North London suburbs. But her friend was aware that she was an expert in these matters, that she must have recognised it and probably thought about the matter later, so that even if she called the police now the evidence would most likely have been disposed of.'

'She mentioned too,' said Maurice, 'that there had been a whole series of thefts, and a lot of discussion about them in the trade. She was also, if you remember, Dorothy, distressed at the idea of giving away a friend, particularly as – if she succeeded in making a charge stick – it would affect his wife as well, and I think she had a great regard for her.'

'Such a dilemma!' said Dorothy Selden in her unemotional way. 'I asked if she thought this man was the head of the ring responsible for the thefts, and she said No, he wouldn't have the knowledge. In fact he had pumped her for information from time to time, and she'd thought nothing of it. But there had been too many thefts for them to be the work of one man only, there must be other people concerned, so she had come to the conclusion that this man was one of them.'

'It didn't occur to her that perhaps he had bought the painting in all innocence, if he wasn't particularly knowledgeable about such matters?'

'That was partly what was worrying her, that she might accuse him unfairly, and then he wouldn't be able to prove his innocence. I think eventually she talked herself into the decision that she ought to speak to him first, in case that was the explanation.'

'And what did you advise, Mrs Selden?'

'I told her she need have no qualms about not telling the police, the matter would be resolved and the man would be punished soon enough.'

'What made you say that?'

'I don't really know.' She sounded genuinely bewildered.

'That sort of thing happens all the time,' said Maurice, shrugging.

'What were Mrs Walpole's reactions to your advice?'

'I couldn't say. As soon as I had spoken I must have gone into trance, and I think you know what happened then.'

'Yes, but at the moment that isn't what concerns us. Mr Selden, can you help us?'

'Mrs Walpole's reaction? She said, "If you're sure of that, dear Mrs Selden, I needn't worry any more." But then she added, as if to herself, "I think I'll have a word with David though, when I see him again. I might be able to help to put him on the right path." '

Sykes turned and looked from one of his companions to the other. 'Chorley's name is David,' said Antony helpfully.

And then, 'Mrs Selden, why on earth didn't you tell us this before?'

'Should I have done so? I didn't know. I never thought it could be important, after all it didn't provide an alternative motive for her suicide.'

There wasn't one of them who wished to enlighten her just then. They expressed their gratitude, each in his own way, and were preparing to leave when she stopped them with a gesture. 'Sir Nicholas,' she said.

'Yes, madam?'

'You've had very little to say today.'

He smiled at her. 'I realise that's unusual, but it was to satisfy Chief Inspector Sykes that we came here.'

'Your mind is still closed to me,' she said. 'But I think you're angry, very angry. There are times when it's not good to blame others for what they cannot help.'

'I'll remember that, Mrs Selden,' said Sir Nicholas, and carefully refrained from looking at his nephew. 'Have you any advice for the rest of us?' And it cannot be denied that this last question was asked with mischievous intent.

'Not exactly advice,' she said doubtfully. 'You are all troubled, and that is not good because if you would only seek help from the other world it would be given to you. Mr Maitland in particular' – she turned to him – 'your mind is torn two ways, and perhaps what I have said this morning will be of some small help to you. What I told you before has happened, hasn't it? The man I spoke of feels great antagonism towards you.'

'You can say that again,' said Antony and ventured a grin, which earned him a sour look from his uncle.

'As for you, Mr Horton, things will go as you wish.'

'What sort of things, Mrs Selden?' Geoffrey asked her.

'I meant that you are a good friend, and that there are people to whom your support is important. As for Mr – Sykes is it? – your mind is closed against me too, I think. You are a materialistic person.'

'Am I?' said Sykes, surprised.

'I don't mean that you haven't your own values,' she told him gently. 'Now I would tell you, follow your instincts. By doing so you will also be doing your duty.'

This time Sykes took her hand in parting. 'I wonder if you could tell me also, madam, whether we shall meet again?'

'Why, surely in court now that you're taking an interest in my affairs.' She paused and thought a little. 'When I think about it I feel that you're right,' she said, 'but I don't understand it.' Then she smiled. 'Can it be that you're a better clairvoyant than I am?'

'So that's that,' said Antony when they were outside on the pavement again and moving towards Geoffrey's car. 'If she's been so sure all along the case would never get to court, it explains why she's never seemed worried. And you must admit she's got you all neatly taped.'

'What about you?' retorted Geoffrey.

'Oh, I dare say. The thing is, Chief Inspector, what are you going to do now?'

'Follow my instincts,' said Sykes smiling. 'You do realise, don't you, that even now she has no idea that Emily Walpole's death was anything but suicide?'

'Yes, which doesn't exactly sort with her mediumistic abilities. I should have thought,' said Sir Nicholas, 'that she'd have been able to tell us that long since. However, if you mean what I think you mean, Chief Inspector, I'd much rather rely on your activities than on the help from the other world she told us was available.'

'On the whole you may be right,' said Sykes seriously.

'Well, look here,' said Geoffrey. 'Antony's theories have been pretty well confirmed by what you've just heard. What are you going to do about it?'

'Just what I said,' Sykes told him. 'There are questions that must be asked, and a whole new line opened to us about the art thefts.'

'The thing is,' said Antony seriously, 'what's Briggs going to say about all this?'

Sykes smiled in his sedate way. 'What the eye doesn't see the heart doesn't grieve over,' he said. 'I shall present him with a *fait accompli*, or with nothing at all.'

So they went back to town and had lunch together before they went their several ways. There was a good deal of talk over what had happened, in which Maitland didn't take too much part. He was mentally storing away Dorothy Selden's words about blaming people for what they couldn't help, for future use as ammunition against his uncle in time of need.

It was after dinner the following Thursday that Antony received a phone call from Sykes. They were alone that evening, and the coffee wasn't quite ready. He went quickly into the kitchen as soon as he had rung off, turned off the light under the pot, grabbed Jenny by the arm and rushed her downstairs, without even remembering to close their own front door. Generally his approach to Sir Nicholas was reasonably circumspect, because if there was one thing his uncle hated it was being rushed. More recently, out of respect for Vera, that had been an added cause for a cautious approach. But that evening he erupted into the study without warning. 'You'll never guess!' he said.

'You're probably quite right about that,' said Sir Nicholas coldly. 'It is not my habit to indulge in indiscriminate speculation.'

Considering this inauspicious beginning, Vera's more hospitable approach was welcome. 'Come and sit down both of you,' she said, 'and Nicholas will get you a drink. What's the excitement anyway,' she added to Jenny as the two of them obeyed her. 'Come into a fortune, or what?'

'Nothing like that so far as I know,' said Jenny. 'But the fact of the matter is, I haven't the faintest idea what he's so excited about. He just grabbed me and rushed me down here, so I'm just as curious as you are.'

Sir Nicholas had got up and made his leisurely way to the table where the drinks were set out. 'I am not curious,' he said, dampingly. But it was noticeable that he poured their drinks with a fairly lavish hand. 'Well?' he demanded coming back to his place by the fire again.

'I thought you might be interested to hear the latest from Sykes,' said Antony.

'So I should be, very interested,' said his uncle. 'But that's no reason for you to come in here—'

'Like a cat on hot bricks,' said Vera uncompromisingly. 'Can't say I blame you for being excited though. Should be myself in your place.'

'Thank you for those kind words,' Antony told her. A belated sense of caution urged him to sip his cognac for a moment before continuing. 'He put the questions in motion that were suggested when Geoffrey and I talked to Briggs, without approaching Mrs Chorley, of course. The picture had been seen in Chorley's study by the charlady on Monday morning. It was standing up against the wall then, face to it, but she was curious and had a good look. On Tuesday morning it had gone again.'

'Was the Selden's house still being watched?' asked Sir Nicholas suddenly.

'Yes, I gather it was. That was the next point,' he added, as his uncle nodded approvingly. 'Sykes confirmed with the chaps who were doing the watching that neither Geoffrey nor I had been anywhere near the Selden's in the intervening period. (I suppose it could still be maintained that I'd telephoned them and told them what to say, but that would be difficult to prove.) He also confirmed with the Verlaines and the Hazlitts, that Sally's story of her mother's reactions on the Wednesday evening was substantially correct. And, of course, that David Chorley had shown a certain uncharacteristic interest in art, which everyone put down, as Emily Walpole herself did, to the fact that he was trying to get round her. There was one other small point: that Emily Walpole had been seen in earnest converse with David Chorley before dinner on the Wednesday. It was Hazlitt who noticed that, and he was surprised because he thought Emily sought Chorley out, and not the other way around. But the clincher was that Sykes was able to learn about the art theft as described by the Seldens. He was able to identify the gallery, to talk to the people who had investigated the robbery, and to get hold of a good set of fingerprints. Armed with those he went round to see David Chorley this morning.'

'At home, or at his office?'

'At home, by appointment.'

'Well, I can see that there would be certain awkward questions to answer, but the man wasn't obliged to give him his fingerprints,' Sir Nicholas pointed out.

'Nor did he. But he couldn't explain about the picture. In the face of Verlaine's denials he couldn't maintain any longer that it had been purchased from the gallery, and he was doing his best to bluster it out when his wife came in.'

'What did Sykes do then?'

'She was obviously perfectly well aware that something was wrong, but flatly refused to leave. He went on with his questions – he had Inspector Mayhew with him, of course – and did his best to establish who was behind this whole business of the art thefts. David Chorley just went to pieces – Sykes said he expected that, he's just the sort of man to do so – so he decided to go away and come back with a warrant. That might make Chorley shut up like a clam or it might loosen his tongue. Either way it seemed the only thing he could do.'

'Seems to me,' said Vera, 'you're playing cat and mouse with us. Know perfectly well what happened.'

'Yes, so I do,' Antony admitted. 'But I don't understand it.' He looked at his uncle again. 'You'll never guess,' he said.

'So you have already informed me. May I remind you, Antony, that my patience is not inexhaustible.'

Antony looked across at his wife but for once got no answering smile. 'I'm just as curious as they are,' she told him.

'All right, but I know perfectly well you're going to ask question after question when I tell you, and I shan't be able to answer any of them. Mrs Chorley called the police about one o'clock – the charwoman had served lunch and then left – to say she had shot her husband.' He paused a moment, and then added in a satisfied tone, 'Yes, I thought that would make you think.'

'From what you told me about the lady – ' said Sir Nicholas slowly, and then broke off and added, 'Sentimental verse!' in a bewildered tone.

'Ought to have known,' said Vera gruffly. 'Question is, why did she do it?'

'I told you I shouldn't be able to answer that,' said Antony. 'I can tell you how, though . . . with her husband's gun. She's always known he had it, but doesn't know where it came from. A war relic, possibly. It hasn't been tested yet, but from the calibre it may well be the weapon used in the attack on me. And there's one more thing, Chorley had already written a letter confessing to Emily Walpole's murder.'

'Why – ?' asked Vera, but this time it was Sir Nicholas who interrupted her.

'Let's leave the why's for the moment, my dear,' he suggested. 'That fits in well enough with something I had to tell Antony, though I didn't see any reason to be quite so precipitate about it as he was with his news.'

'What was that?' asked Antony, and,

'Don't keep us in suspense, Uncle Nick,' said Jenny urgently.

'Mainly that I heard from Geoffrey today, and *he*'d heard from Collingwood. Daniel Walpole has dropped all charges against our client.'

'Well, that's one good thing . . . don't you think?'

'Extremely good from our point of view,' said Sir Nicholas. 'Did Chorley give any details in his confession? For instance, I must admit to some curiosity as to what he did to the Walpole's car.'

'He didn't say, it was just a bare confession, but Sykes felt there was sufficient corroboration from other sources to make it stand up.' He turned to Jenny, smiling again. 'Perhaps you can make a guess about that, love?'

'Uncle Nick doesn't like guesses,' said Jenny flatly.

'In this case I think he might forgive you, if it assuages his curiosity.'

'Do you have some idea, Jenny?' asked Vera curiously.

'Oh yes, I think it was quite simple really. If he jammed the automatic choke so that it wouldn't close . . . that could be quite simply done, and quite simply put right again.'

'That sounds reasonable enough,' said Sir Nicholas judiciously.

'Nonsense, Uncle Nick, you know nothing at all about it. Any more than I do,' Antony admitted after a moment's thought. 'And for all any of us know the whole thing might have been a coincidence, a bit of incredible luck on Chorley's part.'

'Doesn't much matter,' said Vera. 'Admit I'd be happier, though, if I knew what possessed Louise Chorley to kill her husband.'

SATURDAY, 25th MARCH, 1972

I

They weren't destined to know that until the following week-end. Sally Walpole telephoned on Saturday, just as they were sitting down to luncheon, the Maitlands, as usual, having gone downstairs for one of Mrs Stokes's excellent meals. Antony went to the telephone resignedly, wondering how the caller – whoever it was – had traced him to his uncle's. When Sally answered his guarded 'Hello,' it was in a twitter of excitement, so that for the moment he couldn't make out anything she said. 'Wait a bit!' he told her. 'Take a deep breath and start again.'

'I know it's an awkward time to call, Mr Maitland,' she told him, but that was as far as she got by way of apology. 'We're having lunch with Clare and Harry, and he's just told me something I think you ought to know.'

'You've already said all the "thank-yous" that are necessary,' said Antony, not immediately getting her drift. 'More than necessary, in fact. Let's leave it there, shall we?'

'Well, I did want you to know how grateful I am. Think of it, I might have gone on for years being nice to them, giving them Christmas presents, and all the time never knowing – '

'There's no need to worry about that now,' said Antony firmly. 'What did you want to tell me anyway?'

'About Mrs Chorley. You know we were all so surprised – '

'Yes, we'll take that for granted too. *We* were surprised,

218

so I can imagine *your* feelings.'

'You aren't listening, Mr Maitland! It's something Harry told us. You know he's a journalist?'

'I know he's a journalist.' Maitland's tone was a trifle grim. As Clare's husband he was fond of Harry Charlton, but he never could think of him without remembering certain things that he would much rather have forgotten.

'Well then! Louise Chorley is in prison you know.'

'Yes, she gave herself up for her husband's murder. Even if she's retracted her confession –'

'Nothing like that. She told her story to the *Courier*. Of course it won't be published until after the trial, so nobody must know about it. But Harry felt I was a special case, and he didn't mind my telling you.'

'I take it, then, that I'm being sworn to secrecy.'

'Something like that. Though Harry said the whole household at Kempenfeldt Square is completely discreet.'

Maitland thought, that's more than I can say for Harry, who didn't seem to have changed at all in the short time since their paths had first crossed, but wisely he said nothing. After a silence Sally went on, 'Don't you want to know what she says?'

'If you mean Mrs Chorley, of course I do. I am all agog.'

'Now you're laughing at me again. Anyway, it doesn't matter. It was all to do with these people who were stealing art.'

'Don't tell me she was the chief organiser! I don't know that I could believe that, Sally.'

'You needn't try. I didn't mean that at all. She won't breathe his name, or give any hint at all who he is, but apparently she was his mistress for years. And when that detective questioned Mr Chorley, she saw that he was obviously going to break down and tell everything, so she shot him. It's quite simple, you see.'

219

'Simple!' said Maitland. 'You've taken my breath away.'

'Have I? I'm so glad. I thought you might have thought all this out for yourself already,' said Sally.

'Not on your life. Is that all she said?'

'No, there was quite a lot more. She said her husband was first approached about the art thefts because of their friendship with Mother – I suppose it was Mrs Chorley who suggested his name – and that Mother gave him quite a lot of information, not suspecting anything, of course.'

'Did she give any details of how the murder was carried out? Chorley's murder of Emily, I mean.'

'Yes, her husband told her all about it before she shot him. She said Mother asked him about the picture she had seen at his house. That was on the Wednesday evening, when they came to dinner. He said he was as anxious as she was, having come to suspect it had been stolen, and would be grateful for her advice as to what to do. They arranged for him to come to the house on Thursday evening – he gave some reason why he couldn't come early – and that was that!' Sally concluded with something like a sob.

'You can't leave it there,' he protested.

'No, but it's so horrible! He said it was obvious what was wrong with the car, he could put it right in a minute. And he did. Mother was sitting in the Daimler, to try the starter when he told her. He said it only took a moment to make her unconscious, and then ... and then –'

'Don't worry, Sally. I shouldn't have asked you for details.'

'But I want to tell you! A sort of – a sort of exorcism,' said Sally. 'Would Mrs Selden understand that?'

'She might resent it if you tried it on her,' said Maitland, who felt it was time a lighter note was introduced.

'Well,' said Sally, in a very determined way, 'he'd got hold of one of the masks anaesthetists use, as well as the tubing, of course, and the moment he'd fixed it – I don't suppose it took long, do you? – he clamped it over Mother's face, so there'd be no chance of her waking up too soon.'

'You're right, Sally, it is too horrible.' His thoughts about Harry Charlton weren't too charitable just then. 'But, if it comforts you at all, it must have been very quick, she couldn't have known what was happening. I can vouch for that.'

'Thank you. When I started I didn't really mean to tell you all this, but now I'm glad I did.' Sally still sounded subdued, but when he thought it over later he thought she might really feel better for having got all the ghastly details out into the open.

'So am I. And I'm glad you put no restrictions on my telling Uncle Nick and Vera, as well as Jenny, because I think they'd die of suppressed curiosity if I didn't.'

After that Sally let him get back to his lunch. Afterwards, when Gibbs had served the coffee and had taken himself off, he repeated what he had been told. 'Now if you can tell me,' he said, looking from Vera to Jenny, 'what on earth possessed the woman to do anything so drastic, I shall be eternally grateful to you.'

'Easy,' said Vera, 'if she's as you described her to us. A sentimental woman, determined to protect her lover at any cost to herself. To kill the man who might be going to – to spill the beans, and then confess to it, must have seemed the best way of keeping him secure.'

This was too much for Sir Nicholas, even from Vera. He raised his arms to heaven in mute protest, but then he too had a query. 'That's all very well,' he said. 'But you heard of the painting through Mrs Chorley in the first place. Why did she admit so much to you?'

'I think perhaps . . . can I hazard a guess, Uncle Nick, without you jumping on me? I think perhaps she thought I knew more than I did, that Sally had perhaps heard something from her mother that had made me suspicious. In that case, I think she was probably planning a suicide for her husband too, a tacit admission of guilt. In which case she would have been quite in the clear. But then events began to crowd in on her and she took the only way out she knew to keep her lover safe.'

Sir Nicholas thought about that for the moment. 'So now we are only left with two questions,' he said at last, thoughtfully. 'What do we think now about the Seldens, and what does Chief Superintendent Briggs think about us?'

'Her remarks as we left the Hampstead house were illuminating,' said Antony. 'Did Uncle Nick tell you about them, Vera?'

'In detail, I think. An uncomfortable person to know,' said Vera.

'I'll give you that. As for Briggs, I've given up all hope now of ever convincing him of my *bona fides*. Sykes seems happy with the way things turned out, but I wouldn't mind betting the super still thinks I had something to do with it.'

'I shouldn't let it worry you,' said Sir Nicholas. 'With any luck he'll keep his thoughts to himself in future.'

That was something his nephew didn't feel quite so sure of, but he was well enough content that the present difficulties were over, that Jenny had her serene look again, and as for the future, so far as he was concerned, it could look after itself.

II

Only Sir Nicholas said, when he was alone with Vera, 'I wonder how this unknown organiser, the lover of Louise Chorley, feels about Antony's part in all this.' And though Vera answered reassuringly, 'Only doing his job, nobody can object to that,' her husband shook his head dubiously and did not seem convinced. He was perfectly well aware, in addition, that on this subject Vera did not feel quite so brave as she sounded.

Still, the days went by, as days will, and gradually the matter was relegated to the back of both their minds, where it remained a slight, but definite, discomfort.